AN OBSCURE GRAVE

JIM DOHERTY

POLICE OFFICER

PRO SE PRESS

Written by Jim Doherty
Editing by MJ Hendry. Sarah White

Cover by Antonino Lo Iacono
Book Design by Antonino Lo Iacono & Marzia Marina
New Pulp Logo Design by Sean E. Ali
New Pulp Seal Design by Cari Reese

www.prose-press.com

CONTENTS

WHAT JIM'S BROTHER AND SISTER COP/WRITERS ARE SAYING ABOUT HIM AND *AN OBSCURE GRAVE*

"This is a well-researched, addictive collection of true case studies, some sensational, others little known, all intensely interesting. And one, 'The Mad Doctor and the Untouchable,' will no doubt become a terrific movie."
Detective Sergeant Joseph Wambaugh, LAPD (retired), MWA Grand Master, author of *The New Centurions*, *The Blue Knight*, *The Onion Field*, and *Hollywood Station*, on Jim's true-crime collection *Just the Facts*

"*An Obscure Grave* hits with the power and fury of a twister racing across a trailer park. Jim Doherty has created a complex mystery in his first full-length novel to feature his hero, part-time cop Dan Sullivan. More please!" Detective Paul Bishop, LAPD (retired), author of the Fey Croaker series, the "Felony" Flynn series, and Pulp Factory Award-winning novel *Lie Catchers*

"Gritty, realistic story by someone who knows the heartbeat of an officer in trouble."
Detective O'Neil DeNoux, Jefferson Parish, LA, Sheriff's Homicide (retired), Police Book Award and Derringer Award recipient, author of the Dino LaStanza series, the John Raven Beau series, and the Jacques Dugas series

"Police and FBI are stumped by the disappearance of a U. Cal. Berkeley campus beauty. Has she been kidnapped? Is she alive or is she dead? Working only on the fringes of the case, Officer Dan Sullivan ferrets out all the answers with the help of a local clairvoyant. Great story. Great writing. Great read."
Sergeant John Mackie, NYPD (retired), author of the Sergeant

Thorn Savage, Manhattan South Homicide, series

"Jim Doherty's own cop know-how puts us right inside the mind of Officer Dan Sullivan as he risks his life and learns his craft."
Woman Police Constable Joan Lock, Scotland Yard (retired), author of the Inspector Ernest Best series

"What immediately caught my attention was the realism. Jim Doherty's words didn't come across like so many English majors I'd encountered who tested their imagination and literary skills in a genre they knew nothing about. Written in a style that could only be accomplished by someone who walked the walk, Doherty's words flowed easy, making you feel like you were actually there. Intriguing and suspenseful. There were passages where I felt the frustration of the investigators involved. Like most cops or people who deal with life and death, Doherty used a smattering of humor to alleviate the tension. A great read."
Sergeant Don Easton, RCMP (retired), author of the Jack Taggart series

"Jim Doherty writes with a cop's authenticity and with an eye for detail, drawing the reader into his protagonist's way of thinking and investigating crime. Dan Sullivan's pertinent philosophical asides add depth and intelligence to a solid and likeable hero. With touches of romance and paranormal activities, Jim's woven a worthwhile and enjoyable novel."
Special Agent Mark Bouton, FBI (retired), author of The Max Austin series, the Rick Dover series, *The Sacrifice*, and *How to Spot Lies Like the FBI*

"Officer Dan Sullivan is a part-time cop, but he's what his supervisor calls 'instinctive' because like all the best cops he has a 'nose for trouble.' In an *An Obscure Grave,* Jim Doherty has created an authentic feel for what police work is really like and how deeply, often tragically, that work affects the lives of those who are willing to do it. Sullivan is unique and complicated, a refreshing change from the stereotype cop."
Captain Connie Dial, LAPD (retired), author of the Captain Josie Corsino series and the Detective Mike Turner series

"Some people lead more complicated lives than other people. For example, Dan Sullivan, the protagonist of Jim Doherty's *An Obscure Grave,* is putting himself through the University of California at Berkeley by working as a part-time police officer. Berkeley accommodates a vast range of social and political attitudes, with no two residents quite agreeing on anything— except, perhaps, that someone combining the roles of student and cop must be a little odd. Dan notices this, of course, and since he is full of contrarian views, and by no means secretive or apologetic about them, he seldom has anything like a routine day. Then a young woman, an acquaintance, disappears—maybe kidnapped, maybe not—and he is drawn into a tangential role in the investigation. It's only one of the many trains of thought that occupy him, but it doesn't go away, and as his suspicions begin to harden he takes on an increasingly active role. "
Officer Stan Washburn, Berkeley PD (retired), author of *Intent to Harm* and *Into Thin Air*

"When someone who carries a badge and gun for a living writes a mystery novel, you expect it to ooze with authenticity, grit, and realistic action. *An Obscure Grave* is all of that yet more, because Jim Doherty is also a great writer who is able to capture the essence of Berkeley and the U.C. campus, a unique setting as seen through the eyes of a young reserve police officer whose plodding and determined professionalism brings a murder investigation to its rightful conclusion."
Detective Lieutenant Brian Thiem, Oakland PD Homicide (retired), author of *Red Line* and *Thrill Kill*

"Coming from a family of law enforcement officers, long-time cop Jim Doherty spins a tale of murder as if it were a homicide in real life."
Special Agent R.T. Lawton, DEA (retired), author of *9 Chronicles of Crime*, *9 Deadly Tales*, and *9 Historical Mysteries*

"Jim Doherty is an experienced cop who writes like a dream. In his first novel, *An Obscure Grave*, his touch is deft and sure, and his protagonist, Dan Sullivan, is a breath of fresh air in today's crime

fiction. Studying at UC Berkeley while working as a part-time police officer, Dan is a young man with a conscience who loves both his job and crime films, of which he has an encyclopedic knowledge. I couldn't stop reading this and I don't think you will either. *An Obscure Grave* is a winner of a police story!"
Chief of Police David Dean, Avalon Township, NJ, Police (retired), Ellery Queen Readers Award recipient, author of *The Thirteenth Child*, *The Purple Road*, *Starvation Cay*, and the Julian Hall series

"Lovers of mysteries and thrillers have a new hero in Dan Sullivan. He's sort of a combination of Sherlock Holmes and Mike Hammer. I was hooked from the opening paragraph of Jim Doherty's excellent debut novel, *An Obscure Grave*. Do yourself a favor and pick up this novel in what I hope turns into a long series."
Sergeant Michael A. Black, Matteson, IL, Police (retired), author of *Chimes at Midnight* and the Sergeant Frank Leal & Investigator Ollie Hart series

"Jim Doherty's fast-moving and unusual book, *An Obscure Grave*, shows us a hero, Dan Sullivan, dancing to balance his life among Berkeley academics while serving as a part-time reserve officer, digging for clues in a missing persons case. This is where the real-world of policing crashes up against the rarefied world of academe. The ongoing debate about police brutality and accountability resonates throughout this entire story. Doherty shows his skill in handling the topic. His own policing background rings true. So, pick up this rare and well-plotted story. You won't be disappointed."
Investigator Frank Hickey, Manhattan DA's Office – Investigations Bureau (retired), author of the Max Royster series

"In his well-written police procedural, *An Obscure Grave*, Jim Doherty breathes life into his characters. It's easy to envision them and hear their voices. First person narrator Dan Sullivan juggles college courses, a part-time reserve officer job, a co-op position, and time with friends. But never far from his thoughts, and close to his heart, is the young female college student who disappeared

after getting separated from her live-in boyfriend while they were out on a run. What really happened to her? Concerned citizens call in leads for months, but none of them pan out. All the while Dan strongly suspects what actually led to DeeDee's disappearance. He finally hits pay dirt when he meets the right woman, a love interest, who helps him solve the mystery. Doherty weaves his wealth of knowledge, both as a police officer and as a classic movie buff, into the storyline, and tells a compelling story."
Deputy Christine Husom, Wright County, MN, Sheriff's Office (retired), author of the Sergeant Corky Aleckson series and the Snow Globe Shop Mystery series

"What is needed in today's world are police officers like Jim Doherty, who are willing to write the truth about law enforcement, even in fiction, because he has lived the life. I say 'Bravo' for his efforts!"
Lieutenant Dan Marcou, LaCrosse, WI, Police (retired), author of the Sgt. Dan McCarthy series and Law Dogs – Great Cops in American History

"Jim Doherty's first novel, An Obscure Grave, takes Officer Dan Sullivan back to his early days as a reserve officer working his way through college at Berkeley, and treats us to a deep and satisfying dive into homicide police procedure with added forays into film noir and detective fiction. We should all look forward to more from Jim Doherty and Officer Sullivan."
Commissioner Louisa Dixon, Mississippi Dept. of Public Safety (retired), author of Next to Last Chance and Outside Chance.

Dedicated to the memory of my father,
Jim Doherty,
Story-Teller Extraordinaire,
and to the memories of my grandfather,
Investigator Jerry O'Neill,
Southern Pacific Railroad Police,
and my uncle,
Officer Jim O'Neill,
San Francisco Police Department,
whose stories, with a heavy dollop of imagination,
find their way into these pages.
And, as always,
to Katy,
the light of my life.

"It were too gross
To rib her cerecloth in the obscure grave."
William Shakespeare

The Merchant of Venice
Act II, scene vii

ONE

It turns out he killed her in Oakland.

Which means I really shouldn't have been involved.

***

On the day her killer struck the blow that ended her life, DeeDee Merryweather was only 19 years old. An undergrad at UC Berkeley, as I was, she lived in a Co-op, one of a network of student-owned dorms and apartment buildings located around the campus, as I did.

I was a resident of Roylmann Hall on the North Side when it happened. DeeDee shared a room with her boyfriend, Chris Bridges, in Rivendell House, just a bit south of Memorial Stadium at the southeast corner of campus.

Both she and Chris were avid runners who regularly jogged on the Fire Trail in the steep hills east of the main campus. So there was nothing unusual about the two of them taking a run together that autumn afternoon.

The University owns most of that hill and canyon area, maintaining it as a nature preserve, but other police jurisdictions bump against the part that belongs to Cal. The City of Berkeley, the City of Oakland, the East Bay Regional Park District, and Contra Costa County each have a piece of it, too.

Somewhere along the way DeeDee stopped jogging and wandered off the trail. Chris later said they'd had a rather heated disagreement and they'd separated, each going his or her own way to cool down. At some point, she crossed both the University's property line and Berkeley's municipal boundary, and entered Oakland. She most likely wasn't even aware of it. City limit signs aren't posted in wilderness areas. It was on the Oakland side that she met her death. On the Oakland side that her killer struck her down.

It's not likely that he intended to kill her. He'd picked up a discarded hubcap. Maybe, ecologically minded, he intended to properly dispose of it. Berkeleyans, even those with murderous tempers, tend to be concerned about things like the environment. Or maybe he just wanted something to do with his hands. It's even possible that he just happened to spot it at the crucial moment when his temper hit critical mass. It doesn't really matter. The point is it was at hand when he went ballistic.

No one knows what DeeDee said or did to set her killer off. It's entirely possible that even he no longer remembers. But, in the final analysis, it doesn't really matter.

Any homicide cop will tell you that, when you're investigating a murder, knowing "why" is never as important as things like "how," "what," "where," and "when." "Why's" only useful to the degree that it leads to answers for those other questions. And we already have those answers. Or most of them.

We know that, in that moment of rage (when), as they both explored the wilderness of the Berkeley Hills (where), the killer smashed the edge of the hubcap (what) against her temple (how). We may not know why, at least not for sure, but we know the answers to all, or most of, the truly crucial investigative questions.

It almost certainly wasn't intentional, or at least not premeditated. Human skulls are, after all, pretty durable items. They're supposed to be. They're there to provide maximum protection for the brain. But if you hit a skull in just the right place, with just the right force, using just the right tool, you can inflict a fatal injury with a single blow. And that's what happened.

Undoubtedly, he tried to revive her. It was probably several minutes before he even realized what he'd done. Maybe he felt an initial rush of panic, but, if he did, he managed to quickly suppress it so he could take the first steps to cover up his crime.

Using that same hubcap as a makeshift shovel, he dug a grave. More shallow than the standard, but it still must've taken him a while. Digging a hole that's deep enough to accommodate a body, even a petite one like DeeDee's, takes a chunk of time without the proper tools.

2

Once he'd buried her, he left her there, in an unmarked grave, and went home, hoping that the body would never be discovered.

***

As I said, the actual crime took place in Oakland, which should have made the investigation the responsibility of the Oakland Police Department. And it would have been, if anybody'd known for sure that there was an actual crime to investigate and where it actually occurred. But when a couple of other Rivendell residents became concerned that they hadn't seen DeeDee for several days, it was a missing persons report, not a crime report, that they filed with the police.

According to a multi-agency agreement among the various law enforcement bodies serving different parts of Alameda County, when a missing person is reported, the department responsible for the jurisdiction in which the missing person actually lives must take charge of investigating his or her disappearance. That's how Berkeley PD became the lead agency on the case.

Even though it wasn't officially a murder investigation, it would ordinarily have been investigated as if it were. When someone drops out of sight suddenly, leaving no trace, there's a reasonable chance that person's dead, even if there's no obvious evidence, and a reasonable chance that the death wasn't the result of natural causes.

And, had that happened, had her disappearance been investigated as a possible homicide, it's doubtful I would have had anything to do with it. But the killer caught a lucky break when, early in the case, BPD received an eyewitness report indicating that DeeDee wasn't just missing, but had been kidnapped. That pulled the investigation in an entirely different, and entirely wrong, direction.

And, ultimately, that's what got me involved.

Now we know that the abduction report was a false trail. Now we know that DeeDee had already been killed several days before she was reported missing.

And we also know, to the degree that the word "know" can be used in circumstances like these, the answer to the most important investigative question of all.

Who.

But knowing it and proving it are two different things.

TWO

I keep insisting that I shouldn't have been involved, but I suppose you could say that, at least in the sense of being casually acquainted with DeeDee, I was involved before any of it happened.

The first time I ever saw her was eight or nine months before the whole thing began, at the Spring Semester's first regular bi-weekly Co-op Board meeting, which I was attending as the elected director from my house, the tiny, seventeen-member Alexander Hall.

The Berkeley Student Cooperative operates a network of student-owned dormitories and apartment buildings around the perimeter of UCB's main campus. It was founded during the Depression to provide low-cost housing to Cal students who couldn't afford to live in either the University dorms or the Greeks. Residents do the bulk of the labor to keep costs down. So, in addition to the room and board fee charged every semester, Co-opers are required to perform five hours of work every week. Most of these chores consist of things like fixing meals, cleaning bathrooms, washing dishes, the sort of scut work that gets done by paid employees at other student housing set-ups.

That semester, I was fulfilling my workshift requirement as a member of the oligarchy. I got three hours of credit for being on the Board of Directors, which required me to attend all board meetings and to serve on one of the board's committees, and another two for being Alexander's house president, which required me to chair all House Council meetings and to represent the house on the Administrative Committee, the "judicial" branch of the BSC. Compared to cleaning out toilets or scrubbing pots and pans, it was kind of an easy gig. But, on the other hand, being a member of the elected bureaucracy often took more time than one of the more unpleasant jobs, so it kind of evened out.

I'd gotten elected more or less by default. Hal Eakin, the guy who'd had both positions before me, had been appointed BSC Vice-President for Financial Affairs, which meant he automatically got five hours of workshift credit. So, one night at dinner, he called an impromptu house council meeting, informed us about his new job and announced that he was resigning as Board rep and prez.

Problem was no one else was interested in the jobs. After Hal's call for candidates was met with a long, awkward silence, I finally volunteered. Hal, however, who rarely sees eye-to-eye with me, wasn't exactly passionate about the idea of my taking over from him.

"Anybody *else* interested?" he said.

No answer.

"Anyone at all?"

More silence.

He shook his head and, with a sigh of weary resignation, pronounced me the winner of the uncontested "election," and told me when and where the next Board and AdCom meetings were.

I'd been doing it a bit more than six months at that point, and was surprised to find that I was enjoying it.

The meeting wasn't due to start for a few minutes, so I was chatting with Sid Eisbach, a law student who was the rep from Northside Apartments, when I spotted her seated on the other side of the meeting room, next to BSC President Ken Robinson.

She was what Raymond Chandler'd once called "a blonde to make a bishop kick a hole in a stained-glass window." Wavy, shoulder-length, golden hair. Not yellow. Not "wheat-colored." Not "sun-bleached." Not even "honey." But pure spun gold, framing a classically beautiful face, and, as I saw when she stood up, topping off a splendidly curvaceous yet slender figure. If it had been an animated cartoon, my jaw would have dropped to the floor and my eyes would have popped out of my head.

"Who is *that*?" I whispered to Sid.

"Yeah, she's scrumptious, isn't she? That's DeeDee Merryweather. Rich's kid sister."

"*That's* Rich Merryweather's sister? Get out of here. She must be adopted."

"Not as far as I know."

"Go figure. A guy who looks like Rich having a sister who

6

looks like that. Is she a Board rep?"

"No, she's going to be the board's AA this semester. I think Chris Bridges got her the job."

The "AA," or administrative assistant, took the minutes of the board meetings. Basically, a fancy, polysyllabic title for "secretary." Although, in these politically correct times, actual professional secretaries apparently prefer to be called "assistants" themselves. I still haven't figured out what's politically incorrect about "secretary." But let that bade.

Chris Bridges was Rivendell's Board rep.

"Well, wasn't that nice of him?" I said. "Once we're married, I'll insist on naming our firstborn after him."

"It's more likely that they'll name their firstborn after you. They're living together."

"Living together?" I said, my crest in rapid freefall.

"That's what I hear. Rich told me they share a room."

Damn! Shot down before I even got in the air. Before I even got out onto the runway.

"Don't feel too bad, Dan," he said. "It wouldn't have worked out anyway."

"Why not?"

"She lives at Rivendell, so she must be a vegetarian. You're a carnivore."

"I'm an omnivore," I corrected. "I could've adapted."

"You'd still be taking a big chance."

"How's that?"

"Well, say it did work out. In a few years, you'd both be out of school and married, right?"

"Yeah, so?"

"So you'd be running the risk of having a bunch of kids who looked like Rich Merryweather."

***

Well, as they say, girls are like buses; if you miss one, there's always another in a few minutes. So I didn't brood too long over my hopeless crush.

She didn't return as AA after that semester, but she'd developed a taste for oligarchy. During the summer session, she'd gotten elected as Rivendell's AdCom rep. I'd moved from Alexander to Roylmann, and gotten elected board rep there. I wasn't Roylmann's regular AdCom rep, as I'd been at Alexander, but, as the board rep, I'd pinch hit for the guy who was now and then, as he would for me at board meetings, so I occasionally saw her there, though we rarely talked about anything except committee business.

But one night, early in the Fall semester, when the AdCom meeting ended unusually early, several of us, including DeeDee, decided to share a pitcher of beer at the North Side La Val's.

The subject turned to police work, as it often does when I'm around. It seems like anytime I'm present at a social gathering of students, someone's sure to bring up some horror story about a cop who did them, or someone they know, or someone they've heard of, some kind of dirt.

This time it was Kevin Webster, a pre-law from Euclid Hall, complaining about a traffic ticket that a highway patrolman had hung on him about a week earlier. After finishing his impassioned tale of personal injustice, he turned and glared at me.

"What?" I said.

"I just thought you might have some comment, *Officer* Sullivan."

"Well, did you signal when you made the lane change?"

"It was a chickenshit ticket!" he insisted.

"So that would be 'no,' then, right?"

"No, I didn't have my turn signal on," he admitted.

"Well, then you can hardly accuse him of overstepping his authority. Anyway, you said he was CHP. We don't work for the same agency. I don't even know the guy. What's it got to do with me?"

"You're in the same line of work."

"Same line of work, huh? Do you have a part-time job?"

"I'm a waiter at Spenger's."

"And how would you feel about being held personally responsible for every waiter who ever gave a customer bad service?"

"It's not the same thing."

"It sure as hell is. There's more than 800,00 cops in this country. It's not up to me to apologize every time one of them screws up any more than it's up to you to apologize for every waiter who ever spilled coffee on a guest. Anyway, it doesn't sound to me like you've got much to complain about. This guy didn't hit you up for a bribe, use excessive force, or even treat you discourteously. He just cited you for something you actually did. In law enforcement circles they call that 'doing your job.'"

DeeDee suddenly said, "Oh, my God! You're the one!"

"The one what?"

"You're the Co-oper who's a cop!"

"Busted."

"That's *so* interesting! I'd heard there was a cop living in one of the Co-ops but I didn't realize it was you. And you're a student, too?"

"I was a student first, actually. I didn't get hired as a cop until after I'd been at Cal a few years."

"Where do you find the time to do everything?"

"I don't work full-time. I'm a reserve officer."

"What's that?" she asked.

"A part-time volunteer. The law enforcement equivalent of a military reservist or a volunteer firefighter. I get professional experience and make enough on paid details to pay my way through school."

"But you do intend to become a full-time policeman after you graduate?"

"Right now that's the plan."

She went on about how *interesting* having a cop living in the Co-ops was, then asked, "If you'd been the one to pull Kevin over would you have given him the ticket?"

"I don't patrol freeways."

"On a city street, then."

"Hypothetically, you mean?"

"Yes."

"Do I still know Kevin personally in this hypothetical situation, or are we hypothetical strangers?"

"Let's say you know him."

"Then probably not."

"Why not?"

"It's just not important enough to make it worth the aggravation."

"But you might arrest Kevin, or some other Co-oper, for something more serious?"

"Like what?" I asked.

"Say you're called to quiet down a party at a Co-op, and there're people smoking dope. Would you arrest them?"

"I doubt it. I might just confiscate the dope and take their names. If there was someone more senior there, and he was ignoring it, I'd probably just follow his lead."

"Suppose you caught someone growing it in his room."

"What the hell am I doing in his room?"

"Suppose that's where the loud party is. Would you arrest him?"

"I'd probably just confiscate the plant and write up a report. Or I'd call for someone more senior to make the decision."

"Suppose you caught him in bed with an underage girl?"

"How underage?"

"Oh, say she's a freshman who graduated early. Say she's fifteen."

"She's only fifteen and she's at Cal?"

"There's a fifteen-year-old freshman living at Cloyne Court," said Kevin. "He's some kind of math prodigy."

"Okay, so I'll grant it's theoretically possible for her to be fifteen. How old is he?"

"Say he's a senior, 21 or 22."

"And how do I know she's only fifteen?"

"You know her personally."

"Well, if I actually saw what you described, I'd arrest him."

"See, now that surprises me... "

"Oh, give me a break! You've spent the last five minutes trying to maneuver me into some bizarre set of circumstances where I'd feel duty-bound to arrest another Co-oper, and when you finally manage to come up with one, you've got the nerve to say you're surprised? The only thing that surprises you is that it took you so long to contrive the right situation."

"Okay, I was trying to steer you into a dilemma," she admitted. "But, just the same, it does surprise me a little."

"Well, what do you think I should do?"

"I don't know. But you said you'd be willing to overlook a minor traffic matter, so there are situations where you'll give a friend a break."

"Cops are only human. And, no matter how objective we try to be, we're just not going to treat family, or friends, or even casual acquaintances the same way we'd treat total strangers. But you've got to draw a line that nobody's allowed to cross. I think you knew that. You were just trying to find out where mine is. Well, now you know. Child molesting is way over it."

"She's not really a child, though."

"She's certainly not an adult. And he is."

"But there's not that much difference in their ages."

"Christ, DeeDee, we're not talking about 28 and 21. We're talking about 22 and fifteen. That's a *huge* difference. A fifteen-year-old is a lot more vulnerable and a lot easier to take advantage of. Especially when she's living away from home for probably the first time in her life, and all the so-called 'peers' she's trying to fit in with are mostly legal adults. That's precisely why they have laws about things like the age of consent."

She looked thoughtful, admitted I had a good point, and charmingly turned the conversation away from law enforcement's inevitable ethical quandaries and towards other, safer subjects. Like politics and religion. After we all finished our second pitcher, we broke up and returned to our respective houses.

That was the closest thing to a personal conversation I'd ever have with DeeDee Merryweather.

A few weeks later, she turned up missing.

THREE

On my way back to the Public Safety Building, I stopped for a red light at University and San Pablo. The car in front of me had its left turn signal on, its driver apparently unaware of the "NO LEFT TURN" signs posted conspicuously at several points on the signal lights.

I flipped on my unit's spotlight, shined it on one of the signs, and hit the horn a couple of times, in an effort to get the driver to notice that he was about to commit a violation, but it didn't work. When the light turned green he turned left.

I really wanted to let it go. I was heading in to the station to sign off-duty, and I was due to meet Stephanie at the Chinese restaurant near the Cal Theatre in less than an hour. I didn't need any delays. But the infraction was just too blatant to ignore. At the very least, I'd have to give him a warning.

I pulled out after him, switched on my overheads and touched off the siren.

***

Stephanie chewed her bite of pizza as though it had personally offended her.

She'd reamed me out good when I'd met her in front of the movie theatre on University Avenue almost an hour late. I'd hoped that her blow-up, and my apology, would resolve the issue. It didn't.

She hadn't said anything during the movie. I could kid myself that this was out of courtesy to the rest of the audience. Nor had she said anything as we walked to the campus shuttle bus stop in front of the Bank of America, nor during the ride to the stop at the base of Cardiac Hill, nor on the walk up to the North Side La

13

Val's, all of which I could kid myself was on account of she hadn't found the movie worth talking about. But, when we got to the restaurant, she'd uttered exactly one word, and that was to the waiter.

He'd asked her for her ID after I'd ordered a pitcher of beer to go with our pizzas. That always happens. Stephanie, who insists on accentuating her petite build by wearing clothes that are way too big for her, looks about twelve. And even when she produces a perfectly valid ID that proves she's over 21, it's scrutinized with singular skepticism.

When she presented her driver's license to this waiter, she'd said, "Here."

That had been the only word she'd allowed out of her mouth since we'd entered the theatre. And for the last fifteen minutes, she'd been furiously chomping on her food while studiously looking in every direction but toward me. There was no longer any way I could kid myself that she wasn't still seething about my being late.

"Steph, there wasn't anything I could do," I said.

She finally looked at me, which I would have regarded as a minor victory of sorts, except that it was more of a glare than a look, then turned away again.

"I apologized when I got there. I explained what happened. What do you want from me?"

"I want you," she said through clenched teeth, "to be on time. This is getting to be a bad habit."

"Okay, those other two times were totally my fault. I shouldn't have gotten my dates mixed up and missed that show in The City, and I shouldn't have lost track of time and missed the beginning of that book signing. But this time it was police business. What was I supposed to do?"

"If you were on your way into the station, why couldn't you have just ignored it?"

"'Cause it happened right in front of me. And I'd tried to alert him before the light turned green. It would have looked bad if I let him get away with it."

"Then why couldn't you have just warned him?"

"That's all I intended to do. But the guy turned out to have 300 dollars in traffic warrants."

"Well, why couldn't you let him go?"

"You can't let a guy with that many warrants just go. I *had* to serve 'em."

"Well, why'd you have to check him for warrants in the first place?"

"C'mon, Steph, that's just basic officer safety. How do I know he's not one of the FBI's Top Ten or something if I don't run him? Anyway, even when he wound up having so many warrants, I thought I'd still be able to get to the theatre in time, but he couldn't make bail, so I had to book him. That's what took so long."

"Why should that take so long? I remember waiting for you at the station just last month when you were booking that shoplifter. That didn't take very long at all. Why should a thief take so much less time than a bad driver?"

"The thief had a record. The bad driver didn't. That meant we had to create one from scratch. We had to take a full set of prints to send to the FBI."

"You have to send a copy to the FBI for a traffic offense?"

"Everybody who gets booked into a jail anywhere in the United States gets a set of his prints filed at the FBI. That's how a cop in New York is able to find out whether a guy has a record in Oregon. We also, for the same reason, have to send a full set of prints to the State Bureau of Identification up in Sacramento, and two full sets to the Central Identification Bureau over at the Sheriff's Office, plus two sets of palm prints for CIB, plus a full set of fingerprints and a set of palm prints for our own records."

"Even so, if you know what you're doing, taking prints shouldn't take that long."

"Maybe not, but then we have to fax a copy of the prints to CIB to make sure he doesn't already have a county record, and making sure someone's *not* in the system takes lot longer than verifying that someone is."

"You could have called."

"I tried, but you'd already left. You don't carry a cell phone, so what was I supposed to do?"

"Don't try to put this back on me for not carrying a cell phone."

"I'm not blaming you for that. I don't have a cell phone, either. I'm only explaining why I couldn't get in touch. How come this is such a major problem, anyway? We got into the movie, didn't we?"

It probably sounds like we're an old married couple, but, actually Steph and I aren't even interested in each other that way. Stephanie Yee and her roommate, Louise Tillman, are probably my two closest friends. Certainly my two closest at Cal. But there's no romance there. Occasionally, I wonder why not. They're both very attractive, after all.

I met them when we all moved into Alexander Hall the same semester, some two years earlier, and discovered that we shared a lot of the same interests. Old movies, crime fiction, and, of course, good food. Though, since Steph and Lou are vegetarians, it's sometimes hard to find a restaurant that accommodates all our tastes.

We got tight pretty quickly, but were perhaps wary of it getting any more serious in as small a place as Alexander. And later, when we'd all moved to the more populous Roylmann Hall, I suppose our relationships were so firmly cemented into "just friends" mode that none of us ever considered altering it. I guess we valued the friendship too much to risk it for the sake of romance. They say men and women can't be just friends, but the three of us manage it.

At the moment, though, the friendship was a bit strained. I couldn't really blame her for being upset. Possessed, though I am, of many sterling qualities, punctuality's not one of them. I was born several weeks late, and Mom says I still haven't caught up.

This time, though, it really wasn't my fault. Besides, I wasn't that late. We still got in to see the movie. We just weren't able to eat dinner ahead of time, so we were having it now. Neither of us had to be up early tomorrow. What was the big deal?

As I tried to think of something to say that would put her in a more forgiving mood, I picked up the pitcher and poured some of the beer into my mug. Or I tried to. Intent on choosing just the right words, I missed the mug completely and poured the beer onto the table.

I stood up and tried to wipe off the tabletop with some of the napkins, finally gave it up as a bad job, and sat back down. Steph fought the smile that was playing across her mouth, but finally lost the battle, and started giggling. Well, at least the deep freeze seemed to be over.

Someone at a nearby table looked up at us, got up from his seat, and started toward us. At first I thought he might be coming over to complain that our argument was disrupting the other customers, though we weren't really being that loud. Then I recognized Sid Eisbach's trademark shock of dark, unruly hair, and equally dark, curly beard, and figured he was just coming over to say hello.

"Hi, Sid," I said. "Do you know Stephanie Yee?" To Steph I said, "Sid's the Board rep from Northside Apartments."

"How are you, Sid?" she said.

"Fine," he replied. "It's nice to meet you." Turning back to me he said, "Do you know anything about DeeDee?"

"DeeDee Merryweather? Just that she's not available. But I've gotten over it."

"You mean you haven't heard?"

"Heard what?"

"No one's seen her for days. Some of the other Rivendell residents finally reported it to the police. I thought you might know something."

"First I've heard about it," I said. "How long has she been missing?"

"Three days."

"Who made the report?"

"I think Harry Mitchell and Joanne Ward. They're Rivendell's house manager and house president."

"Why didn't Chris make the report? Seems like he'd be the first one to notice she was gone. They are still living together, aren't they?"

"I heard they had a fight. He probably figured she'd gone home for a few days."

"Where's home?" asked Steph.

"Some 'burb on the Peninsula," said Sid. "Atherton or Menlo Park, I think."

"Well, why didn't he try to call her, just to make sure she was okay?" she said.

He shrugged. "I don't know," he said. "To be honest, I don't even know for sure that they had a fight. That's just what I heard."

Steph turned to me. "Will you be involved in this?"

"Why would I be involved? I didn't even know there was

anything to be involved with 'til Sid asked me about it. Anyway, I'm only a reserve cop."

"So?"

"So reserves don't handle missing persons cases. That's Homicide. Well, it's Crimes Against Persons, which includes homicides."

"Why Crime Against Persons?" asked Sid. "She's missing, not dead."

"Well, now that I think about it, I'm not absolutely sure it is CAP, but BPD hasn't got a Missing Persons Detail, so I think CAP gets it by default. Gives 'em a running start if it turns out she's been murdered or kidnapped or something."

"Why wouldn't you have anything to do with it, though?" asked Steph. "They had a bunch of reserves on that 'Stench' rape case a few months ago, including you."

"That was a surveillance detail. They needed a whole lot of manpower to cover it. What kind of massive surveillance you figure they're going to need on a missing persons case? If she doesn't turn up in the next few days, the closest I'll get to having anything to do with it will be listening to updates and BOLO's at the watch briefings."

Sid looked puzzled. "Bolos?" he said.

"It's an acronym for 'Be On the Look Out,'" said Steph. "Hang around this guy long enough and you'll get to be a real expert on police jargon. For example, you might think we're eating pizzas, right now. But what we're actually doing is 'taking a Code Seven.' Have I got that right, Dan?"

"Strictly speaking," I said, "'Code Seven' is just a meal break, not the actual meal itself."

"A meaningless distinction," she insisted.

"Anyway," Sid said, bringing us back to the original subject, "you don't think it's likely you'll have much to do with the investigation?"

"Not a chance. Maybe I'll hear some stuff around the station just before it's made public, but that's about it."

FOUR

For the first week or two following DeeDee's disappearance, I was right. I knew no more about the progress of the investigation than any other Cal student. On the other hand, everybody who knew I worked for the police department assumed I had the inside skinny and turned to me as the resident expert every time the case came up in conversation.

And it came up a lot.

Classes, board meetings, committee meetings, meals. Any place two or more students got together, DeeDee's disappearance was the most popular conversational topic, and if I was there, someone would inevitably ask how was the investigation going? What leads had been developed? How come they hadn't found her yet? Didn't I know *anything*?

It was getting to be a little embarrassing to admit that I knew no more about it than they did. But that was the truth. I had absolutely no role in the case as a cop. Part-time volunteers don't conduct major investigations. Full-time detectives do. And, as a student, my role was pretty much the same as everyone else's. Worrying and expressing concern.

And the more time that went by without any word, the higher the level of worry and concern. Everyone seemed to realize, without it being spelled out, that the longer it took to find her, the greater the likelihood that she'd never be found.

Or never be found alive.

At work there hadn't been any new information since the initial description had been read off at the shift briefings. Nor was there a lot of scuttlebutt around the station. The dicks were following whatever leads they had and, presumably, if there was anything to pass on to Patrol, they'd pass it on.

So, I went through my regular routine, patrolling beats,

directing traffic at football games, taking reports, and making the occasional minor arrest. The investigation affected my professional life (well, let's be honest, my *semi*-professional life) very little.

It was in my life as a student that I couldn't seem to escape the subject. Go to a class, whether the subject was American Literature or Philosophy of Government, and someone brought up DeeDee.

"Finding her isn't a priority because she's a woman," someone would say.

"The police are expending all this energy because she's a blonde white woman," another would counter.

Some thought she'd just run away because the pressure of school had been too much, and others that she'd been romantically swept away by a new love. The usual collection of whackos insisted she'd been abducted by extra-terrestrials. Still others suggested that she'd developed amnesia and was wandering aimlessly trying to find some clue to her own identity. Every soap opera cliché that might explain her being missing was trotted out. Every wielder of a left-wing political ax, and there's no shortage of those in Berkeley, used her disappearance as a grinding stone.

Late one night, in Roylmann's living room, Steph, Louise, and I were seated by the TV looking at an old movie on cable.

Gathered around a six-pack of Henry Weinhard's Private Reserve and a freshly made bowl of buttered popcorn, we were watching an early '60's black and white private eye flick called *The Girl Hunters*, with Mickey Spillane playing his own detective character, Mike Hammer. The plot involved Hammer's sudden climb out of the gutter he's been wallowing in since his secretary's (excuse me, his *assistant's*) disappearance, and presumed murder, years earlier. Fruitlessly trying to drown her memory in alcohol, Hammer suddenly receives information that she might still be alive, and sobers up almost overnight to become the invincible super-sleuth of old. Cheaply made, but surprisingly effective, I'd have enjoyed it if the plot hadn't involved a missing woman.

I was a bit surprised that Steph and Lou, both staunchly ultra-left feminists, had been willing to look at anything involving Spillane. In fact, I'd expected to have to do a little arm-twisting to get them both to watch, but, apparently, just the fact that it was an old crime movie was enough to overcome their political sensibilities.

After remarking that she preferred Stacy Keach to Spillane, a comparison that shocked the hell out of me, not because I necessarily disagreed with it, but because it indicated that Spillane's was not the only Hammer performance with which she was familiar, Stephanie nudged me and asked, "In real life, how likely is it that anyone would still be alive after all that time?"

I swallowed a mouthful of popcorn and washed it down with a pull of beer. "Pretty damned *un*likely," I answered, "unless she went missing voluntarily."

"Why's that?" asked Lou.

"Well, if it isn't voluntary, then she's gone missing because of a criminal act, which makes it either homicide or kidnapping. If it's homicide, then, obviously, the missing person's dead from the start."

"Obviously," she agreed.

"Which leaves kidnapping. And if it's kidnapping, then the responsible only got three options, let the victim go, keep the victim a prisoner forever, or kill the victim. Now what happens if you let the victim go?"

"I guess you're taking a chance that she'll be able to identify you."

"Exactly. And what do you think is going to happen if you try to keep her a prisoner for the rest her life?"

"You'll probably get caught, eventually," said Steph.

"Correct, again. So what does that leave?"

"Kill the victim and hide the body," said Lou. "So you don't think DeeDee's still alive."

"I figured that was what you were probably getting at. I certainly hope DeeDee's still alive. I've got no reason to think she isn't."

"But you just said that if she was a crime victim she was most likely dead."

"In the first place, I wasn't talking specifically about DeeDee. I was talking about a hypothetical crime victim. In the second place, we don't know that DeeDee is a crime victim. She may have left voluntarily."

"Do you really think she left on her own?"

"It's very possible. Most missing persons actually do turn out to have left of their own free will."

"A lot of them turn up dead, though, right?"
"Yeah," I said. "I guess a lot of 'em do."

FIVE

The following Tuesday, I attended a Personnel and Operations Committee meeting at Hoyt Hall. Eileen Roberts, the BSC Vice-President for Operations, ran the meeting. As Operations VP she was POpCom's *ex officio* chairperson.

Besides me, the only other members of the committee in attendance were Sid Eisbach and Chris Bridges. I was surprised that Chris came. He regularly served on POpCom, but I'd just assumed he'd withdraw from public view for a while, at least 'til the excitement from DeeDee's disappearance had died down. He was being enormously dutiful.

Or maybe he didn't really care about DeeDee's disappearance all that much.

Eileen called the meeting to order. With only three members and the chair present, about as much of a turnout as POpCom usually musters, we took care of business fairly quickly. Chris contributed to the meeting in a business-like manner, displaying no signs of emotional turmoil. To me he didn't seem like a lover whose girlfriend had suddenly dropped out of sight, but then it's never happened to me. How did I know what a normal reaction was to such a circumstance?

During a break, I approached Chris.

"You feeling okay?" I asked.

He nodded, not looking at me, intent on the written agenda in front of him, though we'd already dealt with the issue on that page.

"Anything any of us can do."

He looked up finally, and shook his head. "Nothing," he said. He sounded a bit curt. I don't think he meant to, and he must have noticed how he sounded. He added, in a softer tone, "Really, there's nothing anyone can do right now. But thanks for asking."

Eileen and Sid made similar overtures of sympathy which were

JIM DOHERTY

similarly, if not exactly rebuffed, at least not particularly welcomed. Maybe he was signaling that he didn't really want to talk about it, that he wanted to go on about his life normally.

Or, again, maybe he just didn't care that much.

***

After the meeting, Sid invited me up to his place for a beer. He lived in a one-bedroom in the Co-op's Northside Apartments on LeConte, and he apparently had enough seniority that he was able to get it solo.

"How do you rate a one-bedroom of your own?" I asked, looking around the place and feeling envious.

"I'm a second-year law student, and I've been in the Co-ops since I was a freshman. That's more than five years-worth of points."

You get seniority points for every semester you live in one of the Co-op's properties, and a half-point for every summer you spend in one. Your chances of getting assigned to your first choice in Co-ops, and of getting your first choice of rooms once you're in that Co-op, depend on the number of points you've accrued.

"Well, I certainly like the way you've decorated the place. Early nothing."

Sid chuckled and went to his fridge, and pulled out a couple of bottles of Henry Weinhard's. Good. His taste in beer coincided with mine.

"What'd you think of the meeting tonight?" he asked, handing me one of the beers.

"Not as boring as it could be. But that's not what you mean, is it?"

"Well, weren't you surprised Bridges was there?"

"A little, but maybe he's trying to live a normal life, trying to meet his obligations."

"Didn't his attitude seem odd to you?"

"You mean that he wasn't pulling his hair out and weeping all over the place? Maybe keeping it all in is how he's dealing with it."

"Do you really believe that?"

"Well, I sure don't disbelieve it."

24

"But put it together with other things, doesn't it seem suspicious?"

I took a pull on the Henry's and asked, "What other things?"

"What was the first thing you asked when I told you about DeeDee's disappearance last week? You asked why Bridges wasn't the one to report her missing. Well, why wasn't he? Maybe because he already knows where she is."

"Is that what you think?"

"I want to know what you think."

I took another swallow. "Okay, when was the last time she was seen?"

"She and Bridges went up to the Fire Trail to take a run. Bridges came back alone, went straight to their room, and stayed there the rest of the day. Didn't even come out for dinner."

"How do you know all this?"

"I talked to Harry Mitchell about it," he said. "He told me nobody saw Bridges 'til the next morning. According to Bridges, he and DeeDee had a fight up on the trail. He walked off and came back to Rivendell. Nobody's seen her since."

"So you suspect that DeeDee's dead and Chris killed her?"

"Pretty much," he said.

"And, since I'm the law enforcement official with whom you're best-acquainted, you naturally came to me to validate your suspicions?"

"Naturally."

"Well, if she's dead, then most likely she was murdered. And, statistically, you know who most murder victims are killed by, don't you?"

"The people they're romantically involved with."

"Exactly. Wives are killed by husbands and husbands by wives. Girlfriends are killed by boyfriends and boyfriends by girlfriends. Gay and lesbian lovers kill each other. The statistics vary a little, but, all other things being equal, a plus one in the victim's life will get a very close look."

"That's just what I was thinking."

"Then you add in the fact that Chris was the last person to see her alive. Statistically, the last person to see a murder victim alive is also a very likely suspect. And if the last person to see the victim alive is his or her significant other, the odds go way up."

"And he admits they were arguing," he said.

"That ratchets up the probability factors, too."

"So you're saying you think he killed her?"

"No, I'm saying nothing of the sort. What I'm saying is that, if she has been murdered, then Bridges..."

"Yeah?"

"Well, let's just say that's the way the smart money would bet. The thing is there's a whole lot of 'ifs' in that analysis. 'If she didn't leave of her own volition,' and 'if she's dead,' and 'if the death was murder,' and 'if Chris really was the last to see her alive,' and 'if a whole lot of other things we haven't even considered.' And then, it's still nothing but statistical probability. Hell, you're the law student. How much trouble would even a half-ass lawyer have shrouding that in reasonable doubt?"

"Not much," he admitted. "But there's more."

"Like what?"

"Like Bridges' temper."

"First I ever heard of it."

"You weren't at that picnic retreat thing up in Tilden last summer, were you?"

"I was working that weekend."

"Well, Bridges and DeeDee were playing two-on-two volley ball at one point. Now DeeDee was a pretty athletic girl, and Bridges has always been something of a jock." I noticed that he was already referring to DeeDee in the past tense.

He went on, "But the two people they were playing against, Schroeder and Brandon from Rochdale? They play competitively, and Bridges and DeeDee really weren't any kind of a match for them. Every time DeeDee missed a serve or a return, Bridges tore into her like the wrath of God. It was just a dumb volleyball game at a picnic, but he reamed her out for every mistake she made."

"So he's competitive. So am I. So are you, for that matter. Every time you get into a debate at Board meetings, you act like finding the cure for cancer hangs on your winning the point."

"Yeah, but I've never dressed down my girlfriend in public if I lost. It was really nasty to watch. Schroeder tried to get him to calm down and Bridges took a swing at him. Three other guys had to pull him away. It was scary. And all over a game."

"Okay, so it's another piece of evidence on the scale. It's still not conclusive."

"Well, do you think your detectives know about it?"

"Probably. But if they don't, I'll pass it along next time I'm on duty, just to make sure. Now can we find something else, *anything* else, to talk about?"

SIX

I was conscious of not wanting to appear to be the stereotypical, eager-beaver reserve cop, inserting himself into a high-profile case and getting in the way of the pros. So, instead of going directly to CAP with Sid's info, I scrupulously followed the chain of command and reported it to my boss, Sergeant Fred Cutter, the Director of the Police Reserve. He, presumably, passed it on to the Detective Division. If the dicks wanted more information, they'd seek me out.

A couple of days after the POpCom meeting, Chris Bridges' temper became a moot point, superfluous to the investigation.

There had been a pretty massive publicity blitz in the wake of DeeDee's disappearance. Photos on the front pages of the San Francisco and Oakland dailies with "Have you seen this girl?" captions. Radio bulletins. Distraught family members crying for the cameras on the six o'clock news. And all of them mentioned the date and time she'd last been seen, Friday afternoon, September 12th.

When Mrs. Alice Taylor, who'd spent the last two weeks out of town, came back to find the publicity machine still operating full blast, it sparked a memory.

She'd been driving along Grizzly Peak Road, a short distance from the Fire Trail, on the same day DeeDee vanished. She'd passed a blue van parked at the side of the road, overlooking the hill. Spots like this on Grizzly Peak are popular places to park because of the spectacular view of the San Francisco Bay.

A heavyset man with dark, curly hair and a full beard, was standing outside the van, embracing a young blonde woman dressed in a t-shirt, gym shorts, and running shoes, who seemed to be trying to wriggle out of his grasp. She described the young woman as "extremely attractive," and said she seemed to be about

29

the same height and build as DeeDee Merryweather. Shown a picture of DeeDee, she said that "it certainly looked like the same girl." And, after all, how many extremely attractive blonde girls, dressed exactly the same way as DeeDee could there be in that same vicinity at roughly the same time?

Mrs. Taylor hadn't really thought anything bad was going on. Just a guy trying to make a pitch to his girl at a romantic parking spot. But in light of what she now knew about DeeDee's disappearance, the incident she'd blithely driven past took on a far more sinister aspect.

On the basis of Mrs. Taylor's statement, CAP's theory of the case became that DeeDee had been abducted by a sexual predator.

It gave the case a direction to go. It also got Chris Bridges off the hook.

***

All this was in the papers and on the local TV and radio news the day after Mrs. Taylor made the report. And, as expected, the new report fueled new speculation on DeeDee's fate.

It struck me as just a little odd that DeeDee had managed to travel as far as she had. Though they look close on the map, Grizzly Peak really isn't within easy walking distance of the Fire Trail.

Well, maybe the guy stopped to give her a ride after she'd had the fight with Chris, or maybe she'd decided to take a more rugged run, to work off some of the stress and anger of the fight, and had wound up at the top of the hill. It didn't really matter. She'd gotten up on Grizzly Peak somehow.

***

"Do you think they'll find her?" asked Lou that night.

She, Steph, and I were sharing a table in the Roylmann dining room. Most of the other residents had already finished eating dinner, so we had the table, indeed almost the whole dining room, to ourselves.

"DeeDee, you mean?" I asked.

"Of course DeeDee. Who else would I be asking about?"

"Hard to say," I muttered, looking intently at my plate. I'd hoped I'd be able to get through one meal without the subject coming up.

"Well, you're kind of an expert on these types of criminals," said Steph.

"Expert? How do you figure *I'm* an expert?"

"You were on that 'Stench' case."

"Still unsolved."

"The rapes have stopped, so you must have done something right."

Yeah. Or something wrong. But that's another story.

"And there was that child molester who kidnapped the little girl," she went on.

"That wasn't detective work," I said. "I just stumbled onto the guy while I was out on patrol. That hardly makes me an ace profiler."

"It does compared to us," said Lou. "Just tell us if you think this guy still has her alive somewhere."

"It depends, I guess."

"Depends on what?"

"Well, I guess it's possible he might keep her alive as long as she continues to excite him. But if he gets tired of her, or thinks the risk is greater than the reward, he'd probably kill her and go out looking for someone else."

"Excites him?" said Lou.

I wasn't really comfortable talking about this to two women, even if they were close friends. "You know what I mean," I said. "Excites him sexually."

"So you think it's about the sex?"

"Of course it's about the sex. Do you really think he grabbed up a luscious blonde babe because she just happened to be the most convenient victim?"

"Haven't you ever heard of a case of someone being kept prisoner for longer than just a short time?"

"Kids sometimes. Kids can be controlled more easily."

"Never an adult?"

"There was a girl named Colleen Stan who got kidnapped by some bondage freak back in the '70's. He kept her imprisoned for almost seven years. And there was that scumbag in Cleveland.

What was his name, Castro? Managed to keep three girls prisoners in his house for more than ten years. But those were really unusual cases. Almost unique. Most of the time, the victims don't survive."

"So you don't think DeeDee Merryweather's still alive?" asked Steph.

"No I don't. At least, not if she was forced to go against her will."

"That's terrible," said Lou.

"It's not that much less terrible if she's still alive. Would you want her going through the same thing Colleen Stan did?"

"Of course not," said Lou. "But at least if she's alive there's still hope."

I couldn't argue with that.

Steph asked if I was likely to get involved in the case, now.

"Why would I? This is straight investigation. There's no undercover work or surveillance. It's just going to be a case of following up leads, knocking on doors, and interviewing people. I keep telling you, reserves don't do that."

SEVEN

I walked into the Reserve Office the next day, and went up to the duty roster to sign in. Unlike full-time cops, reserves are legally police officers only when they're actually on duty. Off-duty, at least theoretically, we're the same as any other civilian. The official line of demarcation between being on duty and off-duty is a set of initials on that roster. Sign in and you're a cop. Sign out and you revert to ordinary citizen.

It's not really as simple as that. If you're running late, and you forget to sign in, and you go out on the street in uniform for a tour of four hours or a full shift of eight, you haven't been operating illegally. It's just that Sergeant Cutter likes us to observe the niceties.

After I'd signed in, Sergeant Cutter, seated at his desk, beckoned me over.

"Got a minute?" he asked.

"Sure," I said, taking a seat opposite him.

"Be interested in working up at CAP one or two nights a week?"

"Hell, yeah," I answered. "What's it about?"

"The Merryweather girl. CAP's getting swamped with phone calls since the story broke about her trying to fight off that guy up on Grizzly Peak. They can't keep up with them all."

I didn't like where this was going too much.

"And at night," he went on, "when there's nobody in the office, the answering machines fill up the first hour, and a lot of the people who can't get through are calling 911, which ties up the Comm Center when they're supposed to be responding to emergency calls."

"So basically you want me to be a receptionist."

"Essentially," he admitted. "The chief thought a couple of

reserves up in CAP evenings and weekends might take some of the pressure off. And it's better PR if we publicly announce that a cop's answering the calls instead of a civilian employee."

"Well, it ain't exactly *Dirty Harry* or *LA Confidential*, is it? Just kidding, Sarge, I'll be happy to help out any way I can."

It wasn't the big-time but, someday, listing an assignment to CAP would look damned good on a résumé. I wouldn't have to specify that all I'd done was shag phone calls.

"I don't suppose it's a paid detail?" I asked.

"No. That was another reason the Chief thought it would be a good idea to use reserves."

"Well, I'm tied up Tuesday nights with Co-op stuff, and I need to keep the weekends free for football games and Marina shifts. But count me in the rest of the week."

"Thanks, Dan," said Cutter. "Believe it or not, the Chief Nolan asked for you especially."

"Yeah, right."

"He was impressed with the work you did on the 'Stench' detail."

"That's still an open case."

"But you developed the best suspect. And when he wound up feeding fishes the series stopped. So for practical purposes the case is closed, whatever the official line is."

"Well, I can see where that would make me particularly well-qualified to answer phones."

"There's more to it than that. You've got to ask the right questions, draw out whoever's calling, and make sure he's actually given you the information he's trying to impart. There are some regular cops who can't interview witnesses competently, let alone reserves, but you can. It shows in your reports."

"You don't have to sell me, Sarge. I said I'd do it. Just don't try to convince me that the Chief thinks I'm Sherlock Holmes, 'cause we both know that's bullshit."

Several months earlier, a serial rapist the press dubbed "Stench," on account of several of his victims saying he had an obnoxious body odor, had been attacking women in a North Side neighborhood. There hadn't been a discernible pattern to the attacks. The Chief had gotten annoyed when I'd successfully predicted when the next rape in the series would occur, something nobody else, from the Department's most experienced sex crimes investigators to a computer programmer over in The City, had been able to do.

The day after my prediction came true, I was called into the Chief's office for a little Star Chamber session. He hadn't struck me as favorably impressed. Just pissed off. He hadn't liked my explanation of how I'd figured out the pattern. Most of all, he hadn't liked it that, here I was a lowly reserve, and here he was, the big-shot LAPD brass hat come to show us college town dweebs how a police force should be run, and I wasn't acting intimidated.

That interview sent brass plummeting to the bottom of my list of favorite metals.

The Chief's misgivings notwithstanding, a suspect, a very strong suspect, was developed based on my theory. Later, when he'd gotten himself killed, the investigation stalled. Though there wasn't enough evidence to definitely name the suspect as the rapist, the rapes had stopped.

"He really was impressed, Dan," said Cutter. "Said he particularly wanted you on this detail."

Well, maybe he'd come to appreciate solid results. And maybe he just thought I couldn't do that much harm stuck in an office. In any case, I was assigned to CAP, at least on a part-time basis, and I found I kind of liked the idea.

***

"So basically you're just going to be a receptionist with a badge and a gun," said Steph at breakfast the next morning.

"Well, that hasn't been lost on me, but you're the one who's been hoping I'd get involved in the investigation. Well, now I'm involved."

"Yeah, but I thought you'd be doing actual investigating."

"Like I told you before, they've already got actual detectives for that. Maybe, if I'm there, a key tip will get reported that might have slipped through the cracks otherwise. Wouldn't that be a valuable contribution?"

"I suppose."

"Then why are you acting so disappointed? They're just not going to make me the lead investigator on this thing. And, what's more, they shouldn't. I'm lucky to get any kind of role at all."

What was probably bugging her, at least subliminally, was that there wasn't any role for *her*. During the Stench case, she'd made an off-hand suggestion that led me to figure out how Stench had been picking which nights he'd hit. She'd had a bit of a Nancy Drew complex ever since.

Fielding phone calls didn't fuel her crime-solving fantasies. It was scout work. It was to law enforcement what scrubbing floors and cleaning bathrooms was to living in the Co-ops, necessary but unglamorous drudgery.

But, hell, if she'd read more of the cop autobiographies I collected, and less Sayers and Christie, she'd know that most cases are solved by applied drudgery, not by inspired brilliance.

And every now and then applied drudgery points the way to inspired brilliance.

EIGHT

I worked the CAP phone assignment the following Monday evening. As expected, it was dull, stultifying dull, work.

A typical phone tip went like this. Someone would call in and tell me that he'd seen a blue van on the freeway.

"Which freeway?" I'd ask.

"I don't remember. One of those freeways leading up to the bridge."

"Which bridge?"

"The one that crosses the Bay."

"They all cross the Bay, sir. Was it the Oakland Bay Bridge or the Richmond Bridge, or one of the others?"

"Which one goes through the island with the tunnel through it?"

"The Oakland Bay Bridge?"

"I guess."

"And you say it was one of the freeways leading to that bridge?"

"Yeah."

"But you don't know exactly which one it was?"

"Nah, I don't really remember."

"Did you see what kind of van it was?" I'd ask.

"What do you mean, 'what kind?' It was a van."

"I mean was it a Ford or a Dodge or a Chevrolet?"

"Oh, I don't know."

"Well, did you get the license number?"

"No, I didn't see that."

"Did you see the driver?"

"Didn't notice who was driving. I just noticed the blue van."

"When was this?"

"Two weeks ago."

You think I'm exaggerating? Not a bit. Most of the calls I got were just about that useful. No wonder they didn't want to tie up real detectives with this chickenshit. Hell, they didn't even want to tie up civilian employees. Why should they when there was a whole long line of reserve cops eager and willing to put up with it, free of charge, just to be able to say they'd been assigned to CAP?

And I was at the front of the line.

***

The Tuesday afternoon following my exciting new assignment, I went to a second-floor classroom in Wheeler Hall for my "Male Roles in Society" class. I was running late. My previous class was scheduled to end at the same time the "Male Roles" class was scheduled to begin, and the buildings they're held in were far enough apart that I always had to sprint to make it.

I've got no one to blame but myself for Tuesdays being so crowded. I try, if I can, to schedule my classes for Tuesdays and Thursdays, so I can have Mondays, Wednesdays, and Fridays off. Since I don't carry a full load (which means it'll probably take me seven years to get my damned degree instead of the usual four) that's not as difficult as it sounds, but it makes for a long class day. In addition to the classes, I've got either a Board meeting or a Personnel and Op Committee meeting every Tuesday.

Roylmann's a bigger house than Alexander, with a larger pool of work shift hours, so being Board rep there earned me credit for a full five hours instead of the three I'd previously gotten at Alexander. That meant I didn't have to make up the other two by going to AdCom meetings or presiding over the House Council. Still, it made for a hectic Tuesday.

The two-hour "Male Roles" class was listed as a lecture section rather than a discussion section, but, in practice, it was a back-and-forth discussion. The chairs were all arranged around the classroom in a rough circle, so that we all faced each other, rather than in rows. Professor Gottfried mostly just steered the course of the conversation instead of actually lecturing.

On that particular day, however, the professor was absent, replaced by a guest lecturer named Dorothy Remsberg, who was some kind of anti-rape activist.

Women, by and large, aren't rapists, and, this being a class on male roles, I figured men were about to take it on the chin. You know, one of those statistical sleights-of-hand in which someone proves that since 99.999999 percent of all rapists are males, then 99.999999 percent of all males must be rapists.

Actually, given my expectations, Ms. Remsberg was pretty even-handed. She spoke briefly at the beginning of the class, describing herself as a psychological counselor who worked with rape victims (she called them "rape survivors"), talked a bit about her organization, East Bay Women Against Sex Crimes, and listed some of the preconceptions about sex crimes that still persist despite the increase in public awareness.

She did not suggest that all men were rapists, as I'd been a little afraid she would, though that still seemed like the inevitable conclusion one had to reach when a class session of a course on male roles is devoted to rape.

After talking for about ten minutes, she opened up the floor to questions and discussion.

"You've talked about how violent rape is," said one woman student. "But lots of women fantasize about rape, don't they?"

"Of course."

"Why would a woman fantasize about something that's so awful?"

"A woman's rape fantasies aren't really about rape. They're more along the lines of 'Leonardo DeCaprio refuses to take no for an answer.' But the woman's still in control, because it's her fantasy. In real life, rape is about the loss of control."

"So from the rapist's standpoint," asked another woman, "it's not about sex it's about control."

"Control, violence, and hostility to be precise. Sex plays no real part in it."

Ah! The Gospel According to Susan Brownmiller. Though I've never been persuaded to adopt that particular Faith, I decided not to respond. But poker's never been my game, and my disagreement apparently showed.

She looked at me and said, "You don't accept that?"

"I didn't say anything."

"No, you didn't. But the expression on your face makes it clear that you don't agree. Do you think rape's *not* a crime of violence?"

"Of course it's a crime of violence. And hostility. And control. Just like you said. But you specifically added that rape wasn't about sex. And from the rapist's point of view, I think that, more often than not, sex is exactly what it's about."

"Are you saying that you believe that rapes occur because rapists are just unable to restrain their sex drive?" she asked. There seemed to be just a hint of sarcasm there, but, feeling defensive as I did, I might have imagined it.

"No, I think, for the most part, they can restrain it just fine. They just choose not to. What I *am* saying is that, just because it's about violence and hostility, doesn't mean it's not also about sex."

"I don't think you're seeing the point."

"No, ma'am, you're not seeing the point. I think we can all agree that rape's not about love. But it sure as hell *is* about sex. If it was just about violence, if it was just about intimidating and controlling somebody weaker, the criminal could cave in some old man's head with a lead pipe. Instead he specifically picks out a woman. And what does he force her to do? Have sex."

"But he's using the sex as a weapon."

"Sex used as a weapon is still sex. And saying sex has nothing to do with rape is ignoring the obvious."

"But that puts it back on the woman," said another student.

"How does it do that?" I asked.

"All that stuff about how she brought it on herself by the way she was dressed, or by being out alone at night, or something, and giving somebody who just wanted sex an opportunity."

"Okay, let me make this clear. A woman's got an absolute right not to be raped. Dressing a certain way, or being out after a certain time, doesn't mean she's waived that right, any more than leaving your car unlocked and your keys in the ignition means you've given up your right not to have your car stolen."

"Well," said another student, "I think leaving your car keys in the ignition of an unlocked car is just stupid."

"It's certainly ill-advised," I agreed, "but it doesn't give a criminal the right to make you a victim by stealing your property. It does make it easier for him to victimize you, but that's another subject."

"Then what exactly are you talking about if it's not the victim's behavior?" asked Ms. Remsberg.

"I'm talking about what motivates the criminal. I mean, look, we do call them *sex* crimes, after all. We call the people who commit them *sex* offenders. Yet we're supposed to believe that sexual desire has nothing to do with it? That's like saying greed has nothing to do with theft. Jesus, Mary, and Joseph, how's he supposed to get hard enough to actually complete the crime, if he's not turned on? Saying it's not about sex is nothing but a lot of politically correct bullshit that just defies common sense. Susan Brownmiller and *Against Our Wills*, notwithstanding."

Ms. Remsberg looked surprised by my last comment. Apparently, she hadn't expected me to be familiar with Ms. Brownmiller's book.

Another woman, a short, dark-haired zealot who invoked Marx or Che or Mao every time she was recognized, got the floor and went into a tirade about rape being a politically motivated plot by men to keep women in their place, and marriage was just institutionalized rape, and all sex with men was a form of rape whether the woman thought she was consenting or not.

She broke off her tirade for a moment, and turned to me and said, "What have you got to say about that?"

"Why do you ask?"

"I was responding to what you said. I'm giving you a chance to respond to what I said."

"It wasn't really clear to me what anything you said had to do with my original point."

"You were talking about what motivates the man," she said. I noticed she referred to the hypothetical predator as "the man," not "the rapist" or "the attacker."

"Yeah."

"Well, my point is that men are motivated by their desire to keep women down, that's all. It's all political. I'm giving you a chance to respond in the spirit of a free exchange of ideas."

"Well, since you insist on a response, I don't think you're really interested in the free exchange of ideas. I think you're interested in using this class period as a forum for *your* ideas, and, no offense meant, but I already get a bellyful of leftist rhetoric every single day just living in this town and going to this school. You want to sound off, go right ahead. I won't say a thing to stop you. But, if it's all the same to you, I'll just politely not participate."

The leftist student (which, now that I think about it, is almost, if not quite, a redundant phrase at Cal) muttered something about male hierarchical privilege being an outmoded paradigm and some other stuff about class warfare, but ran out of steam when her comments failed to generate much response from the rest of the class, either positive or negative. Before relinquishing the floor she brought up a new subject.

"We've talked about women's rape fantasies," she said. "I want to hear what kind of rape fantasies you men have."

I kept my mouth resolutely shut on that one, too, if you don't count exasperated muttering under my breath. But a couple of the other guys bit and sheepishly described theirs.

"I don't really *hurt* the girl," one guy said. "It's just like it's a *game*, see, and, she won't admit it out loud, but we're *both* enjoying it."

The other guy said something similar. I was trying to look neutral, but, as I said, I've got a lousy poker face which is why I don't play cards much. I must have rolled my eyes, because Ms. Lefty turned toward me and said, "I suppose you don't even *have* rape fantasies?"

"Fantasies where I rape a woman, you mean?"

"Yeah."

"That's right. I don't."

"C'mon, *all* men dream about taking a woman by force. All *straight* men, anyway," she added, her eyes softening as she looked at the gay men in the class.

"I don't," I repeated.

"I think this gentleman's probably telling the truth," said Ms. Remsberg. "My guess is he doesn't have rape fantasies. He has rescue fantasies."

"What do you mean?" asked Lefty.

"He doesn't fantasize about attacking women. He fantasizes about saving women from being attacked."

I didn't say anything. The fact was, however, that she'd hit uncomfortably close to the mark.

"I'm correct, aren't I?" she insisted.

"I'd just as soon my private fantasies stayed private, if you don't mind," I said.

She nodded, and let the subject drop. Instead she picked up my original point.

"His fantasies aside, he makes a good argument for the position that sex crimes are motivated, in part, by feelings of sexual desire. And if we look at some of the more famous sexual predators, there's evidence to support his point. Ted Bundy's victims, for example, were not only all very attractive, but all fit into a very specific physical type, right down to the way they wore their hair. And the young woman who was kidnapped a few weeks ago, DeeDee Merryweather, was also a very beautiful young woman. Do you think maybe there's some merit in his point?"

I wished she hadn't have brought up DeeDee. Sure enough, as soon as she was mentioned, the floodgates were opened, and everyone was talking at once about what must have happened to her.

"She must be dead by now."

"He's still keeping her prisoner."

"They're out of the country."

"I heard the guy's a procurer for a white-slave ring, and she was sold for several million dollars."

And, inevitably, "The police aren't doing enough to find her."

It just goes to show you how much her disappearance had infected the whole community. It was always there, lurking under the surface, and if you scratched it just a little, it erupted like a bad rash.

The comment about lack of adequate police response brought a question from Ms. Remsberg.

"What would you have the police do that they're not doing?"

"I don't know," said the person who made the complaint. "But everyone knows the police aren't sympathetic to crimes against women."

"I've been a rape counselor for years," Ms. Remsberg replied, "and I certainly don't know anything of the sort."

"But I've always heard about cops being uncaring when they're dealing with rape victims or battered wives or other female victims."

"Police officers deal with a lot of heartache, and they do tend to shut themselves up emotionally. And the worse the crime, the more they shut themselves up. It's a syndrome I know well. Rape counselors can be the same way. It's a defense mechanism, a way of coping with the ugliness. But it doesn't mean we're not sympathetic."

"So you think they're doing everything they can?"

"I'm sure they're trying to, but I have no idea of precisely what steps they're taking." She looked at me again. "This gentleman might know, though."

The rest of the class turned toward me.

"You're a cop?" Lefty asked.

Now I know how a closeted gay man feels when he's been outed. Understand, I'm not the least bit ashamed of being a cop. I'm damned proud of it. I just don't like it becoming an issue. And in a class like "Male Roles in Society" it was bound to.

"You are, aren't you?" asked Ms. Remsberg.

"Well, yeah," I said. "I am actually. But I'm a uniformed cop, not a detective. I can tell you that the Department takes DeeDee's case very seriously, but I don't know too many more precise details about the investigation than any of you." Strictly speaking that wasn't altogether true anymore, so after a pause, I continued, "I can tell you that the Department's assigned several extra officers to work exclusively on the case."

That those officers were all unpaid reserves, whose contribution to the case amounted to nothing but taking phone tips, and that I was one of those officers, was, I decided, information they didn't need.

As usual, once my job became public knowledge, the subject quickly shifted to police work. And, predictably, the "horror stories" about discourteous traffic cops, officious crowd control officers, indifferent responders to domestic disturbances, etc., etc., etc., all got trotted out. One guy went on for some time about how it bothered him to have a uniformed force walking around in a supposedly open, democratic society "armed with guns."

He looked at me directly and said, "You seem like a nice enough guy, but, I've got to tell you, it really, really bothers me to think that you have a job that involves carrying a gun. A gun you're fully prepared to use against other people."

He shook his head, but didn't go on. Apparently, confronted with the singular incongruity of someone he found reasonably likeable holding a job that involved the carrying of a deadly weapon, he was simply at a loss for words.

Naiveté, thy name is pacifism.

"Any response?" said Ms. Remsberg.

"Nope," I said.

That actually seemed to have more of a prophylactic effect than my arguing with them would have. Maybe there was a general realization that just ganging up on me like that wasn't quite fair. After a few moments of silence, one woman who'd been quiet to this point spoke up.

"You do admit that policemen sometimes do bad things, don't you?"

"Of course."

"Don't you think cops should be held to a higher standard of behavior?"

"Yes, I do. And when cops do wrong I think they should be punished. But there'll always be some cops who're brutal, and some who're corrupt, some who're lazy, and some who're just plain incompetent. It's an unavoidable consequence when your hiring pool is the human race."

Ms. Remsberg brought the class back to the subject of rape, and law enforcement, as a general topic, didn't come up again.

After dismissing the class, she approached me.

"Good class," I said, partly because it really was a good class, and partly, since I could see she was uncomfortable, to let her know there were no hard feelings.

"I'm sorry about what happened," she said. "When it occurred to me that you must be a policeman, I assumed that everyone in the class already knew about it."

"Well, eventually everyone probably would have. Professor Gottfried already knows what I do. Having a cop in this class would have been too good an opportunity for him to pass up. How did you know, anyway?"

"In my job I work with a lot of cops, and you have many of the typical characteristics. You're exceptionally self-confident. Particularly for an undergrad. Almost arrogant, in fact. You're impatient with political rhetoric, particularly when it's leftist. Your opinions about sexual violence, and crime in general, for that matter, were obviously well-informed. If not necessarily correct. And when they didn't meet with immediate agreement, you weren't intimidated, but stood your ground, and articulated your position well. And you as much as admitted that, rather than fantasizing about victimizing women, your fantasies involve saving them."

"So what you're saying is that you profiled me?"

"In a manner of speaking."

"Then you're not psychic?"

"Of course not."

"That's good. I don't believe in psychics."

And, at that point, I didn't.

NINE

"Crimes Against Persons. Sullivan," I said.

Damn, I liked the sound of that! Taking the tip reports was, as I said before, dull as dirt, but I have to admit that I got a charge every time I answered the phone with those words. One of this assignment's few perks.

Being in plain clothes was another. Having an excuse to wear my pistol in my seldom-used shoulder holster was yet another.

But the whole *Miami Vice* fantasy of sitting around a detective squad room looking stylishly macho dissolved as soon as I actually started talking to the people who were calling in.

That night, I was working the CAP assignment with Reserve Officer Bob Bower. A few days had passed since my public "outing" in the "Male Roles" class. We'd been on duty about fifteen minutes, and this was the first call.

"Yes," came the voice at the other end. "My name's Peter Kase. With a 'K.' I'm calling about that kidnapped girl."

"Yes, sir. Do you have some information?"

"I certainly do."

I tapped my pen against the desk a few moments while I waited for him to speak his piece. I decided he must need prompting.

"What kind of information do you have, sir?"

"Well, I'm pretty sure she's already dead."

I sat up in my chair. He had my attention, that was for sure.

"How do you know that, sir?"

"See, I've been trying to focus on her all night."

"Focus on her?"

"Yes, home in on her essence, you see. And I haven't been able to."

"You haven't?"

"No. And I can always home in on someone's essence when I

47

concentrate. The only time I haven't been able to is when the person's dead. So you see, she must be dead, or I'd be able to home in on her."

I'd already relaxed once he'd said the word "focus." This was just another of what I'd come to think of as "Twilight Zone" calls, based on the caller's supposed psychic information rather than hard info.

"You're always able to home in on any person in the world, as long as they're alive?" I asked.

"Well, of course I have to know they actually exist. I can't just home in on some anonymous hypothetical person. But once I know a person exists, I can always home in on them."

"Okay, what do you mean 'home in?'" I asked, as I made notations on a blank tip sheet form. "Do you mean you can read their minds, or you can remotely view them, or what?"

"Well, just sort of sense their presence. I tried it with this Merryweather girl, but I wasn't able to get any sense of her. I wouldn't be able to tell you much, even if I could, other than that she's alive. Unfortunately, I wasn't able to focus on her, you see, so she must be dead. I thought you should know."

"I see. Let me ask you this. It's kind of late at night. Would you be able to focus on her if she was asleep, just the same as if she was awake? Or would her being asleep block you off the same as if she was dead?"

"You know, I never thought of that. Let me make a few tests and I'll get back to you."

"Yes, sir, you do that. We'll be right here at the phones."

I hung up the phone, and looked over at Bob, a short pudgy guy about a year or two older than I. Already out of Cal, he's working on his Master's at Golden Gate University over in The City. Like me, he was in shirtsleeves, his gun visible in a shoulder holster.

"They're coming out early tonight," I said. "I wonder if it's a full moon."

"This is California," Bob answered, looking up from the papers he was reading. "The kooks don't need a full moon to come out. And Berkeley is California squared."

"Cubed," I said, chuckling. "At least they provide some entertainment value. That's more than most of the callers do. What are you looking at?"

"The initial report on this case. Jeeze, this Bridges guy must be a real piece of work. He's damn lucky his girlfriend got kidnapped."

"Yeah, he sure is. If the girl I love is ever snatched off the street in broad daylight by some psycho pervert, I'll be sure to go out and buy me a mess of lottery tickets."

"I mean he's lucky somebody saw her being kidnapped," he said. "He'd already be a pretty good bet to have done her just being the boyfriend, but the way he handled the whole disappearance is suspicious as hell."

"How do you mean?"

He pointed to the report. "Says here they go out running together that morning, but he comes back alone, goes straight to their room, and doesn't come out 'til the next morning."

"I knew that already. What else?"

"Next day a few of the other residents ask him where DeeDee is. He doesn't say he has no idea. Instead, he lies through his teeth, and says she's not feeling well, and she's staying in bed. Then he makes a pretense of bringing her meals to their room."

I got up and looked over his shoulder at the report. "That I hadn't heard," I said. "The story I got is that they had some kind of fight up on the Fire Trail, and he stomped off in a huff."

"That's what he finally admitted the next day when the other residents pressed him."

"Why didn't someone make a report then?"

"He said he figured she'd gone home to her folks for a few days and he was so embarrassed that he didn't want to admit that she'd probably left him. They didn't make a report 'til her parents called after not hearing from her."

The phone rang. Bob picked it up and I went back to my desk.

"Crimes Against Persons. Bower... Cecilia Beckwith. Can I have your address?"

He wrote that down.

"You say you're a psychic, ma'am?... I see. A high clairvoyant... And you have a vision of her being held in a deserted warehouse in San Jose."

As he talked he clicked his pen open and closed as if to work off the tension that was building.

"You're sure it's in San Jose and not some other city?... Like Gilroy or Santa Clara or some other town in the same area... Because they've all got their own separate police departments, ma'am. If you're absolutely sure it's San Jose I can just call the San Jose Police, but if it might be in some other nearby city, I have to call them each up, you see?"

An edge was coming into his voice despite the effort he was making to sound pleasant.

"Okay, then, you're sure it's San Jose... That's still a pretty big city... Can you be any more specific?... You know, like an address or at least a street... No, ma'am, I'm not doubting your psychic abilities... Excuse me. High clairvoyant abilities... No, it just helps if we have complete information... I'm sorry you feel that way... No, you don't have to call the San Jose Police yourself. We'll do that... No, I'm not saying you can't call the San Jose Police, too. I was just trying to save you the trouble... All right, then. Thank you for calling."

He hung up and looked over at me, and shook his head.

"I don't know how you manage to act like you're taking these flakes seriously," he said.

"Law enforcement's been using psychics for a long time."

"Yeah, and how often have they come up with something useful?"

"That's not the point. The point is when they do come up with something useful, and the cops ignore them, it's the cops who look stupid."

Not wanting to look stupid, he phoned the San Jose Police and passed on the tip. They told him there weren't any deserted warehouses in San Jose. The space was too valuable to leave vacant. But they'd check it out.

The phone rang again. I picked it up.

"This is Peter Kase," said the caller. "With a 'K.' I spoke to you earlier about not being able to get a sense of Miss Merryweather?"

"Yes, sir. Do you have some new information?"

"Well, you suggested that she might just be asleep, so I tried to focus on my wife. She's asleep upstairs. And I wasn't able to. So it's possible Ms. Merryweather is just sleeping, not dead. I wanted to let you know right away."

"Well, we certainly appreciate your calling back, Mr. Kase. I'll be sure to add a note to your tip sheet."

"Happy to be of assistance, Officer."

I hung up and said, "Christ, that was a big help, all right. She might be dead, but she might just be asleep. That's the third psychic call in less than a half-hour. There really must be a full moon tonight."

"That one was the same guy calling back," said Bob. "He only counts once. And mine wasn't a psychic. She was a high clairvoyant. Anyway, you handle 'em a lot better'n I do."

"What else in that file jumps out at you?"

He looked down at the report again.

"This whole notion that he thought she must have gone home to Mommy and Daddy," he said.

"What's wrong with that? Her folks live close by. And she's away from home for the first time. If she was having problems, why wouldn't she go home for a few days to sort it out? Lots of students do."

"Yeah, but he supposedly left her up on the trail in just a t-shirt and gym shorts. All her street clothes were back in their room. And so was her purse, with her money and ID. Even if she was going home, wouldn't she go back to her room first?"

"Her brother lives in Rochdale Apartments. She could have gone to him, explained why she didn't want to go back to her room, and hit him up for a loan or a ride home."

"But she didn't."

"Yeah, we know that now, but, at the time, it wouldn't have been that unreasonable for Chris to think so."

"Well, maybe, but I still say he's damned lucky someone saw her getting nabbed."

Two separate lines started ringing simultaneously. Bob picked one up. I answered the other.

"Crimes Against Persons. Sullivan."

"Yes, how are you? My name's Letitia DeCorsio. I have some information about that poor girl."

I started filling out a tip sheet. When I had her personal info down I asked, "What information did you have, ma'am?"

"I talk to those who have departed this life."

Great. Yet another message from Rod Serling country.

"I see," I said. "Have you spoken to DeeDee? Is that it?"

"Oh, no. I talk to the *departed*. I'm a medium, you see."

You sound like a small, I thought, particularly in the brain. I stifled a laugh.

"So she's not dead?"

"No, not in the least."

"But if you talk to people who've died, how do you know this?"

Bob had hung up. I signaled him to pick up his phone and listen. This was too good not to share.

"Well, my special contact is a Japanese gentleman. He has told me about the poor girl's fate."

"And what has he told you?"

"Well, that ruffian in the truck? He was a white slaver, and after he captured her, he sold her to some Japanese gangsters."

"Yakuza, you mean?"

"Precisely. I'm sure I don't have to tell you how prized a beautiful blonde girl is over there."

"I have heard that," I said. "Do you know where she's being held?"

"Well, in Japan, of course."

"Can you be more specific? Is it Tokyo or Kobe or Hiroshima or one of the outlying islands?"

"Well, you see, my contact's command of English isn't so very good, and I don't speak Japanese, so when we commune, we often have a hard time making ourselves understood."

Bob buried his head in the desk and shook with silent laughter.

"But he's sure she's in Japan at this moment," I said.

"Oh, yes."

"Well, thank you very much for taking the time to pass this on, Miss DeCorsio. We'll be sure to follow up."

I hung up.

"What did you have?" I asked Bob.

"Just someone who saw a big, bearded guy on the street."

"Where was this?"

"New York."

"New York?"

"Yeah, he was in midtown Manhattan last week, and he saw this guy who reminded him of the forensic sketch they've been showing in the papers. So he waited until he got back home to the Bay Area, and then he called us."

"He waited until he was back to tell us about a guy he saw on the street 4,000 miles away a whole week ago."

"That's right."

"And they say people are unwilling to get involved."

The phone rang again.

"Crimes Against Persons. Sullivan."

"Yes," came a female voice at the other end. "I'd like to... look this is going to sound silly... but it's possible I may know something about that missing girl."

I pulled out a blank tip sheet and started to fill it out.

"Why do you think it will sound silly?"

"Well, because I don't really have any rational reason for knowing what I do."

Another psychic. At least this one had a sense of just how ridiculous it all sounded. She also had a nice-sounding voice. Youthful and vibrant.

"Could I get your name and address before we start?" I asked.

"I'd really prefer not to. Is that okay?"

"Sure," I said. "That's perfectly all right." A little unusual, though. Generally, the psychics (or mediums, or "high clairvoyants," or whatever) I talked to were very particular about making sure I got their names right. If they called in a tip that played out, it meant a jackpot in positive publicity.

Apparently, she really did want to be anonymous. Caller ID indicated that she was calling from a payphone.

"The thing is," she said, "I live in the same neighborhood as DeeDee Merryweather."

"Do you know her?"

"No. I've probably seen her, but I've never met her. See, the Co-op she was in, Rivendell House, is near the apartment building where I live."

"I see."

"Well, this is the part that's going to sound silly, but when I was little, I started being able to sense when things were going to happen before they happened. And sometimes I could sense things that had already happened."

"Like what?"

"If I could be near something that belonged to whoever what I sensed had happened to, or was going to happen to, I'd get a kind of vision of what the event was. Or if not the event, maybe its aftermath."

"Could you give me an example?"

"Once, in a parking lot, I brushed against the car parked next to mine, and I suddenly had a vision of a man in a hospital being operated on. Just a flash. It was gone as suddenly as it appeared. The next day, there was an article in the local paper about how a man had suffered a heart attack while driving his car and crashed it into a fire hydrant. He was taken to the hospital for emergency surgery. It happened an hour after I'd brushed against the car."

"Okay. So what you're saying is you think this was the guy you saw in your vision."

"He *was* the guy. The paper had a picture of him for the article, and I recognized him from my vision. And they had a picture of the accident, and I recognized the car I'd brushed against."

She was taking a lot more time to convince me than most of the "Twilight Zone" tipsters I'd talked to. They usually just assumed they'd be believed. This caller, on the other hand, expected skepticism. As if she herself was a bit skeptical of her gift.

"Okay. Have you been able to use your power to get a fix on DeeDee?"

"Yes."

"How?"

"Well, like I said, she lives near me, so I went by the house she lived in. It doesn't always work when I want it to. It usually just comes up unbidden, but if I try to concentrate, it just doesn't work. Well, it didn't this time, either."

"Then how did you get a fix on her?"

"I walked around the house, and even up and down the steps, but nothing happened, so I figured I wasn't going to be able to get a vision. As I was walking away, I brushed against a motorcycle, and that's when it came."

"What kind of a motorcycle was it?"

"A Honda. It was blue. I don't know the model, though, and I'm afraid I forgot to get the license."

This was interesting. Chris's ride was a blue Honda bike. And I'd seen him and DeeDee on it any number of times.

"Well, what did you see? In your vision, I mean."

"I didn't *see* anything really. It was more like a sense. I smelled dampness, and I felt darkness all around."

"Like you were enclosed in a box or something?"

"The dampness smelled like moist dirt. I think maybe she was buried."

TEN

For the next week or so, I didn't work the phone detail. I resumed my regular routine, class, meetings, patrol, and, when I could get them, paid details.

The following Sunday, I worked the Marina Detail. The Berkeley Marina is a landfill peninsula jutting into the San Francisco Bay at Berkeley's extreme west end. It's home to several hundred boats (some of them the primary residences of their owners), a chandlery, a bait shop, a hotel, and three restaurants. Every weekend, the Marina's carved out into its own separate police beat, a beat that's patrolled by reserve officers. Every Friday and Saturday night, from 1900 to 0300, and every Sunday afternoon from noon to 2000, at least one, and usually two Berkeley reserve cops drive around the Marina playing neighborhood cop.

I work enough Marina patrols and other paid details every year that I'm able to support myself. In fact, I'm probably the only reserve cop in Berkeley for whom paid details are bread and butter. The rest of the reserves, most of them anyway, have regular jobs, and, for them, an occasional Marina shift is just gravy.

At that, I was only able to support myself because I was attending a state college, getting a partial scholarship (*very* partial), receiving small payments from a trust fund my dad's deceased father set up for my education, and living in a Co-op. As it was, I barely managed to put together enough to cover the University's fees and textbooks, and the Co-op's room and board, and still have a little left over to walk around on.

But since I did support myself by working as a policeman, I tended to regard myself, perhaps to a greater degree than most of the other reserves, as a professional cop.

I tooled around the Marina, but my thoughts weren't on alert patrol. They were on the girl I'd talked to during my last tour on the Crimes Against Persons assignment.

I wondered how seriously I could take her. In her vision, if it could be called that since she didn't really get any visual perceptions, DeeDee was buried. So, logically, she must be dead.

Of course, as she was quick to point out, she was experiencing this psychic sensation from the inside out, so to speak, and, since she couldn't actually see that person, she couldn't say for sure that it was DeeDee she sensed.

But, she wondered, who else would it be?

I'd dutifully taken down her tip, and tried to keep her on the phone for a few more minutes. She'd sounded really attractive, though my ability to guess what someone will look like from his or her phone voice is about as unreliable as anyone else's.

I also found talking to a supposed psychic who seemed a bit uncomfortable with her abilities, even embarrassed about them, kind of, well, refreshing. All the others I'd talked to seemed to have their egos tied up with their supposed extra-sensory powers.

This one, though, sounded like someone I'd like to get to know better.

***

After driving around the Marina for about an hour, I parked at University and Seawall, then picked up the car mike and keyed it.

"673," I said. 673 is my badge number, which, per BPD communications procedure, makes it my radio call sign, too.

"*673,*" came Control's response.

"I'll be on foot on the Fishing Pier."

"*10-4.*"

The Berkeley Fishing Pier is a sort of continuation of University Avenue past Seawall into the Bay. Or at least it would be if cars were allowed on it.

Actually, it's wide enough, and sturdy enough, that it can be driven on if the barriers restricting the pier to pedestrian traffic are removed, which, as a police officer, I'm allowed to do. But it was a nice day, so I decided to take a stroll, instead.

Walking the pier is mostly a PR, "Officer Friendly" type of activity, but that day I actually found a little police work to do.

Three Vietnamese fishermen were pulling crabs out of the Bay, using wire traps. They were putting their catch into one of two large, plastic buckets. One of the buckets was open. The other had a towel covering it.

I approached them and looked in the open bucket. All of the crabs inside were roughly five inches or longer in diameter. The California Fish and Game Code requires that any crab less than four and a quarter inches has to be thrown back. None of the crabs in the open bucket violated that provision.

The three fishermen looked nervous, shifting from one foot to the other, and avoiding my eyes. I suppose that could've been a function of growing up in a police state.

On the other hand, they might've had a reason for being nervous.

I pulled back the towel covering the second bucket. Inside were a number of crabs, all of them much smaller than the ones in the first bucket.

"These don't look like they're up to code, gentlemen," I said. "Let's make sure."

I pulled out a ruler from my jacket pocket that I carry on Marina duty just for this purpose. As a municipal police officer, enforcement of the Fish and Game Code isn't really my primary responsibility, but there are fewer than two hundred game wardens covering the whole state of California, and the last time I saw one of them patrolling the Pier was never, so I've made a point of learning the F&G laws.

There turned out to be seventeen crabs in the second bucket, the largest one barely four inches in diameter. That made seventeen separate violations of the Code.

"We'll throw them back, Officer," said the youngest one. He had no accent that I could discern, and he was more self-assured than the other two. Either he'd come to this country at a very young age, or he was a native-born American.

"Throw the ones in the other bucket back in first," I said.

"But those are all legal."

"Yeah, I know. Throw them back in anyway."

"You haven't got any right to make us do that," he said. "We've been here all day. That's a long, hard day's work there. You can't just make us throw them back when they're all legal."

"I know they're all legal," I said. "Throwing them back is your punishment for keeping the others."

"What are you being so hard-nosed about it for?"

"Hard-nosed? I think I'm being uncommonly generous. In fact, I'm so generous, that, out of the goodness of my heart, I'm going to give you a short lesson on criminal justice in the great state of California."

I reached into my shirt pocket and pulled out my badge case, and slid a Miranda card out from behind my police ID.

"First let me read this to you," I said.

I rattled off the litany. Of course I knew it by heart. Probably most of you do, too. But the three fishermen were, if not under arrest, in custody of a sort, at least for practical purposes. So before I could talk to them any further, it was a good idea to give them the warning so I'd be able to use any guilty admissions they made, if it became necessary. And if I read it to them, instead of reciting it from memory, no one could ever suggest later on that I'd left something important out.

"Do you all understand that?" I asked when I'd finished.

They all said they did.

"Okay, let me ask you something before we go any farther. You guys are all working together on this, right?"

They all admitted that it was a group effort.

"You catching them for the family restaurant?"

"Yeah," the youngest one said.

"Okay, now if you had all the crabs mixed together, you'd maybe have a chance of convincing me that you weren't aware of the law that said crabs had to be a certain width. You've all got commercial fishing licenses displayed, so that argument might sound just the tiniest bit disingenuous, but it's an argument you could at least make."

"What's your point?"

"My point is that, instead, you put the legal crabs in one bucket and the illegal ones in the other, which you then covered up. That indicates to me that you knew exactly which ones were legal and which ones weren't. You follow?"

"Not really."

"Sure you do. Game wardens never walk this pier. And nine days out of ten, neither do local cops. So you'd probably be safe.

And even if it was the tenth day, most cops wouldn't bother to check the size of your catch. And even if this was the one time in a thousand a cop did check, he'd most likely give you the benefit of the doubt, and just make you throw the small ones back."

"So how come you're not doing that?"

"Because you tried to make it easier on yourself. You figured if a cop did come along and made you throw back the small ones, you'd save yourself a bit of trouble if they were already separated out. So you put the illegal ones in a separate bucket, and then tried to hide 'em, proving, not only that you were aware of the law, but that you knew what the likeliest consequence was if you actually got caught."

"So you're making us throw our whole catch back because we put the small ones in their own bucket."

"I'm making you throw it all back because putting the small ones in their own bucket proves you knew exactly what you were doing."

"I still say you haven't got any right."

"Strictly speaking, you're absolutely correct. So I'll give you a choice. You can throw the whole catch back, and I'll let you off with a warning. Or you can insist on exercising your right to keep the legal crabs, in which case I'll arrest the three of you and book you all on seventeen separate counts of criminal conspiracy."

"What do you mean criminal conspiracy?"

"You were working together," I said. "You all admitted that after I read you your rights." I reached into another jacket pocket and pulled out a small tape recorder.

"I've got it all down here," I said.

"You can't record us without our knowing about it," the kid protested.

"Get real," I said. "I told you that anything you said could be recorded and used against you. It *was* recorded, and it *is* being used against you."

"Well, so what? All we said is that we working together and we were catching crabs for our restaurant."

"Yeah, but that's the point. You were working together. That makes catching all those illegal fish a criminal conspiracy. And here's the best part. Catching and keeping an illegal fish is only a misdemeanor. In this case, it's seventeen misdemeanors, but it's still just a bunch of petty offenses."

"So it's no big deal."

"Big enough. You'd probably all have your fishing licenses yanked and there'd be some pretty stiff fines. But that's the least of your problems. Under California law, a criminal conspiracy is always a felony, even if the crime being conspired is itself only a misdemeanor. So that means I've got the three of you on seventeen separate felonies. That means hard time. San Quentin or Pelican Bay time."

"San Quentin? For not throwing some undersized crabs back?"

"No. For entering into a conspiracy in which you deliberately planned not to throw them back. And if the DA decides to file each charge separately, you could get life after just three convictions, under the 'three strikes' law, and still have another fourteen felony charges hanging fire. So I leave it up to you gentlemen. Throw the catch back in or go to jail and get booked on seventeen separate felonies."

Technically, what I'd told them was the truth. As a practical matter, though, it wasn't likely that the DA would actually prosecute them for criminal conspiracy, even if, in a formal legal sense, I had a solid case. But they didn't know that. After thinking about it for a few moments, they threw the catch back into the Bay.

"Thank you, gentlemen. Now would you each show me some ID?"

They each showed me their fisherman's licenses. I copied the information onto three field interrogation cards, handed them back their licenses, and said, "Don't ever try this again. The next time I catch any of you guys with an undersized crab in your catch, I will arrest you. Clear?"

They nodded.

I started to walk away. A young woman who'd been observing the proceedings intercepted me before I got too far.

"I think that was just terrible," she said.

"Catching all those undersized shellfish, you mean?" I said, though I knew very well that wasn't what she meant at all. "You're right. It's a blight on the environment."

"I'm talking about what you did to those poor men."

"Which part do you find terrible, Miss? Saving all the crabs or not arresting those men when I had them cold on nearly twenty felonies?"

"It was just mean of you to make them throw back their whole catch after all their hard work."

"Okay, in the first place, I didn't make them throw it back. They decided to do it after I explained what the alternative was. In the second place, if I'd arrested them, which I had every right to do, their whole catch would have been confiscated anyway, and their licenses revoked. This way, at least the crabs got a second chance, the ones that were still alive, anyway, and so do the fishermen."

"I still say you were being petty and mean. Haven't you got anything better to do than harass some hard-working immigrants? I mean here's that poor DeeDee Merryweather still being held somewhere by some maniac. Why aren't you out looking for her instead of making such a big issue out of a few shellfish?"

Jesus, even in the arcane realm of game enforcement I couldn't seem to escape DeeDee's shadow. She was already the only thing any of my friends or acquaintances wanted to talk about. Now even complete strangers were coming up to me just to point out how badly law enforcement was failing her.

***

After completing my foot patrol of the Fishing Pier, I went back to the station to write up a short report on my encounter with the three fishermen. Ironically, one of the reasons I'd made them throw their catch back instead of arresting them was to save myself some paperwork. I'd intended the three stop cards to be the only written record of the incident.

But after getting treated to a lecture on "hard-working immigrants" by Little Miss Social Justice, I'd gotten the impression that, while she hadn't actually made any threats, she might just beef me with Internal Affairs and/or the Police Review Commission, so I decided I better get my side fully documented.

And, anyway, even if she never made a personnel complaint, a report would record them having been previously warned if I ever caught them at it again.

After completing the paper, I returned to the Marina and was immediately sent to one of the docks to handle a noise complaint.

***

Not all the crafts moored on one of the Marina's docks are seaworthy. Or even river or lake-worthy. As I said, a fair number of people lived on their boats, and one or two of those aquatic houses were just that. Actual houses built on a floating platform.

Two minutes after receiving the call, I was knocking on the front door of a particularly elaborate two-story "houseboat," a kind of boxy Victorian mansion that looked like it might actually have more floor space than the suburban three-bedroom home I'd grown up in.

The door opened and a young man, well-lubricated, looked out. "Yeah."

"Your TV's too loud, sir," I said.

He considered that for a moment, then said, "Come again?"

"Your television. It's turned up too loud."

He frowned as though he found the information difficult to absorb all at once.

"TV?" he said.

"Yeah. It's on too loud."

"Too loud?"

"That's right."

He thought about it some more, frowned some more, then said, "Oh. The *TV's* on too *loud.*"

"Exactly."

"I'll go and turn it down, then."

"That would be a good idea."

"Thanks, Off'cer."

"That's okay. Just keep it down from now on."

The complaint had come from the resident of another boat farther down along the dock. I went down to make contact with him.

This one was a real boat. A good-sized one, but a boat, built for traveling on water, rather than a floating fantasy bachelor pad.

"Anyone home?" I called out.

"Who's that?" came a voice.

"Berkeley Police."

A slight pause, then, "Is that Dan Sullivan?"

"Yeah."

"Hold on a second, I'll be right up."

After a few moments, during which I guessed he was pulling on some clothes, the boat's resident emerged topside and said, "Come on up."

"Rich," I said. "When did you move down here?"

"After the news about my sister broke."

"You gave up that studio at Rochdale?"

"No, I've still got it, but I can't get a moment's peace there. Reporters always calling. Mom and Dad have had the boat docked here for years, so I decided to stay here 'til the weather gets too cold or the news dies down."

At first glance, Rich Merryweather didn't look like the kind of guy who could have shared genetic material with DeeDee. Short and rotund, his face is so chubby the eyes appear to have been sunken into the rolls of fat, giving him a porcine appearance. He's got a pleasant smile and a friendly manner that keeps him from seeming truly ugly, but even his closest friends would admit that he passed homely several miles back. The odd thing was that, when you placed him next to DeeDee, you could actually see a discernible family resemblance.

"Yeah," I said. "Must be hard to get through the days, wondering what's happened."

He nodded. "Actually, the reporters weren't even the worst of it. All the other people at Rochdale were always coming around."

"I'm sure they were just trying to be supportive."

"They were. But all I really wanted was to be left alone. I went back home for a few days to be with Mom and Dad, but I couldn't afford to miss so much school. So here I am."

"Yeah, I can imagine," I said, just to be saying something that would hold off the awkward pause we both knew was coming.

Despite our best efforts, the dreaded awkward pause descended. We both stood there nodding and shrugging, not knowing what else to say.

"Yeah," I said, then I nodded some more. "Anyway, I talked to that guy you called about. He said he'd turn down the sound. He was pretty polluted. I don't think he realized how loud he had it turned up."

"I figured it was something like that. He hits it pretty hard on

Sundays. But I've got a paper due tomorrow, and I don't need the distraction. I tried to handle it myself, but he just cursed me out."

"Well, that's what we're here for." God, how many clichés could I spout in one conversation?

Yet another awkward pause. Rich broke it this time.

"Have you heard anything?" he asked.

"Honest to God, I haven't, Rich. I take phone tips up at Crimes Against Persons one or two times a week but the regulars do the follow-ups. I'm sure if they find out anything substantial they'll let you or your folks know."

"I suppose." He paused, then went on, "Have you seen Chris at all?"

"At board meetings. And we're both on the Personnel and Operations Committee. I was kind of surprised to see him attending the meetings, to be honest, but some guys hole up in boats and some guys go to meetings."

I looked away for a moment, embarrassed.

"I'm sorry. I didn't mean that there's anything wrong with staying here. Or with going to meetings, either, for that matter. I just meant that people have different ways of dealing with worry."

"No need to apologize," he said. "I'm just wondering how much he's really worrying."

"What do you mean?"

"Well, you know he didn't treat DeeDee very well, don't you?"

"I heard he blew his stack at the retreat last summer. Are you saying that wasn't an isolated incident?"

"DeeDee admitted to me once that he'd hit her a few times."

"You're kidding?" I don't know why that surprised me, particularly given what I'd already heard about Chris and DeeDee's stormy relationship. Besides, I'd responded to dozens of domestic disturbances, so I should've known how common it is. I guess I wasn't as hardened as I liked to believe. As I liked others to believe. I could still be shocked when I learned that people I personally knew were involved in those situations.

"No, I'm not kidding at all. She never went into details. Just showed up at my place one night crying, with a mark on her face where he'd slapped her."

"Jesus."

"Yeah, she was so young, she didn't really know how to handle it. I told her to leave him, but she felt it wouldn't be fair to the other residents once the rooms had been assigned."

"She was going to stay with a guy who smacked her around to keep from upsetting the room assignments? When the hell was this?"

"Just after the semester began."

"Well, for Christ's sake, nobody would've had time to settle in at that point."

"That's what I told her."

"Anyway, if he really did swing on her at that volleyball game, why'd she stay with him in the first place?"

"She could have stayed with me at the studio 'til the summer was over. But Chris could be really charming when he wanted to be, and she was just a kid."

Just a kid. Of course Rich and I were all of three or four years older.

"I'll tell you one thing. I was sure he'd killed her 'til that lady reported seeing her kidnapped like that."

I nodded.

"Well, I'd better get back on the street," I said. "I'm keeping your sister in prayer, Rich."

It didn't seem like much, but it was what I could offer. People do seem to appreciate it when you tell them that, even if they're not particularly religious.

"Thanks, Dan. I just hope it's not already too late for prayers to do her some good."

ELEVEN

For the next month or so I shagged phone calls at Crimes Against Persons one or two evenings a week. Tips were starting to decline as time passed and attention waned, but they were still coming in faster than they could be followed up.

Most people were now of the opinion that DeeDee would never be found, and once they reached that conclusion, they began to lose interest.

We (which is to say, the Berkeley Police Department) were still faithfully chasing down any and all leads. The FBI, via its Oakland Resident Agency, was also investigating because of the kidnapping angle. But they found nothing useful under any of the rocks they turned.

Copies of the forensic sketch of the suspect made from Mrs. Taylor's description were still posted all over the Bay Area, particularly in the East Bay. I was amazed to discover just how many dark-haired, bearded, heavyset men I was seeing now that I was on the alert for them. And blue vans were even more ubiquitous than heavyset, bearded men.

As interest began to die down, somebody got the idea of taping a re-enactment of the abduction at the actual site where Mrs. Taylor had seen it. A blonde, shapely civilian clerk in the BPD's Support Services Division played the part of DeeDee and a burly, bewhiskered Police Service Assistant who worked as an ID tech portrayed the responsible.

Using the footage from the taped reenactment, a one-minute commercial was put together, with the chief providing a voice-over narration of the events and appealing to the public for any information. The commercial was played on local stations all through the latter part of the fall and into the winter.

The number of tips getting phoned in started to climb again as a result of the ad, but no useful leads developed.

The Department having to negotiate for ad time on Bay Area TV channels was an indication of just how much media interest in the case had died down. Rich Merryweather was even able to move back into his South Side apartment.

**

On the morning of the second Saturday in November, the mind of the average Berkeley resident wasn't on DeeDee's disappearance. It was on football. Cal's Golden Bears were hosting the University of Washington's Huskies at the Memorial Stadium. Neither team was ranked, but, since it was the last home game of the season, a big crowd was expected. And a win by Cal would give them momentum for next week's "Big Game" with Stanford on the Cardinals' home turf in Palo Alto.

I was assigned to a fixed traffic post at the intersection of Piedmont and Channing, a bit southwest of Memorial Stadium and, as it happened, a bit southwest of DeeDee's Co-op, Rivendell House, as well. Mainly my job was to redirect traffic away from the area. Lots of out-of-towners try to get as close to the stadium as they can, so local residents are issued windshield stickers so they can come and go with a modicum of convenience while outsiders are pointed in other directions.

I'd just finished explaining all this to a motorist from Washington who professed to be "shocked, shocked that drivers aren't being allowed to drive on public streets just because they happen to be from another state."

"I understand how frustrating it must be, sir. But whether you find it shocking or not, you're going to have to turn your car around and go back the way you came."

He started in again, serving me up another ration of shit. There wasn't that much traffic so I let him run on for a bit, nodding and smiling agreeably, until two more cars came up behind him. At roughly the same time, a girl stopped at the curb and waited, as if she wanted to talk to me.

I held up my hand against the onslaught of rhetoric, and said, "That's enough now, sir."

"It's not nearly enough. I may not live in this state, but I'm a taxpayer, too, you know."

"I know you are, sir, but so are the people behind you. I don't have the time to listen to you anymore. I need you to move your car now."

Instead of driving off, he began to get revved up again. Before he could get started I cut him off.

"Sir, you may not realize it, but the San Francisco Bay Area has no less than five separate Public Broadcasting channels."

"What the hell's that got to do with anything?"

"It means that, whenever I feel like a debate, I can watch *The McLaughlin Group*. Now move your car or get a ticket."

"I don't like your attitude."

"Yeah? Well, I'm sure that'll lose me several nights' sleep. In the meantime, you've been presented with your options, and you've got five seconds to make up your mind."

With a growl he made a u-turn around the traffic circle and drove off. The two waiting cars were both residents who I waved on through.

Once traffic cleared I was approached by the girl who'd been waiting at the curb to speak with me.

"Officer," she said, "I have a friend coming to visit today. Will she be able to get through to my place?"

"Where do you live, Miss?"

"Prospect Avenue."

The same street that Rivendell was on, I thought.

"Well, technically I'm not supposed to let anyone through unless they have a sticker or they can produce an ID that shows they live in the area."

"If I waited here for her, and then rode in with her, would my driver's license suffice?"

I noticed that she referred to her friend as "her," which I found rather pleased me.

She was an extraordinarily attractive girl. Small and slender, she had an elfin face that most would call "cute" or "pretty" rather than classically beautiful. Her shoulder-length hair, tied into a business-like ponytail, was blonde with reddish highlights. Not quite enough to designate her as an official redhead, more what my dad would call a "strawberry blonde." A small pattern of freckles across her nose added to her "girl-next-door" appeal. And that had to be the map of Ireland that I was seeing in her sparkling blue eyes.

"Sure," I said. "That'd be fine."

"Can I just wait here for her, then?"

"That'd be even better."

We both stepped back onto the curb. While I kept an eye out for any approaching vehicles, I asked, "Do you go to Cal?"

"Yes."

"What's your major?"

"Film Arts."

"Really? Do you want to get into movies?"

"Maybe. I haven't made up my mind. But I've always loved film."

"You're not sure if you want to make a career in it, but you're majoring in it?"

"Lots of people who love books become English majors while they're figuring out what to do with their lives. I thought I could do the same thing with movies."

"What kind of movies do you particularly like?"

"All kinds. Anything from romantic musicals to westerns. Lately I've started developing a taste for American crime movies from the '40's and '50's."

"Film *noir*, you mean?"

"Yes, exactly," she said, smiling. "You're familiar with the term?"

"Just a bit," I said. This was too good to be true. A very pretty girl who was a movie buff. And she'd recently discovered that she likes old-time crime movies.

Mom always assured me that going to Mass faithfully every Sunday would pay off.

I had the sense that I'd met her before, but she didn't look the least bit familiar to me. I'd have definitely remembered.

"The visual techniques they used were truly awesome," she said. "Lots of directors try to capture that same mood now with those 'neo-*noir*' films, but it just doesn't seem the same in color."

"You actually like black and white movies?"

"Very much. Why?"

"I find that a lot of people our age won't even give a black and white movie a chance. I took a girl to a movie last summer at the

Pacific Film Archives. It was a film *noir* double bill. *The Big Sleep* and *Murder, My Sweet.* All she did after we got out of the theatre was complain about how old-fashioned the black and white movies looked, and why couldn't they have colorized them."

"Blasphemy!" she said.

"Absolutely," I agreed.

"You go to the Archives a lot?"

"Quite a bit. I'm not much for a lot of that obscure foreign stuff they show, but I'm always up for a classic American film."

"Don't sell the foreign stuff short," she said. "Some of the greatest American filmmakers came from Europe and learned their craft there."

"Including a lot of the *noir* directors like Fritz Lang and Robert Siodmak."

"That's right," she said, obviously delighted at being able to talk about movies with someone else knowledgeable.

She looked at the name tag pinned to my uniform shirt.

"Sullivan," she said.

"That's right."

"Are there any other Sullivans in the Berkeley Police?"

"There's an O'Sullivan. But I'm the only one whose family 'dropped the O in the ocean,' as they say."

"What's that mean?"

"A lot of Irish immigrants dropped the 'O' or the 'Mc' prefix from their family names when they came over to the States. It was back in the 'NINA' days, and they were trying to avoid sounding so overtly Irish."

"The Nina days?"

"'*No Irish Need Apply.*' A lot of Irish immigrants had trouble finding work when they first came over. You could say that the Irish were America's first persecuted minority. With the obvious exceptions of black people and American Indians. You ever hear of a film *noir* called *Crossfire*?"

"I've heard of it, but I haven't seen it yet. I thought it was about anti-Semitism."

"It is. But the lead character's an Irish-American cop played by Robert Young. Toward the end of the movie, Young gets to give a big soliloquy tying post-war anti-Semitism to anti-Irish and anti-Catholic prejudices that his own family suffered in earlier generations. It's a great scene."

"I never knew about any of that. I'd never heard of the 'NINA' days before."

"Yeah, and you sort of look like you should have. What's your name?"

"Megan."

"Megan what?"

"O'Hara."

It suddenly occurred to me where I might know her from.

"Why were you asking about any other Sullivans in the BPD?" I asked.

"I just was wondering."

"Did you ever have occasion to talk to an Officer Sullivan before today?"

She looked up at me nervously. I tried to smile reassuringly so she'd know there was nothing to be afraid of.

"You're the reluctant psychic, aren't you?" I said.

"The reluctant psychic?"

"I was working the phone lines at Crimes Against Persons a few weeks ago and a girl called up and told me she had some kind of vision that DeeDee Merryweather was dead and buried. That was you, wasn't it?"

She nodded and looked away. "Do you have to give them my name, now?"

"Not if you don't want me to. I would like it for private use, though."

"Private use?"

"How many nice, pretty Irish girls who like film *noir* do you figure I get to meet? Of course your name won't do me much good without your phone number."

"You're asking me for a date?"

"At this precise moment, I'm asking you for permission to ask you for a date at some time to be specified later. But going out with you is what I had in mind, yes."

"Going out to do what?"

"You know, the usual. Dinner and a movie, that sort of thing."

She folded her arms, and looked at me appraisingly, and nodded.

"Let me borrow your pen," she said.

She wrote down her name and phone number on the back of one of my business cards. The friend she was expecting drove up at that point. She entered the car, showed me her license to keep everything kosher, and road back up the hill.

It was going to be a beautiful day.

TWELVE

Oddly, or coincidentally, or maybe fatefully, it was at that same football game that I started to develop my own suspicions about Chris, though, looking at it objectively, I have to admit that it wasn't because of anything that really gave me any solid foundation for suspecting him.

Once the before-game traffic posts close down, all officers, city and campus, are assigned posts inside the stadium. We have the option of taking a meal break during either the first half or the second half. Everyone's required to be inside during half-time.

Of course, you're free to stay inside during both halves if you choose to, but you'll only get paid for one half. And if you stay inside during both halves, you're required to stay on your feet, even though one of those halves is supposed to be your free period.

I usually stay inside during the first half. If it looks like it's going to be an exciting game, I'll stay in for the second, too, and just grin and bear having to stand. If it's a boring game, I'll go to a restaurant near wherever my after-game traffic post is going to be, and have a bite.

When game time approached that day, and the dispatcher announced to all game detail units that they could fold their tents, I went to my assigned post in the stadium, getting there in time to snap to attention and salute the flag during the "The Star-Spangled Banner."

It was between the last few bars of the anthem and the opening kickoff that I spotted Chris Bridges, seated in the middle of the Cal cheering section with his arm around a girl who most definitely wasn't DeeDee Merryweather.

She was the same general type physically, though. Blonde, attractive, shapely. Her hair wasn't quite the same shade as DeeDee's spun-gold, and her figure wasn't quite as curvaceous, but, if you were giving a capsule description of DeeDee for a police radio broadcast, Chris' date would've fit that description as well as DeeDee herself.

Well, I guess that shouldn't have surprised me too much. If he was with DeeDee because he liked the way she looked, then I guess it was only to be expected that, when DeeDee was out of the picture, he'd gravitate toward someone similar-looking.

The thing was who was he to decide that DeeDee was out of the picture? Sure, the odds seemed to be against her still being alive, but we were light-years away from developing any conclusive evidence that she was dead.

And even if she was dead, didn't he owe her a period of mourning? Of remembrance? Of respect for what they'd been to each other? Maybe they weren't married, but they'd been a couple. Didn't that count for something?

And if it didn't count for anything with him, should I infer anything sinister in that?

I guess I'm an old-fashioned guy, but Chris's being with another girl, while the search for DeeDee was still being pressed with full vigor, really offended me. There are military wives from the Vietnam era whose husbands are still listed as "Missing in Action," whose fates are unknown, but who've remained faithful for years, for decades, just on the pitifully small chance that their husbands will someday return. Chris Bridges hadn't even made it to three months before he was seeking out new territory to conquer.

The whole first half, I barely looked at the game. I was too preoccupied with staring at Chris and fuming.

Bob Bower had the post next to mine. As the first half wound down, I walked over to him.

"You planning on staying here for the second half?" I asked.

"Yeah. Why?"

"I was going to go grab a bite. If you want to join me, I'll buy. I just saw something that I need to talk to somebody about."

"What'd you see?"

I pointed out Chris Bridges and his date.

"That's DeeDee Merryweather's boyfriend," I said.

Bob looked at the girl appraisingly.

"Didn't take him long to find a replacement, did it?"

"No, it sure didn't. And it kind of brings that point you made about him into sharper focus, doesn't it?"

"Which point was that?"

"About how lucky he was that someone saw DeeDee getting kidnapped."

"I'm not sure I see what you're driving at."

"If he was still regarded as a suspect, wouldn't going out with another girl so soon after DeeDee's disappearance be yet another suspicious circumstance?"

"True enough," he said. "Okay, I'll let you buy me lunch."

***

Bob took a bite out of his hot dog, chewed, swallowed, and said, "I see your point, Dan, but when you come right down to it, all it proves is that he's an asshole. Hell, I'm not even sure it proves that."

We were seated at the counter in Top Dog on Durant, a small lunch spot that boasts of having the best hot dogs in the world. I was enjoying a hot link while Bob had a milder garlic sausage.

"Why not?" I asked.

"Well, think about it. What's he supposed to do, enter a monastery until, if, and when DeeDee's found? It's not his fault she got kidnapped."

"Don't you think he owes her a certain amount of fidelity?"

"Maybe, if she's still alive."

"There's no proof she's dead."

"No, but we both know that's the most likely possibility. So does he. Should he take a vow of celibacy just 'cause no one can absolutely prove what everyone's already pretty sure of?"

"Even if she is dead, doesn't he owe something to her memory?"

"Christ, Dan, this isn't the Victorian era. There's no such thing as a period of mourning these days. And even if there was, they weren't even married."

"He was supposed to be in love with her."

"Maybe he was, but now she's gone, and he's doing the only thing he can do, getting on with his life. At least that's an argument that he could make. If he had to. Which he doesn't."

"What do you mean?"

"It's like I said before. He's just damned lucky someone saw the kidnapping. As things stand now, he doesn't have to explain anything."

Maybe not. But that didn't keep me from wanting an explanation.

The dispatcher announced the two-minute warning a few minutes later, and we both walked over to our after-game posts. I was a few blocks south at Haste and Telegraph, manning an unchallenging "push-button post," one that would require me to do nothing except manually work the signal lights.

Bob was right, I decided. We knew DeeDee was kidnapped, and we knew that the guy who did it didn't look a thing like Chris, so Chris' being with another girl didn't prove anything.

Except, as Bob said, that he was an asshole.

THIRTEEN

I felt a little nervous as I waited for someone to answer the ringing phone on the other end of the line.

"Hello," came a female voice.

"Megan?" I said.

"This is her roommate."

"Is she home?"

"Yes. Who should I say is calling?"

"Tell her it's the traffic cop who likes movies."

"The traffic cop who likes movies? Okay."

After a few moments a second voice came on.

"Dan?"

"Yeah. Hi, Megan. How're you doing?"

"Just fine."

"Good. You busy Thursday night?"

"Thursday?"

"Yeah. I usually work weekends."

"Oh. Well, yeah I'm free. What'd you have in mind?"

"The PFA has got a film *noir* double bill. *T-Men* and *He Walked by Night*."

"What are those?"

"Cop movies. A small studio called Eagle-Lion put 'em out in the late '40's. John Alton was the photographer on both of 'em."

"Really? One of my professors was just mentioning him. That sounds like fun."

"Good. How about if I pick you up around five?"

"That's fine."

"Great. I'll see you then."

We both said something about how we were each looking forward to the evening and rang off.

I swear to God, the lamest phone conversations in the history of electronic communication occur whenever a guy phones up a girl for the first time.

***

"Who was that playing the head of the crime lab?" she asked me.

"Which movie?"

"*He Walked by Night.*"

"That was Jack Webb."

"You know, I thought it was him, but he looked so young. And so *skinny*."

"How familiar with Webb are you?"

"Oh, you know. I've seen reruns of *Dragnet* on cable. Never thought much of them, though. They seemed pretty lame."

"Actually, there was a time when Webb was thought to be to television what Orson Welles was to movies."

"You're kidding."

"No, honestly. He did it all, just like Welles. Produced, directed, wrote, and acted. He was regarded as a genius. Fact is he got the idea for *Dragnet* after doing this movie."

"How come he waited 'til the '60's to put it on?"

"He didn't. The show you see on cable is a revival of something he did years earlier. It started off as a radio show in 1949 and moved to TV in '51. If you like film *noir*, you'd really enjoy those early television episodes. It was one of the first dramatic TV series to be done on film, and he used a lot of the same visual techniques that *noir* movies did. But by the time he came back to do the color episodes, he was burning out, and it showed in the finished product."

"You've seen the original shows?"

"I've got a few of 'em on DVD. Got some recordings of the old radio shows, too."

"You'll have to let me see some of them."

"Anytime. Some of 'em are available on YouTube, if you don't want to wait."

"Had you seen both movies before?"

"Yeah. But the one that really blew me away the first time I saw it was *T-Men*. The camera angles and the dark shadows and everything just hit me right in the gut. I was in eighth or ninth grade, I think, and I was flipping channels on TV. I had no idea what film *noir* was. Fact is it was still a few more years before I ever actually heard the term used. But I date my knowledge of what film *noir* is from the first time I saw that movie."

The weather was fairly gentle that evening. What Pete, my grandfather, would call a "soft night." So we'd walked from her apartment to the Pacific Film Archives theatre in the University Art Museum, and, after the show, to the South Side La Val's on Durant. By the time the second movie had ended, it was nearly ten, and we were both starving. Fortunately, I had no classes the next day and her first wasn't 'til noon, so we didn't have to hurry. It was now a bit past eleven PM, and we were finishing off the combo pizza we'd ordered.

I offered to pour her another glass of beer. When she shook her head, I poured the last of it into my own mug. As I took a sip, I tried to think of something witty and original to say.

"Who are you really and what were you before?" I asked. "What'd you do and what'd you think, huh?"

Witty perhaps, but not the least bit original, as Megan quickly realized.

"*Casablanca*," she said immediately.

"Correct."

"So are you starting a new game where you recite a piece of dialogue and I guess where it's from?"

"No way. If I wanted to, I could skunk you on that every day of the week and twice on Sundays. I just wanted you to tell me about yourself."

"There's not much to tell. I'm 19. Born and raised in and around San Diego. Dad's in insurance. Mom's a teacher. My older sister's married. My younger brother's still in seventh grade. I grew up loving movies."

"Well, we both know there's more to you than that."

"I kind of wondered whether you'd bring that up."

"Bring what up?"

"You know, the psychic visions."

"Oh. I didn't mention that because you seemed so uncomfortable about it. That wasn't what I meant when I said there was more to you than that."

"What did you mean?"

"Where did you go to school? What kind of books do you like to read? What kind of music do you like to listen to? How is it that you weren't involved with someone else when I asked you out? Stuff like that."

"You're not interested in the psychic stuff at all?"

"Mildly, I suppose. But, it's not really the facet of your personality and life that most interests me."

"Why's that? Most people are very interested when they find out. Didn't you think I was telling the truth when I called you that night?"

"Sure I did, but I also thought you were very uneasy talking about it. First dates are awkward enough without deliberately stepping into minefields."

She looked at me for a few seconds, then said, "You really *aren't* particularly interested, are you?"

I shook my head.

"You know, that's quite unusual in my experience."

I shrugged.

"What can I say? I'm an unusual guy."

"But you do believe I have psychic powers?"

"I didn't say that. I said I thought you were telling the truth, which isn't quite the same thing. I can believe you're sincere without believing you've actually got the powers you think you have."

"So you think I have no powers."

"I didn't say that, either."

"So what is your opinion?"

"I guess I'm agnostic. Not just about you, but about psychic phenomena in general."

"And you really don't care whether I talk about them or not?"

"Hey, what is this, some kind of test? Do I pass if I don't care and prefer to admire you for yourself alone? Or do I pass if I'm interested in nothing else but your psychic ability because it's the most important thing in your life?"

"I'm not trying to put you on the spot. It's just that I've gone out with a lot of guys and, once they found out, that's all they ever wanted to talk about."

"I'm interested in you personally. How many guys were ever

interested in whether you were right-handed or left-handed?"

"What do you mean by that?"

"I mean you don't have any choice about which hand is dominant, but it doesn't really affect the kind of person you are. If you really are psychic, it's just something innate. Something you have no control over, like being right or left-handed."

"Okay, but even if you're not interested as a guy, aren't you a little interested as a police officer? It was my calling in a psychic tip that brought us together."

"Actually what intrigued me wasn't the tip you called in. It was that you didn't want to leave your name."

"An air of mystery?"

"Not really. See, a lot of people claiming to be psychic call in. And they always make a point of leaving their names and addresses and phone numbers and email addresses. That way, if the case is ever solved, they'll be able to claim that they were consulted on the case, and if anyone looks it up, there it'll be on one of the tip sheets in black and white. And if anything they say is borne out, they'll be able to claim that they gave the cops the case-breaking lead. They're all publicity hounds. You weren't."

"And you don't think any psychics have ever been really useful to the police?"

"Maybe sometimes. But, at best, the record's spotty. And even when they turn out to be right, it's mostly in retrospect."

"What do you mean?"

"I mean that a lot of so-called psychic insight seems to amount to shooting an arrow into a wall and then waiting for someone to come along later and paint a bulls-eye around it. Let's say the cops are looking for a body, and someone calls up and tells 'em, oh... say that the murder victim they're looking for is near a body of water. And when the corpse finally turns up, sure enough, there's a lake, or a river, or a pond, or an ocean nearby."

"Isn't that evidence that he really might have some kind of second sight?"

"Maybe, but so what? Two thirds of the entire planet is covered in water. When you think about it, there aren't all that many places a body could be found that aren't near *some* body of water, depending on your definition of 'near.' How big a help is that? Sure it sounds convincing. But after the fact."

"So if it's not my psychic powers that interest you, what does?"

"Take a look in the mirror. There're plenty of reasons for any guy to find you interesting."

She smiled. "You've got a lot to learn about women if you think looking in a mirror reassures us."

"Even Helen of Troy had a flaw or two. Flaws just make you human. Now tell me how you became the human you are?"

"You first," she said.

"Okay," I said. "But I'm every bit of 23, so it's a much longer story than yours."

FOURTEEN

"Did you always want to be a cop?" she asked.

"When I was real little I played cops and robbers, like all boys do. But I think I was nine or ten when I made a conscious choice."

"As early as that?"

"Genetic imperative," I said. "Being Irish, I either had to go into the cops or the priesthood, and I didn't think I could hack lifelong celibacy."

"That's what happened when you were ten? You decided you were going to grow up to be an ethnic stereotype?"

"No. What really happened was, once we hit the fourth grade, we were allowed to borrow one book from the school library every week. One week I checked out a book about the US Secret Service. Lord, it was absolutely beautiful to look at. This great pulpy cover, a guy in a trench coat and fedora standing in the shadows, and smaller inserts of counterfeiters getting busted and car chases and presidential assassinations getting thwarted. Let me tell you, I snapped it right up."

"Just the cover impressed you that much?"

"Absolutely. Up 'til then, I'd been reading about the Hardy Boys and the Three Investigators and Encyclopedia Brown and all the other kiddie detectives, but this was about real, grown-up cops fighting real, grown-up crime. And it was all true stories."

"No wonder you like *T-Men*. And that's what decided you?"

"It's what started me on that track. Over the next few months I was checking out every book in the school library that involved law enforcement. One week I'd get out a book about the FBI, the next week one about Scotland Yard, and the week after that one about the Canadian Mounties. Sister Helena, my fourth-grade teacher, was getting so alarmed by all the cops and robbers book reports I was turning in, she wrote a note to my folks about it. Of course, she and I never got along. She was always writing notes to my folks."

"And by the end of the fourth grade?"

"I felt I had a vocation. A true vocation."

"Was anyone else in your family in law enforcement? Your dad or your grandfather?"

"Both of them, as a matter of fact. Dad was a military policeman in the Army and later he was in the San Francisco Police. Pete was a railroad detective for the Southern Pacific."

"Pete?"

"My grandfather."

"His name is Pete?"

"No. His name is Frank. Pete's just the nickname all his grandchildren use."

"Why's that?"

"Oh, he always uses 'Pete' as a kind of generic nickname for whoever he happens to be talking to. Like some guys use 'Mac' or 'Bud.' My oldest cousin, Robby, imitated him as soon he was able to talk, and pretty soon they were calling each other Pete. When the rest of us came along, 'Pete' just stuck."

"What do you call your other grandfather?"

"Dad's folks both passed away before I was born."

"Oh, I'm sorry. So Pete's your mom's father?"

"That's right. And Pet's Mom's mother."

"'Pet?'"

"Pete got called Pete because that's what he calls all his grandchildren. Pet got called Pet because that's what *she* calls all her grandchildren. Her pets. To our generation they were always Pete and Pet."

"That's sweet."

"Well, mildly interesting, anyway."

"I imagine growing up as a cop's son, and a cop's grandson really did impose a kind of, what did you call it? Genetic imperative?"

"Not really. I didn't actually grow up a cop's kid. Dad had already been off the Job for several years by the time he married Mom. I didn't know he'd ever been in law enforcement 'til I was in high school. And Pete was retired by the time I came along. For years all he ever told me was that he'd worked for the railroad. He

never specified that he'd been a railroad cop."
   "How did your mom and dad meet?"
   "Pete invited Dad to dinner after Dad took a bullet for him."

FIFTEEN

"Your dad was shot?"

"Yeah. It was about, oh, twenty-five or thirty years ago now, I guess. Pete was pinned down in a shootout. Dad backed him up and caught a slug."

"Do you know the whole story?"

"I've put most of it together over the years."

"Well, tell me."

So I did.

***

Pete had been with the Railroad Police for nearly thirty years at that point [I told her] When he first came to the US from County Cork, he'd settled in Butte, Montana, where he'd worked as a miner. But the mines were starting to play out, and he didn't like it much anyway. He signed on as a deputy sheriff in a neighboring county for a year or two, and found he enjoyed police work. But the deputy's job didn't pay much, and by this time he'd married a local girl named Julia Murphy, destined to become Pet, and they'd racked up a couple of kids, with a third on the way.

Well, he needed something that paid better, so he moved his family to Portland, Oregon, and got a job as a security guard on the riverfront there. That's where Mom was born.

The harbor job was a union position, and it paid better than being a deputy back in Montana had, but going from being an actual cop to a security guard is kind of like going from being a priest to an altar boy.

So he started looking around for real police jobs and heard about an opening with the SP. In most states, including California, railroad cops are actual peace officers, with full law enforcement authority, and Pete had always been a train buff, so it seemed like a perfect fit. He applied, and got the job, and he and his family were on the move again. This time to San Francisco.

Well, after a number of years as a uniformed patrolman, he'd impressed his superiors as a solid, reliable cop, and, eventually, was appointed a plainclothes detective. A typical immigrant's success story. Hard work, determination, and perseverance had taken him from being a poor kid in a poor rural section of a poor country to being nothing less than Investigator Francis Xavier Jeremiah Lowney, scourge of all evildoers who dared to prey on innocent train passengers. And wasn't he proud as a peacock!

On this particular night he was staked out in the train depot at Third Street and Townsend. Once one of the most beautiful buildings in The City, it had fallen on hard times. A few years after all this took place, the building was torn down and replaced with a much smaller station a block or so south.

There'd been a number of complaints about pickpockets in the depot, and he was trying to spot the responsibles.

Pete's self-image notwithstanding, the fact of the matter is that, most of the time, railroad policemen are concerned with protecting the company's property, not the company's passengers. So, generally, his job involved looking into thefts, burglaries from freight cars, embezzlements, things like that.

Not that there were never what were called "crimes against persons" on railroad property. In fact, there were plenty. Two hoboes camped on railroad property might have a violent falling out that ended with one or the other getting knifed. A passenger might get mugged walking from his or her late-night train to the parking lot. That sort of thing. Usually, however, violent felonies were turned over to the local city police or county sheriff, leaving the railroad cops free to handle the "crimes against property" that directly affected the railroad.

That didn't always sit well with Pete, who felt that, as a cop, his main job was to protect the public, and that, as a railroad cop, his main job was to protect the members of the public who used the railroad.

So when he got the stakeout assignment, he jumped at it. Spotting dips was a specialty of his. And over the years, he'd managed to attain a 92% conviction rate on the pickpockets he'd caught in the act.

He'd been on twelve hours at that point. The problem with stakeouts and surveillances is that, most of the time, you're watching things that aren't happening. What I mean is you're waiting for something to happen, some crime to be committed, but until it happens, you're intently observing perfectly ordinary, everyday activity by perfectly ordinary, law-abiding citizens. It's dull as hell, and if you've put in twelve hours without any result, exhausting.

Pete was really hoping to get a hit that night. The SP had already, some years earlier, happily given up its interstate rail passenger service to the quasi-federal AMTRAK agency, which had its own police force. It was trying to do the same with the commuter rail service it operated between San Jose and The City, hoping to push it off onto the California Department of Transportation. When that happened, and Pete was sure it would eventually, protecting passengers, protecting actual people, would no longer be even a small part of his job.

Well, by that time, he'd probably be retired anyway. After more than thirty years in law enforcement, counting the stint as a deputy sheriff, he was nearly ready to pull the pin, anyway. The kids were all grown, the oldest ones married with kids of their own, and he and Pet had a bought a couple of adjacent lots up in Sonoma County's redwood country that they planned to build on when the time came.

But it would be nice to put a few more felons away before he finally turned in his badge. Nice to have a last hurrah. Or two or three.

I'm not sure what time it was, but a crowd was gathering in the station. There were more trains south to the suburbs that time of day than there were north into The City, so I presume it was a crowd of people waiting for the next train headed down the Peninsula.

Pete suddenly spotted a crook he recognized. He always called him "Fingers." That's all. Never referred to him by any other name, just used the street moniker he'd picked up.

Fingers was a hype who supported his habit by stealing wallets and purses and, evidently, he was damned good at it, which is why he was called "Fingers." Most pickpockets work in teams, one to distract, the other to dip. Fingers was good enough that he could do both by himself.

This was rather surprising, when you stop to consider that junkies tend to be nervous and twitchy, particularly when they're jonesing, and being nervous and twitchy is not a quality that guarantees success in the pickpocketing field.

Fingers, however, managed to avoid this handicap. He was skinny and unhealthy looking, like a lot of addicts, but he always dressed well, in a nicely-pressed suit and tie, so, if you didn't look closely, he appeared to be one of the commuting businessmen waiting for the train home. And he was adept enough at his chosen profession that he was usually able to keep a step or two ahead of the withdrawal symptoms that would've doomed to failure most junkies who attempted this particular criminal specialty.

It was his bad luck that he happened to be plying his trade at the same place my grandfather was plying his, and his worse luck that my grandfather recognized him.

Pete kept him under observation for a few moments and was rewarded when he saw the dip "accidentally" bump into a citizen. The victim's wallet was out of his pocket in less than a second. Pete saw Fingers discreetly slide his hand into an overcoat pocket as he apologized to the man he'd jostled.

"Stop right there, Fingers," Pete called out. "Sure it's the Limb of the Law I am, and it's arrested y'are, so just be comin' along quietly now, there's a good lad."

(Okay, maybe he didn't say it in quite that exaggerated a stage Irishman brogue, but it makes a better story when I tell it that way.)

Now pickpockets are not generally violent criminals, but picking pockets is a felony, even if what you steal would normally only amount to a misdemeanor. It counts as grand theft under the California Penal Code because, even if you only get a buck or two, you've invaded the victim's personal space to accomplish the theft. It's not as bad as robbery, but it's worse than just plain stealing.

And Fingers had already fallen three times. Now in those days California didn't actually have a "three-strikes" law, but habitual felons weren't looked on kindly, and Fingers knew that, with a fourth felony conviction, he'd be going to the joint for a long time. He wasn't a young man, and he didn't want to die in prison. So he'd taken to doing something he never would have considered when he'd first started out as a thief.

He'd started carrying a gun.

Pete was still about six feet away from Fingers when he called out the warning. Fingers reached into his waistband, pulled his weapon, and cut loose. Pete hit the prone as soon as he saw Fingers bringing the piece to bear, and rolled, clawing desperately at his shoulder holster for one of his own revolvers.

When Pete dropped to the floor, Fingers turned, ran out of the depot, and headed south on Townsend. For a guy who'd been on the junk for more than two decades, he was pretty fast.

Pete, on the other hand, was nearly 60, and it had been several years since he'd last been in a foot pursuit. But he was still in great shape and he had plenty of stamina. Fingers might be able to beat him on the short sprint, but as long as Pete kept him in sight, the thieving junkie had no chance over a stretch of distance.

Pete tried to let his dispatcher know what was going on, but when he'd started in police work more than three decades earlier, personal two-way radios were regarded as science fiction stuff you only saw on the pages of a *Dick Tracy* comic strip. He'd never gotten used to the idea that the batteries had to be recharged and that they might not last over a shift of more than twelve hours.

Unable to get any response, he shoved the belt radio back into its holder, swearing, and concentrated on keeping up with Fingers. His primary weapon, a chrome-plated Colt Python .357 Magnum with a pearl handle, was clutched in his right hand. His back-up, a matching chrome-plated, pearl-handled Colt .38 Detective's Special, was still snugged into a belt holster at his right hip, butt forward for a cross-draw. As a patrolman, he'd been content with a much less flamboyant Smith & Wesson four-inch .38 Model 10, but when he'd been promoted to investigator, he'd celebrated by purchasing a couple of weapons with what he called "style."

This was the first time he'd ever actually had to use one of them.

Periodically, Fingers would turn and snap off a shot while continuing to run. Pete stopped every ten or twenty steps, and returned fire. Pete's shots came closer, since he was actually taking the time to stop and aim, but Fingers was still a moving target, and Pete had learned to shoot one-handed. The two-handed isosceles grip or Weaver grip, either of which might have steadied his aim, were alien to him.

Fingers turned into the railroad yards among the freight cars. Pete kept after him.

***

"Where does your father come into the story?" asked Megan. "Right about now."

***

Though Pete hadn't been able to communicate his situation to his dispatcher, the SFPD communications center at the Hall of Justice was getting plenty of emergency calls about the two men trading shots near the train depot.

The Southern Pacific Railroad Police was a pretty large force. At one time, before the SP got absorbed into the Union Pacific, it had more than a thousand officers. But it was also pretty far-flung, spread over a half-dozen or more states.

So when an SP cop found himself in trouble, he wasn't necessarily able to call on someone from his own force for back-up. The nearest unit might be fifteen or twenty minutes away. Sometimes much more.

Which meant that he had to rely on local officers from the surrounding city, county, or state agencies to cover him in a critical situation.

When the "shots fired" call went out over the air, the nearest SFPD unit to the scene was being driven by Officer Steve Fanelli. Officer Daniel Sullivan, my dad, was riding shotgun. They began a Code 3 response. That's with lights and sirens going.

Dad's family had been in the real estate business for several generations, and it had been assumed that, when Dad grew up, he'd get a real estate license and take his place in the family firm.

Some years earlier, though, he'd completed an overseas combat stint in the Army as an artilleryman, which had left him with a Purple Heart when a rifle slug drilled through his left forearm., and a sense of having no real direction in his life other than a firm conviction that he did not want to be a realtor.

When he came home to serve out the rest of his enlistment stateside, he signed up for Military Police training. Like Pete a generation earlier, he discovered that law enforcement suited him, and, after his discharge, much to the dismay of his father and uncles, he took the SFPD test and enrolled at the Police Academy instead of the University of San Francisco's business school.

Dad had been out on the street for about a year and half at this point. He was past his probationary period, having successfully completed both his basic training course at the academy and his prescribed stint of field training. Officially he was no longer a rookie, but he was still far from being a veteran.

Fanelli pulled the patrol car up to the yards, and both officers exited, alert to the sound of shots. They suddenly heard a volley coming from behind a row of freight cars. There was a second long row of cars on the parallel track on the far side. Fanelli ran south about the length of four cars, drew his weapon, and slowly entered the corridor between the two rows by climbing between cars.

Dad, armed with the shotgun, was at the end of the row. He didn't have to climb between cars, just work his way slowly around the end, and wait for Fanelli so they could simultaneously enter from both sides of the shooting and flank the combatants.

Dad peeked around the corner of the freight car to assess the situation. One man was on the roof of a car on the next track shooting down at a man who'd rolled under the same car for cover and was trying to return fire from his back. Unfortunately for him, his right hand was pointed toward the inside of the car, so he had to shoot left-handed or risk exposing himself to the fire of the guy on the roof.

The rooftop gunman was shouting something at the man on the ground.

"You'll never take me alive, copper!" he screamed.

Well, maybe those weren't his exact words, either. It does sound a little too Jimmy Cagney for real life. But whatever he said, it was enough to make it clear to Dad that the man on the roof was the bad guy and the man on his back under the freight car was the policeman.

Dad racked a round into the twelve-gauge, raised it to his shoulder and yelled, "Police! Drop the gun!"

That, I think, is pretty darned close to what he actually said.

Fingers, who, of course, was the man on the roof, twisted around and cranked off a shot at Dad. Dad fired a blast of double ought buckshot at Fingers. Having never actually been under fire before, at least as a cop, he reflexively racked and fired three more rounds without thinking about it. This emptied the twelve-gauge. He ducked behind the freight car and drew his handgun.

Fanelli, meanwhile, had taken cover between two cars and was also firing at Fingers.

Fingers was sufficiently concealed on top of the car that none of the double ought pellets Dad had fired, and none of the handgun rounds fired by Fanelli or Pete had hit. But with the odds now three to one, he decided that flight was a more sensible course than fight. He rolled to the other side of the freight car. Dad peered around the corner of his car just in time to see him doing this and quickly ran between the cars in the next row to intercept him.

Fingers was still descending the ladder leading from the top of the freight car when Dad took a quick glance around. The gunman's hands were both occupied in holding onto the ladder. He'd stuck his pistol in the waistband of his pants.

Dad took dead aim and said, "Don't move!"

Fingers froze, looked down at Dad, and, with his right hand still holding onto the ladder, tried to pull his gun with his left hand. It got caught in the fabric of his shirt and pants.

"Don't try it," said Dad.

The gun came free with a ripping sound. Dad opened up, firing four shots, all of them hitting home. Fingers fell to the ground.

Pete and Fanelli had both climbed through the line of cars to the row where Dad and Fingers were. They found Dad covering Fingers, approaching him cautiously.

Dad was pretty pumped by this time, and when he heard the other two officers behind him, being so jumpy, he whirled around to make sure they weren't a threat.

"It's us," said Fanelli.

Fingers, though seriously injured from both his wounds and the fall, wasn't yet out of action. While Dad was distracted he started to raise his gun.

"Look out!" said Pete.

But Fingers managed to get off a shot that caught Dad in the left knee. He collapsed, but managed to put his last two shots into

Fingers before he hit the ground.

Pete, the Python in his right hand, and the snubbie in his left, began firing two-handed like a cowboy in the movies until both his weapons ran dry while Fanelli emptied his own gun into the pickpocket.

Fingers had avoided prison the hard way.

***

"That's an absolutely amazing story," said Megan.

"Yeah. And except for a few lines of dialogue, it's all true."

"Did your father recover?"

"Mostly. His police career was over, though. They might have kept him on limited duty. With work and therapy, he might have even been able to work his way back to field duty. But he was young and impatient, and desk duty, even for a few years, didn't appeal to him."

"What did he end up doing?"

"Well, his father and uncles were on him like bees on honey, insisting that this was a sign from God that he shouldn't have joined the cops, and he was meant to be in the family business. They even had priests in to visit him in the hospital and counsel him about his duty to his family, which always struck me as dirty pool. But, ultimately, they got their way. Dad finally decided that if he had to work in an office it might as well be the family office."

"And you never knew any of this?"

"Like I said, I didn't even know he'd ever been a cop 'til I was 12 or 13. Over the next few years I put the story together from bits and pieces he, and Pete, and Mom told me at different times."

"That's too bad, since it seems like that's what he really wanted to do."

"Well, there's a happy ending."

***

Pete went to visit Dad while he was in the hospital.

"Lad," he said, "It's that heartsick I am. If only I hadn't distracted you, he'd have never been able to get off that shot."

"It wasn't your fault, Mr. Lowney," said Dad. "I shouldn't

have let myself get distracted, but it wasn't anyone's fault but the guy who shot me."

"Well, it's that glad I am that you see it that way," said Pete. "D'you think they'll be springing you by next month?"

"Most likely."

"Come around to the house on the 21st, then. M'second oldest, Frank Jr., is getting out of the Air Force and starting at USF Law School. We're throwing a party for the lad to celebrate."

"Well, thanks, Mr. Lowney, but I wouldn't want to intrude on a family function."

"Lad, it's m'life y'saved. As far as we're all concerned, y' *are* family."

***

"Well," I said, "Dad did end up going to that party and it turned out Frank Jr. was an old acquaintance. He'd been a couple of years ahead of Dad, but they'd both gone to high school at St. Ignatius. Not close friends or anything like that, just enough to nod at each other in the corridors, if that. But after Frank got out of the service, he and Dad got to be really tight. In fact, from just about that point, each one always counted the other as his best friend. And Dad got even closer to another of Pete's kids."

"Your mother?"

"Exactly. Pete and Pet's younger daughter, Peggy. She and Dad went together for several years and then decided to get married. They almost weren't able to get a marriage license, though."

"Why not?"

"Because Dad didn't know what Mom's name was?"

***

See, they went into City Hall to get their license and the clerk behind the counter was filling it out. He turned to Dad, and said, "Your full name, Sir?"

"Daniel Michael Sullivan."

The clerk turned to Mom and said, "And yours, Miss?"

"Margaret Brigid Lowney."

100

Dad turned to her and said, "Margaret? Your name's Margaret?"

"Yes."

"I thought your name was Peggy."

"It is. Peggy's a nickname for Margaret."

"No, it's not. The nickname for Margaret is Maggie or Margie or Margo or something like that."

"Those are all nicknames for Margaret, too. But the one I use is Peggy."

Well, as far as the clerk could tell, he was about to give a marriage license to a couple who didn't even know each other's names. He almost refused to issue it.

***

"But they managed to persuade him that they knew each other very well, and that Mom's formal name just hadn't come up before. So, they got married, and, in the course of time, had three kids."

"Which brings us to you."

"Born in St. Mary's Hospital, baptized at St. Paul's Church in Noe Valley where I lived for the first three and a half years of my life. We moved down to San Bruno, a 'burb on the Peninsula, about two years or so after Mom had my brother Joe. A few months later she had Pat. When I was five, I did a year in a kindergarten at the local public school. Then eight years with Franciscan nuns in grammar school. Four with Jesuit priests in high school. The last five years at Cal slowly working towards a bachelor's degree."

"What's taking you so long?"

"I'm self-supporting. It takes longer that way. But I can't complain. I'll always count being a sophomore as three of the best years of my life."

"*Doonesbury.*"

"Can't get anything by you. Now it's your turn."

SIXTEEN

"Well," she said, "my story's nowhere near as exciting as yours. My mom and dad met in college, dated the whole time they were undergrads, and got married after they received their degrees."

"And?"

"That's really about it. Dad got a job with an insurance company. Mom got a job teaching sixth grade. They had three kids. I was the second."

"Do they both still work?"

"Mom stopped when she had kids. She went back after my younger brother started high school. Good thing, too. Dad's on an extended leave right now."

"Why's that?"

"He had a heart attack a little while ago. Kind of minor as heart attacks go. But no heart attack is really minor."

"Is he okay now?"

"Yes, he's getting better. He had a bypass operation early in September. I went back to be with Mom when the surgery was scheduled. I was gone for more than a week. I'm still playing catch-up in my classes."

"He's still taking time from work, though?"

"Yes. He won't be going back for at least another month. But the sick leave is all used up and Mom's teaching salary is all the income they have right now."

"I'm glad he's on the mend, though. But back to you. Where'd you go to school?"

"Local public schools."

"So you were a CCD kid?"

"Just in grammar school. Once I got confirmed, Mom and Dad stopped sending me."

"You sound like you've kind of gotten out of the church-going

103

habit."

"Not entirely. I go more often than Christmas and Easter, but not all that regularly. Mom's not Catholic, and Dad's a little casual about it. I guess you could say I was never in the church-going habit to begin with. You?"

"Hey, you know what the Jesuit motto is? 'Give us the boy and we'll return the man.' Well, they returned me. I'm right there at Mass on all Sundays and holy days. Well, most Sundays and holy days."

"Newman Hall?"

"Sometimes. My freshman year I lived in the University dorm unit on Haste, and I went there all the time. But I'm on the North Side now. The Graduate Theology Union's got an interdenominational chapel a short walk from my Co-op that has a Catholic Mass every Sunday. And since it's not a regular parish service, there's no collection plate. Best of all possible worlds."

"A man of parts. Career cop. Devout Catholic. Perennial student."

"Not perennial," I protested. "It's just taking me longer to get my degree than the standard four years. I told you, that's what happens when you're working your way through."

"What's your major, then?"

"Legal Studies. And that's as much as I'll say about me for the moment. I've already told my story. We're talking about you now."

"Okay, what else do you want to know?"

"What kind of books do you like?"

"All kinds. I went through a period where I wouldn't read anything but books about girls and their horses."

"Did you ever graduate to Dick Francis?"

"Who?"

"Guy who writes about boys and their horses. Never mind. I shouldn't have interrupted."

"Where was I?"

"Girls and their horses."

"Right. I like a lot of popular authors. I'm embarrassed to admit it, but I actually loved *Valley of the Dolls* when I was in high school."

"Oh, God. You're kidding. Where did you find that?"

"My mom had an old paperback. I know it's trash, but I loved all the movie stuff. See, I was already getting into movies. Not just the stories they told, but the techniques and the history and the, oh, what would you call it? The trivia, I guess."

"Like who was the actor who played Sam Spade before Bogart, that sort of thing?"

"Sort of. But more who won what award, who was the first director to use a particular technique, how did musicals grow as a genre after sound was introduced."

"The statistical lore."

"Pardon?"

"Dad's a big baseball fan. After his family and the Church, what he's most devoted to is the San Francisco Giants. In baseball, they'd call what you're talking about the statistical lore. The history of baseball in terms of all the minutiae and achievements over time. What was so-and-so's lifetime batting average? Who pitched the most no-hitters in a World Series? You're talking about the statistical lore of movies."

"Statistical lore," she said. "I kind of like that."

"So what's your all-time favorite movie?"

"Oh, I'm just a 'go-along with the crowd' type, there. *Citizen Kane*."

"With a name like O'Hara, I was half-expecting you to say *Gone with the Wind*."

"Not my favorite, but I think it's a great movie."

"So you lean toward unpretentious American genre crowd-pleasers rather than self-consciously arty films?"

"Oh, yes," she said. "Definitely crowd-pleasers."

"A girl after my heart. So let's break it down. What's your favorite musical?"

"*Singin' in the Rain*."

"Another safe choice. Are you really that typical, or do you just like to avoid controversy?"

"Maybe I just like the film," she said. "What's your favorite musical?"

"*Seven Brides for Seven Brothers*. But *Singin' in the Rain*'s a very close second. Come to think of it, with the whole silent movie background, I can see why it appeals to you. Favorite western."

"*Dances with Wolves*."

"*Dances with Wolves*?" I said. "That's not old enough to be a favorite movie. You haven't got enough historical perspective."

"It's older'n *me*!" she replied.

"Yeah, but you're not that old."

"Old enough to have some historical perspective, at least from a personal standpoint. Anyway, it got the Oscar for Best Picture."

"Like that's a guarantee of quality. You know what the only western to get the Best Picture Oscar before *Dances with Wolves* was?"

"What?"

"*Cimarron*."

"*Cimarron*? Never heard of it."

"My point exactly. It got Best Picture of the Year and hardly anyone remembers it anymore. You're a self-described student of film's statistical lore, and you're not even familiar with it."

"Okay, so what's your favorite western?"

"*My Darling Clementine*. Though I have to admit it takes a mighty suspension of disbelief to accept a big, robust guy like Victor Mature as a man dying of tuberculosis. Still, he was one hell of a Doc Holliday."

"I thought you might say *She Wore a Yellow Ribbon*."

"If I was allowed to pick more than one movie, I'd probably say the whole Cavalry Trilogy, but I have a difficult time choosing between that, *Fort Apache*, and *Rio Grande*. I tend to love whichever one I happen to be watching at the time best."

"So basically, then, you don't think there've been any decent westerns except John Ford's."

"I didn't say that. I love *High Noon* and that's Fred Zinnemann. I love *Shane* and that's George Stevens. I love *Seven Men from Now* and *The Tall T* and those're Budd Boetticher. I love *Red River* and *Rio Bravo* and those're Howard Hawks."

"And every one of them made before 1960."

"*Ride the High County*. Sam Peckinpah. *Hang 'Em High*. Ted Post. *True Grit*. Henry Hathaway. The remake. The Coen Brothers. *Unforgiven*. Clint Eastwood."

"Okay, but I still like *Dances with Wolves* best."

"Fine. It's a good movie. But so was *Cimarron*. If it's still remembered fifty or sixty years from now, you can have a big laugh at my expense. Favorite spy movie."

"*North by Northwest*," she said. "Yours."

"*Notorious*. Unless you count *Casablanca* as a spy movie."

"Intrigue and suspense, certainly. I guess you could count *Casablanca*. If you do, I might have to change my vote."

"If you exclude *Casablanca*, it's interesting that we both chose Hitchcock pictures. And both of them starred Cary Grant."

"Yes. Maybe we should've said favorite non-Hitchcock spy movie."

"You might have a point there. Hitchcock does seem to be in a class by himself."

"Almost like he's his own genre."

***

Well, we spent the next hour or so talking about our favorite movies. She said that *The Departed* was her favorite cop movie. I, being a loyal son of the San Francisco Bay Area, said it was a toss-up between *Bullitt* and *Dirty Harry*. She said *Chinatown* was her favorite private eye movie. I opted for *The Maltese Falcon*. She said her favorite horror movie was *The Bride of Frankenstein*. I said that, as a Jesuit high school alum, I naturally had to go with *The Exorcist*. *2001* was Megan's favorite science fiction movie. *Star Wars* was mine. She insisted that *It Happened One Night* was the best romantic comedy. As a John Ford partisan, I held firm for *The Quiet Man*.

I'd gotten a second pitcher of beer and Megan'd had two more mugs during this time. Maybe that was more than she was used to drinking. Or maybe she just felt comfortable being out with someone who was more interested in talking about movies than in her supposed gifts.

In any case, she started to open up.

"I was just a kid when it started," she said.

"Liking movies, you mean?"

"No. Just a kid when all the, you know, the mumbo-jumbo started."

"Ah. You know, you don't have to talk about that."

"Suddenly that's just what I do want to talk about."

"Okay."

"My mom was looking for something. An earring or something

like that. I was maybe seven or eight. And I saw it under her dresser. Only I wasn't even in her room. But I saw it there inside my head."

"I see."

"We all thought I just got lucky." She paused to yawn, and looked at her watch. "Later than I thought. Anyway, we all thought I just got lucky. But things like that kept happening. Not when I tried to make it happen. Just when I least expected it."

I nodded.

"People started treating me differently when they found out. So I stopped telling people. My ex-boyfriend back home found out. Made him act all weird. That's why he's my *ex*-boyfriend. That's why I transferred up here from UC San Diego. Nobody knows up here. Even my two roomies don't know. Just you, Dan. And you don't treat me differently."

"I probably would if I was more of a true believer," I said.

"But you're not," she said. "Oddly enough, that seems to be what I find most attractive about you."

"And here I was hoping it was 'cause I look so much like Errol Flynn."

"Your mustache helps. But he was blond and you're dark-haired."

She yawned again, and said, "Getting late. I think you'd better take me home now, Danny Sullivan. You may not have classes tomorrow, but I do."

I walked her back to her apartment. She left me standing outside the front door after a quick kiss.

Shouldn't have bought that second pitcher. Maybe, if we'd left La Val's earlier, she'd have invited me inside.

Live and learn.

SEVENTEEN

Notwithstanding that ill-advised second pitcher, it didn't delay getting invited into Megan's place by all that much.

I phoned her the next day to make the customary and obligatory "had a great time last night" call, and she responded with the customary, though not quite so obligatory, "offer of reciprocation," asking me over that Sunday for a home-cooked dinner followed by a movie she needed to see for one of her classes.

"What are you making?" I asked.

"Roasted chicken."

"Sounds great. I'll bring a bottle of chardonnay. What movie are we seeing?"

"*High Noon*. It's on a list of recommended movies in my class on 'Depictions of American Society in 1950's Filmmaking.'"

"One of my favorites," I said. "Have you already got a video or can I pick one up?"

"If you could pick one up that'd be a big help."

"DVD okay?"

"Perfect."

"About six?"

"Make it five."

That gave me something nice to look forward to. In the intervening two evenings, however, I was signed up for a couple of Marina details.

Friday night's was uneventful, but Saturday's gave every indication, at least at first, of being momentous.

It all began with what seemed to be a routine drunk driving stop.

Of course, the use of that term "routine" is discouraged. Every traffic stop is different, and every one potentially dangerous, simply because you have no idea who's behind the wheel of any car you pull over nor what kind of threat they may pose. Thinking of car stops as "routine" can make you complacent. And complacency can get you killed. Still, there was no obvious reason to think of the guy I saw weaving back and forth across the traffic line on University Avenue as anything but what he seemed to be, someone too intoxicated to be operating a motor vehicle.

He was driving a navy Dodge Ram Wagon, which is to say a dark blue van, automatically making him a figure of more than usual interest, but, as I'd had cause to discover, there were thousands of blue vans in California. There was nothing to indicate that this was the particular blue van every cop in the Bay Area was on the lookout for.

Not at first.

The plate had come back clear of wants and warrants, and was attached to the vehicle it was supposed to be attached to, so I flipped on the roof lights and punched a short yelp on the siren to pull him over, then asked Control to send me a cover car, not so much because I felt threatened as that I wanted a second officer present as a witness when I administered a field sobriety test to determine just how drunk the guy really was.

I approached the driver side door to ask for the license and proof of insurance. The guy behind the wheel was a husky, bearded white male adult.

Now a blue van was one thing, but a blue van driven by a heavyset guy with a beard was something else. He was definitely going to bear a bit more investigation.

Bob Bower, the other reservist on Marina duty, rolled up behind me a few moments later.

He was struck by the coincidence, too.

"Let's just give him the field sobriety," he said. "Either he's the one or he's not. If he is, at least we'll have his picture and prints on file. If he's not, it'll be one less DUI on the street."

I agreed. I ran the driver, George Trenton Neville, through PIN (the Bay Area's Police Information Network), CLETS (the California Law Enforcement Telecommunications System), and NCIC (the FBI's National Crime Information Center), to see if there were any warrants out for him. No hits. A criminal history check also failed to turn up any information. If Neville was a bad guy, he had, so far, managed to operate below law enforcement's radar.

I had him step out of the van to begin the series of tests that would indicate his level of inebriation.

As I opened the door for him to step out I spotted the top of a magazine cover underneath the driver seat. The letters "BOND" were visible.

"What's that?" I asked Neville.

"Jus' a magazine," he said.

"Okay if I take a look?"

I reached in. The magazine was called *Bondage Babes*. The cover depicted a young blonde woman, nude, who'd been tied to a chair and gagged. Apparently struggling to escape her captivity, she was looking into the camera with an expression of simulated fear. Similar photographs illustrated the inside pages.

Neville had a bondage fetish.

Now it was a lot more than just a blue van, or even a blue van driven by a heavyset man with a beard. Now it was a blue van driven by a heavyset bearded man who was turned on by pictures of beautiful young women who'd been abducted and tied up.

Still a long way from "Probable Cause," the level of proof I'd need to actually take Neville in and book him for kidnapping DeeDee, but it more than made the cut for PC's baby brother, "Reasonable Suspicion," the level of proof needed to hold him temporarily at the scene for an investigative stop.

But, as Bob pointed out, if I didn't have evidence enough to arrest Neville for kidnapping DeeDee, I had a very good chance of being able to develop enough to take him in on another charge altogether.

I told Neville to stand on one foot. He couldn't manage to do it for more than a few seconds before he started to stumble.

I had him stretch out his arms and try to touch the tip of his nose with his eyes closed. He missed consistently.

I had him walk a straight line, heel to toe. He was unable to stay on the line for more than a step or two.

I had him recite the alphabet out loud. He managed to get all twenty-six letters in the right order, but almost immediately lapsed into singing the nursery rhyme tune little kids are taught to help them memorize the correct sequence of letters.

I had him print out the alphabet in block letters on a blank sheet of notebook paper. The letters he wrote were crooked, he couldn't stay on the lines, and he omitted two letters. When I had him sign and date what he'd written, he got the date wrong.

No doubt about it. Neville was drunk. A blood/alcohol test would clinch it.

I cuffed him up and, with Bob's help, loaded him into the back seat of my patrol car. Then, after locking up his van, I headed back to the station to administer an Intoxilizer test.

Neville blew better than a 0.12 twice. Half again what I needed to establish a legal presumption of intoxication.

That made his arrest legally solid, but it didn't mean he'd had anything to do with DeeDee.

Nevertheless, that certainly would bear looking into.

Once Neville was booked and locked in a cell, I went down to the patrol sergeants' office and spoke to Gary Church. As the senior sergeant on duty, he was, in the absence of the lieutenant, the acting watch commander. Since it was the weekend, there was no one on duty in the Crimes Against Persons Detail. Whether or not anyone from CAP should be called in would be up to him.

Gary Church was a tall, rangy guy with more than twenty years on the Job. His lined face gave him the appearance of an old-time frontiersman. A champion pistol shot, he was the BPD's top gun and, on that account, had been designated the Department's "Senior Firearms Instructor."

I laid out my suspicions of Neville for him.

"On top of everything else," I said, "he lives in an apartment on College near Durant, just a few blocks from DeeDee's Co-op. He might have seen her a dozen times or more. Hell, he might have stalked her."

"Yeah, it sounds good," he said, nodding. "How'd you happen to see that skin magazine, anyway?"

"Part of it was sticking out from under the front seat as he got out of the van."

"Okay, that's plain view. But that's still nothing more than being in possession of a dirty magazine, which doesn't happen to be a crime." The unspoken part of his sentence was, "though it ought to be." Gary Church is old-school when it comes to things like porn.

"Maybe it's not a crime," I said, "but it does show what kind of things turn him on. Did you ever hear of Harvey Glatman, that serial killer in Los Angeles back in the '50's?"

"Think so. Wambaugh mentioned him in one of his books, didn't he?"

"That's the one. They called him 'The Lonely Hearts Killer.' He used to kidnap women, tie them up, and rape them. Then he'd take pictures of them while they were bound and gagged just before strangling them to death. They found the photos when they searched his home. Along with several thousand dollars worth of bondage porn that he'd spent years collecting before he went on his murder spree."

"I'm not disagreeing with you, Danny," he said. "Believe me, I'd love to get a closer look inside that van. Or better yet, his house. I'm just wondering if there's any legal way we can do that. The porn's not enough."

"Doesn't quite come up to PC," I agreed.

"Not for the kidnapping. But maybe we can search it for evidence of the deuce."

"We're already solid on the deuce charge. He blew an oh point twelve."

"Yeah, but suppose it wasn't just booze he was on? Then maybe we could search the van for drug paraphernalia. And anything else we found we could use. Even if all we found was a roach or a homemade crack pipe, that'd be enough to get a warrant for his crib, which is where we'd be most likely to find anything related to DeeDee, anyway."

I saw where Gary was going. His reasoning was predicated on several different legal doctrines.

To make a search of any premises for evidence of a crime (presuming that you don't have the permission of the owner of the place to be searched), you need two things.

The first is "Probable Cause," a set of circumstances that, considered in their totality, would lead a reasonable person to conclude that evidence of a crime was likely to be found in the place to be searched.

The second is either a search warrant or what are called "exigent circumstances." A search warrant is, of course, nothing more than a document signed by a judge who, having reviewed an officer's assertion of Probable Cause, has concurred with the officer's judgment that it does, in fact, exist and, in consequence, has approved the search. A cop who thinks he has PC may or may not be right, but once a judge agrees that he has PC, which is what he's saying when he signs the warrant, that cop's judgment is already validated before the case ever gets to court.

Making a search based on exigent circumstances is a much dicier situation, legally. It means that events are breaking too fast for the officer to take the time to apply for a warrant. Maybe a crime is in progress, or someone is in immediate danger, or the officer reasonably believes that if he waits to get a warrant, the evidence will be moved or destroyed. If the officer makes such a search, then not only is his assertion of PC going to be very carefully scrutinized, since he didn't run it by a judge first, but his assertion of exigent circumstances will also be closely examined, since it's that assertion that justified his immediately making the search without taking the time to get a judge's approval.

Unless the officer is searching a vehicle.

Under something called the "Carroll Doctrine," named for a pair of bootlegging brothers in Michigan back in the 1920's who made a habit of tooling around the state in a souped-up Olds loaded with illegal liquor, exigent circumstances can be automatically assumed if the premises to be searched are some sort of moveable conveyance such as a car, a boat, or a plane.

So, if we could develop PC to search Neville's van, the fact that it was a van automatically gave us exigent circumstances. And if we found evidence of a crime in the van, that would give us the PC we needed to get a warrant for his home.

The problem was one porn magazine was nothing like enough PC to search either his van or his home for evidence relating to DeeDee's kidnapping. Which is where another legal principle, known as the "Plain View Doctrine," came into play.

The Plain View Doctrine means just what its name implies, that a cop can seize evidence of a crime if it's in his plain view. He can't barge into a private home in search of a marijuana plant just on a whim, for example, but if the homeowner stupidly puts the marijuana plant in his front picture window where it's visible from the street, and the officer sees it while he's walking his beat, then he can enter the home and seize the plant, without bothering to get a warrant, because it was in his plain view.

And it also works with actual searches. Let's say you've got a warrant to search a house for stolen diamonds and, in the course of making that search, you open a desk drawer and find a kilo of heroin inside. Even though that heroin wasn't listed on the warrant, doesn't even have anything to do with the crime you're investigating, you can seize it, and use it as evidence, because it was in a place you had a right to look, thanks to the warrant, and it's come under your plain view.

You have to be careful that the place you were looking was actually a place you had a right to look, though. If the item listed in the warrant, say, a stolen wide-screen television instead of stolen diamonds, then you couldn't look in that drawer because you'd have no reasonable expectation that a large item like a TV could actually be hidden there.

In this case, assuming we could establish that Neville was intoxicated by dope as well as booze, we could search the van, without a warrant, for evidence of drug use.

At least Gary seemed to think so.

If we found any such evidence, we could use it to get a warrant to search his home. And if, in the course of searching either his van or his home, ostensibly for dope evidence, we found anything that connected Neville with DeeDee's disappearance, we could use that, too, even though DeeDee was never, at least on paper, the focus of the investigation at all.

The whole house of cards hinged on getting some evidence that Neville was high as well as drunk. But since he'd chosen the breath test, which only tests for alcohol, we wouldn't be able to prove it by the chemical analysis evidence.

"Hal Bocatelli's on Crimes Against Persons this year," I said.

"Yeah, so?" said Gary.

"So he used to be on TAP and SIB, and he's taken the DEA course on identifying people under the influence."

TAP is the Telegraph Avenue Patrol, a high-profile foot beat that BPD and UCPD run as a joint operation. A city cop and a campus cop are partnered up and assigned to aggressively patrol the South Campus, with special attention paid to the drug violators who run rampant in that area. SIB is the Special Investigations Bureau, the Department's vice/narcotics squad.

Hal Bocatelli, as a veteran of both special assignments, and a graduate of the federal class on recognizing subjects who are under the influence of illegal substances, was legally qualified to judge whether or not Neville had any other recreational chemicals coursing through his bloodstream besides alcohol. If he was able to say that Neville was stoned as well as soused, that'd be our ticket to ride. And since his current assignment was CAP, he'd be right on hand to take over if we found anything against Neville more damning than a half-smoked joint.

Gary gave him a call.

***

When we laid everything out for Hal, he went up to the jail, had Neville brought out of his cell, and examined him closely. Gary and I went back to the sergeants' office.

I was beginning to wonder how legally shaky the ground we were preparing to walk on was and said so to Gary.

"Why's that?" he asked.

"Okay, suppose Hal examines Neville and decides that he has, in fact, been using drugs. And suppose we find some dope in his car and use that to get a warrant to search his crib. And suppose, finally, that, in the course of ostensibly searching for additional evidence of drug use, we do find what we both know we're really looking for, evidence that Neville was behind DeeDee's kidnapping. Are you sure we'd be able to use it?"

"Plain view doctrine," he answered.

"Theoretically sure. But the underlying presumption of the Plain View Doctrine is that finding the evidence in plain view was serendipitous."

"Was what?"

"A fortunate surprise. But, in this case, the proposed search for drug evidence is just a pretext to search for clues about what happened to DeeDee. Would it be admissible once it came out that it was what we were really looking for all along?"

"Why should that come out? And even if it did, you know courts have been allowing cops to use pretexts when they're investigating crimes."

That was true. Courts do allow some pretextual actions by

police. Say you're following a guy you suspect is carrying dope (sorry to keep coming back to that example, but, hey, this *is* Berkeley, and drug cases loom pretty large) in his car. You want to investigate, but lack PC. Then the guy makes a right turn without signaling, so you pull him over, using the traffic violation as an excuse to investigate the suspected drug possession. That's allowed, as long as there actually was a traffic violation supporting the original stop.

"I see what you're saying, Sarge. But you're combining two different legal concepts."

"Why should that be a problem? If the courts allow pretextual stops, and they allow plain view seizures, why is it such a big jump to conclude that a pretextual search to get a chance at a plain view seizure would be allowed?"

"Because it's uncharted territory, which means it's sure to get challenged. And this is Alameda County, and Alameda County has a whole bunch of judges who never met a defense motion to suppress evidence that they didn't like."

"We're not violating any of this guy's rights."

"No, but we're making an end run around them and, if Neville's lawyer, whoever that turns out to be, makes a convincing argument, we won't be able to use any evidence we find."

"Okay, maybe you're right. Can you think of any other way to get it?"

I couldn't. And, fifteen minutes later, theory became practice when Hal told us that, in his expert opinion, Neville was not just drunk, but high as well.

EIGHTEEN

The three of us, Hal, Bob, and I, went back to the Marina, where Neville's van was parked off of University Avenue. A quick toss turned up a roach clip, with the tiny remnant of an almost completely smoked joint still attached, and a glass crack pipe, with burnt residue at the base. Not much, but it counted as drug paraphernalia, and was enough for us to reasonably infer that more such items were likely to be found in his home. In other words, it was probable cause.

Getting the warrant took a little longer, but, all things considered, particularly allowing for the fact that it was a Saturday evening, it took Hal very little time to write up an affidavit applying for a warrant to search Neville's apartment, to run it by a deputy district attorney, and then to find a judge willing to sign off on it.

Two hours after finding the paraphernalia in his van, we were entering Neville's apartment, ostensibly to look for more evidence of drug violations, but actually to see if there was anything there that could connect him to DeeDee's disappearance.

It took us another three hours to thoroughly search the apartment. We'd found a few more comparatively innocuous items that made it clear that Neville was a frequent user of dope, but nothing that indicated anything more than private use. And, more importantly, nothing that tied directly to DeeDee's case.

There were dozens of porn videos, both DVD and VHS, as well as magazines, paperback novels, and comic books, all devoted to graphic depictions of bound and gagged women. We confiscated it all.

There was a huge pile of newspapers in one corner of the kitchen.

"Grab all those," said Hal. "Maybe he's keeping them to clip out articles about the case."

They were added to the seized property.

There were a number of blank VHS cassettes, all of which apparently had been used to record material for later viewing. We didn't stop to see what was on them, but we did pack them all up. Perhaps, like Harvey Glatman, he'd used these cassettes to create a photographic record of DeeDee's captivity, before doing her in. In the meantime, our ostensible reason for taking them was that, sometimes cassettes are used to hide drugs or other drug-related paraphernalia.

He had a laptop computer on a coffee table in the living room. We grabbed that to see if he was keeping track of DeeDee's case on the 'Net, as well as to track his use of porn websites.

But really, we were grasping at straws. Aside from a tiny amount of illegal substances and a few items of drug paraphernalia, there was nothing in the place that indicated Neville was guilty of being anything but an indifferent housekeeper.

Yeah, we found plenty of evidence that he had a bondage fetish, but so did lots of other guys. There wouldn't be so damned much of it, if there weren't a market for it. And possessing the stuff wasn't illegal, as long as it didn't involve children, or actual deaths weren't depicted. In fact, as bondage porn went, it was pretty vanilla. Taken with his physical appearance, and his personal ride, both such a close match to DeeDee's abductor, and the fact that he lived so close to DeeDee's Co-op, it was loosely consistent with the kind of guy who'd kidnap a girl and get his rocks off by keeping her captive.

But the operative word there was "loosely." For practical purposes, it was such a tenuous connection as to be all but nonexistent.

Nevertheless, we bundled it all up, along with the unlabeled cassettes, the laptop, and the old newspapers, and took it back to the station.

***

Before booking the stuff into evidence, we had Neville brought from the jail to the CAP office. He'd sobered up during the hours since his arrest, and was able to answer questions. Hal, being the detective, conducted the interrogation. I was allowed to sit and quietly observe. Bob returned to patrol, since no one had been covering the Marina during this whole time.

After Mirandizing Neville, Hal began by asking him how much he'd had to drink before getting behind the wheel of his van. Neville admitted finishing off the better part of a 750 ml. bottle of vodka, mixed with lime juice.

"Was there anything backing that up?" asked Hal.

"What do you mean 'backing that up?'"

"I mean were you using anything else besides the booze?"

"I made me a J and smoked it."

Hal nodded.

"We searched your apartment," he said. "Found more evidence of drug use there."

"Why'd'ja search my apartment? D'ja have a warrant?"

"Of course."

"You went and got a search warrant over a chickenshit deuce rap? What're y'all being so hard-nosed for? Y'already had me on the breath test! Why'd'ja need any more evidence?"

Hal changed the subject to keep Neville off-balance.

"Tell me about the magazine in your van."

"Oh, shit. C'mon, man. I ain't proud o' that, but it ain't illegal."

"You like seeing women tied up and helpless, George?"

"Man, it's just a... whatcha call it... a fantasy. Some guys like black underwear. Some guys like stockings and garters. I like ropes and gags."

"You ever tied up a woman, George?"

"No, man! I toldja, it's just a fantasy. Lotsa people go to conventions where they dress up like *Star Wars* or *Star Trek*. Don't mean they shoot people with phasers or cut 'em up with lightsabers. It's just a fantasy."

Hal pulled out the unmarked VHS cassettes.

"Y'know, George. People have been known to hide things in these cassettes. My warrant gives me the right to break these open and check."

"Ah, man, don't do that. That's just stuff I've saved, haven't gotten around to looking at yet. Go ahead and play 'em yourself, if you don't believe me."

"You're giving me permission to look at these videos to make sure they're not being used to hide anything?"

"Yeah. I'd rather you did that than break 'em apart."

"Anything on 'em we're likely to find interesting?"

"Maybe if you're into old movies. It's just stuff I recorded off of TCM and channels like that."

"None of these are movies you made yourself?"

"No. All I got's a player. Don't have a camera. What would I be making movies of, anyway?"

"Well, you like this bondage stuff so much, maybe you decided to roll your own."

"Why would I do that?"

"Maybe there was a local girl you were attracted to, and you wanted to see how she looked in ropes and gags."

"What're y'talking about, man?"

"You live in the same neighborhood as DeeDee Merryweather, the girl who went missing from the Fire Trail on Strawberry Canyon a few weeks ago. Real pretty blonde with a great figure. Just like a lot of the girls in your magazines."

"Is *that* what you think? You think I'm the one snatched DeeDee Merryweather?"

Hal showed Neville a reproduction of the forensic sketch portrait of DeeDee's captor.

"Look at this, George," he said. "You look so much like the guy in this sketch, you might have been the one posing for it. Your ride is a blue van. And you live less than a block away from Rivendell House, DeeDee's Co-op. Plus it turns out you fantasize about kidnapped girls. What would you think?"

"For Christ's sake, you've seen my crib. Where would I keep her if I'd kidnapped her?"

"And what about all these old newspapers? You saving 'em all to clip out stories about the case? Y'gonna make a scrapbook out of your press clippings? A lot of criminals do that, you know."

"Are you *serious*? I just haven't gotten around to taking 'em down to the recycling bin, that's all. You really figure everyone who's lazy about throwing away their old newspapers is a criminal?"

I was no experienced interrogator, God knows. Nevertheless, to my ears, at least, Neville's denials had the ring of truth. Hal had stopped asking questions, and was just staring at him. Silence makes some suspects uneasy. When the conversation stops, they feel compelled to fill the silence, and sometimes say something not to their advantage.

But not this time.

Neville just sat there thunderstruck, as if it'd never even occurred to him that anyone would think he'd had a thing to do with harming DeeDee.

When he finally did speak, it turned out that he had a very good reason for believing he was above suspicion.

NINETEEN

Megan hit the button on the remote that ejected the DVD from the player and turned down the sound on the TV as I picked up another homemade chocolate chip cookie from the tray on the coffee table and took a bite. It was Sunday evening, and we'd just enjoyed an hour and a half of nail-biting suspense watching Gary Cooper single-handedly face down Frank Miller and his outlaw gang over the objections of his pacifist wife, Grace Kelly.

"So what did you think?" she asked.

"It's great," I said, shrugging. "It's always been great. I told you it was one of my favorites when you invited me over."

"Yeah, but what did you think about the depiction of the town?"

"Visually, you mean? Stark and sparse. Kind of the way you'd expect a remote frontier town to look. It kind of resembled photography from that era. I think I read somewhere that Zinnemann was deliberately going for that kind of look."

"But the townspeople, how about them?"

"What about 'em?"

"This is a class on depictions of American society in film. I'm supposed to be able to comment on what this movie's depiction of the townspeople has to say about the national character."

"Well, then you're out of luck, 'cause what the film has to say about the national character, at least if the residents of Hadleyville are your template, is a lie."

"What do you mean a lie?"

"I mean something that isn't true. I'm not particularly upset by it. It's fiction after all. But it wasn't an accurate depiction of the way the citizens of a frontier town would have reacted to a situation like that."

"How do you know that?"

"I know for the simple reason that the historical record shows that citizens of frontier towns reacted to those kinds of situations just the opposite of the way the townspeople in *High Noon* did."

"Like how?"

"Okay, it's 1876, and the James gang has just ridden into Northfield, Minnesota, to raid the town. As soon as they make their presence known, everyone in town rises up, grabs their guns, and shoots down just about everyone in the gang. Frank and Jesse are the only ones to get away. And just barely, at that."

"That's only one example. You can't build a whole historical record from one example."

"Fine. Same year, Sam Bass and his gang try to rob a train when it stops at Hutchins, Texas. One train crewman manages to get away from the depot without being seen by the gang, runs into the center of town, and sounds the alarm. Within minutes, a group of townspeople have formed a makeshift posse, and are rushing to the train station to drive off the gang before they're able to complete the robbery. There's maybe twenty thousand dollars in the express car, but the gang only gets away with about ninety bucks in silver."

"Any others?"

"Yeah. 1892. The Daltons and their gang ride into Coffeyville, Kansas, where they plan to rob two banks simultaneously. But they've bitten off more than they can chew. Once again the whole town responds, and almost every member of the gang is captured or killed. The only one who gets away is a guy who got cold feet and decided not to ride into town at all."

"How do you know all this stuff?"

"It's common knowledge. You can find it in any history of the Old West. Check it out if you don't believe me."

"Oh, I believe you. What I can't believe is that you have all that stuff right at your fingertips."

"Yeah, but on the other hand, I have no idea what the balance is on my checking account."

"Very funny. Do you think Carl Foreman knew all this? The screenwriter?"

"I know who Carl Foreman was. The general events, I suppose. I'd be willing to bet he was aware of what happened at Northfield and Coffeyville, 'cause they'd both been dramatized in maybe a dozen movies by the time he wrote the script for *High Noon*. Actual dates and such, maybe not. What difference does it make?"

"Well, if he knew what frontier communities were really like, why would he give such an unflattering portrayal of them?"

"Who knows? Maybe that was the way the town was depicted in the short story."

"What short story?"

"'The Tin Star' by John Cunningham. The story the script was supposedly adapted from. I've never read it, but maybe he was just following the original story. That's one possible explanation."

She frowned, and said, "One possible explanation?"

"Well, he was a communist. At least he had been. Maybe he was trying to draw some comparison between the selfishness of the townspeople and the inherent selfishness of capitalism. When his party affiliations became public, that's what a lot of people thought, that the whole script was just commie propaganda. Of course, Foreman claimed that he'd left the Party years before he ever wrote *High Noon*."

"But he still got blacklisted, even though he said he left, didn't he?"

"Yeah. He got subpoenaed to testify before the House Un-American Activities Committee prior to *High Noon*'s release. Gave 'em the standard 'I left the Party because I was disillusioned with Stalin and totalitarianism, yadda, yadda' line. But when he was asked to name other people in the Party, he refused."

"You don't think it was right for him to refuse?"

"He was trying to have his cake and eat it, too. If he were a committed communist, and he refused to name names, that'd be one thing. He'd be wrong, but at least he'd be consistent. And honorable, according to his own lights. But for him to say that he'd come to believe communism was wrong, a threat to the country, antithetical to freedom, and all that, but then refuse to name anyone else who was involved in this dire threat, well, sorry, I just don't think he gets to have it both ways. Anyway, getting blacklisted didn't hurt him much, as far as I can see."

"What do you mean?"

"He moved to England. A few years later he got hired to co-write the script for *Bridge on the River Kwai*. Yeah, he didn't get to use his own name, but he got paid a pretty decent chunk of change. A few years after that he's plainly listed on the credits as the writer and producer of *The Guns of Navarone*. Hell, he's practically got his name above the title in that one. *High Noon*, *Bridge on the River Kwai*, and *The Guns of Navarone*. Plus *Champion* and *The Men* before the whole blacklist thing started. Plus *Young Winston* years afterward. Three Best Picture nominees, one of 'em the winner, one Oscar for Best Screenplay, and five more nominations. Quite a career for a guy who's supposed to have been blacklisted."

"He never got to actually possess the Oscar he won for *Bridge on the River Kwai*. He was never publicly acknowledged as one of the screenwriters, nor listed as one of the winners, until after he died."

"No, but *he* knew he won. And so did most people in the industry. It was an open secret. So it was still a great bullet point on his résumé."

"But getting back to the original point, you really think *High Noon* was communist propaganda?" she asked.

"I never said I thought so. I said that's what a lot of people thought after his past came out. Duke Wayne for one. Howard Hawks for another. Harry Cohn at Columbia for a third. On the other hand, Ronald Reagan and General Eisenhower, neither of whom could ever be accused of being commie sympathizers, both admired the film very much. And the Soviet Union officially condemned it because it, quote, glorified the individual, unquote, which severely undercuts its commie status. Hell, if Foreman hadn't've been a known communist, or former communist, or whatever the hell he was, the whole script probably would've been seen as a Christian allegory."

"How do you mean?"

"Think about it. You've got a guy, hailed as a savior by the whole community, who's taken on heavy responsibilities. Then a crisis looms, a crisis that'll likely get this guy killed, and suddenly all his friends desert him and he's left to do his duty all by himself. Doesn't that sound familiar?"

"When you put it that way, yeah."

"And there're also a lot of elements that suggest an essentially conservative political orientation. Remember, Frank Miller's a known murderer, but he's free to wreak vengeance on Marshal

Kane because of a criminal justice system that didn't have the balls to punish him properly. Twenty years later, *Dirty Harry* was preaching the same message. Now that I think about it, that one also ends with the hero tossing his badge away in contempt. Probably a deliberate homage. Which is French for 'rip-off.'"

"So what do you think the real reason was?"

"Suspense. It suited the story he wanted to tell. He wanted the marshal to face the outlaws single-handed, and, in order for him to have to do that, the town had to desert him. Simple as that."

A news bulletin was just coming on. The announcer was saying something about a suspect being questioned in the DeeDee Merryweather disappearance. Megan turned the sound up in time to hear him say that the suspect had been released and that details would be forthcoming on the regular eleven o'clock news program.

"I just hate it when they make it look like a breaking news bulletin and it turns out to be a commercial for the late news," she said. Turning to me, she asked, "Do you know anything about this new suspect?"

"Yeah," I said. "All about him. Fool's gold."

"What do you mean?"

"That what Pete calls it when you have a suspect who looks perfect, but just happens to be totally innocent. You put in a lot of time and effort trying to make a case, and he turns out to be the wrong man. Just like prospecting for gold and finding pyrite. Fool's gold. Probably picked it up from when he was a miner."

"From the way they talked about it just now, I got the impression that the police thought he was the right man but just didn't have enough evidence to hold him."

"Oh, we've got evidence. But all it proves is that he couldn't have done it."

"Why's that?"

"'Cause he was in Maine for two weeks in September, and it was in the middle of those two weeks that DeeDee turned up missing."

"So he's got an alibi?"

"Rock solid and iron-bound. Hell, calling what he's got an alibi is like calling the Pacific Ocean a bit moist. He flew out seven days before she disappeared, flew back seven days after, and was seen every day he was there. It was somebody else that Mrs. Taylor saw, and it was some other van she saw him standing by."

She could tell I wasn't really enjoying the topic, so she dropped it and we went back to talking about the movie.

But, subliminally at least, I suspect things were still percolating in my mind. I think I was probably starting to edge a little closer to the notion that we were following the wrong trail.

I mean, a profile's just a profile. And lots of people can fit a given profile. But there couldn't be that many who fit it as closely as Neville.

Yet Neville was totally innocent. Did that prove anything? Did it at least indicate anything?

Yeah, God knows there were thousands of blue vans in California. And thousands of heavyset, bearded men, too.

But how many of those heavyset bearded men who drove blue vans also lived in the same neighborhood as DeeDee Merryweather?

And how many were bondage freaks?

To say nothing of so closely resembling the sketch they could have, as Hal had said, posed for it?

There just couldn't be that many guys who fit that profile that perfectly. And if someone who was such a perfect fit could turn out to be so completely innocent, then maybe, just maybe, the profile was wrong.

All wrong.

And if the profile was wrong, what were we left with?

All subliminal, like I said. None of it considered thought. But those subconscious notions were starting to get ripe for a nudge to the surface.

TWENTY

For the rest of the semester, I made a point of fitting as much time with Megan as possible into my regular routine of classes, Co-op meetings, patrol tours, and Crimes Against Persons shifts.

We'd grab quick lunches between classes. We had study dates at each other's homes. We went to parties together. We went to a whole lot of movies together. We even went to Mass together once or twice.

She'd gone back to San Diego for the Thanksgiving weekend. A difficult to endure preview of what the upcoming semester break would be like without her.

She stayed for a few days after final exams ended so we could spend as much time together as possible before she went home for the Christmas holidays.

"Will you be back in time for New Year's?" I asked.

"I will," she said. "Count on it."

***

For the first few days after she went back to San Diego, I found it pretty hard to take an interest in anything.

I was working full-time during the weeks leading up to Christmas, which was fortunate since it kept me occupied with things other than Megan being away.

The paid traffic posts had ended with the passing of football season, but another seasonal paid detail, the Christmas Foot Patrol, powered up in the weeks preceding December 25th, and I'd signed up for forty hours a week.

This is probably my favorite detail. It's just old-fashioned neighborhood cop work. A visible walking patrol along Shattuck Avenue in Berkeley's downtown shopping district. You stop in a few stores, visit with the owners, and discourage thieves just by your presence. You walk up and down the sidewalk and smile at all the shoppers, who invariably smile back, glad to see something as anachronistic as a foot patrolman at Christmastime. You stop in one of the many banks, initial a little sign-in sheet that shows how often the police have made a check, and pass a few minutes with the bank guards, some of whom are retired cops who have a career's worth of wisdom to pass on, and some of whom are cop wannabes who invariably act grateful that a real cop is condescending to speak with him as though he's a brother professional.

I tell you the Christmas detail is the biggest ego-building assignment in the BPD. And I get paid for it.

And with Megan out of my life for several weeks, my ego needed some building.

***

Though there's a PR aspect to the Christmas detail, the real reason they have us out there is because, at Christmastime, there's a heightened need for cops on the street. So it's not all smiling and nodding and acting nice for the citizens. Occasionally, there's some actual police work to do.

So far, I'd taken some theft reports, arrested a drunk or two, responded to some disturbances, and settled down a few disputes between customers and shop owners.

I hadn't encountered anything violent, though. Facing a violent offender is always a possibility when you're wearing a uniform and a badge, but it's also the tip of the iceberg. It really doesn't come up that much. So the call I got on the afternoon of December 21st surprised me.

"*Car 11,*" came the voice of the desk officer in the Comm Center.

"*11.*" That was Officer Fred Davidson, the regular beat officer on mobile patrol in the area.

"*245 in progress at the UA Theatre, 2274 Shattuck. 673, 666, and 645 also respond. 11, you'll handle the case.*"

666, Officer Nick Huang, who we jokingly called the "Devil's Spawn" because of the badge number he'd gotten saddled with, and 645, Officer Doris Brandon, were the other two reserve cops on the downtown foot patrol detail.

"245" is the California Penal Code section for "Assault with a Deadly Weapon."

"*11, from Durant and College,*" came Fred's voice.

"*10-4, 11,*" said Control.

I keyed the remote mike of my belt radio and said, "673, on foot from Shattuck and Bancroft."

"*10-4,*" said Control.

"*Triple-Six, from Shattuck and Miliva,*" came Nick's voice.

"*10-4, Triple-Six.*"

"*645, from Shattuck and Dwight.*" That was Doris.

"*10-4, 645.*"

I was only a half-block south, so I'd almost certainly be the first one to arrive. I keyed my mike again.

"673, any further details?" I cursed myself as soon as I allowed the question over the air. He'd put out further details as soon as he had them. He didn't need prompting from me. Asking for the information like that was something a rookie or an amateur would do.

"*673, your suspect's a white male, early to mid-twenties, armed with a knife. No other information at this time.*"

"10-4. 673 is 10-97."

That was radio-ese for "arrived at scene."

I peeked around the corner of the theatre alcove, saw nothing. Nothing going on in the lobby either, at least in the part I could see through the doors.

The girl in the box-office didn't know anything about knife attacks occurring in the theatre. I went into the alcove to the front doors and waited for cover to arrive.

The UA's been around for decades. Starting out as a single-screen theatre, it began sub-dividing in the '70's to compete with the multiplexes that were becoming so common. A series of renovations over a period of years had transformed the venerable old movie house from a single-auditorium theatre to one with seven screens.

Which might just make it a bit hairy. If this assault was going on in one of the seven auditoriums instead of the lobby or snack bar, we were going to be dealing with darkness, crowds, and all sorts of other dangerous variables. To say nothing of finding the guy in the first place.

Nick Huang came up beside me a few moments later.

"Triple-Six, 10-97," he said into his remote mike, then, to me, "See anything?"

"No. You want to wait for more cover, or go in?"

"We better go in."

I agreed. We informed Control, pushed through the entrance, and approached the guy behind the snack bar.

"You make the call?" I asked.

"Yeah," he said. "They're upstairs. I don't know how it started, but when one of them pulled a knife, I decided I better not try to break it up myself."

"Good choice," I said. "How many are there?"

"Two."

"Okay." I informed Control that the disturbance was on the second floor, and that a knife was involved, then started up the stairs with Nick, our weapons drawn.

As we climbed, we started to hear loud voices.

"Who the hell you think you are, dissin' me?"

"Just stay away from me."

"Teach you some respect's what I'm gon' do. Take that blade away from you and cram it so far up you ass you be able to pick you teeth with it."

I was at the top of the stairs at this point, Nick right behind me. The one with the knife was a small white male. His weapon seemed to be just a folding pocket model, like a Scout knife or a Swiss Army knife. He had it opened and was holding it in front of him as he backed away from the other guy.

This other guy was a big, heavyset black male, late teens or early twenties, wearing what looked like gang colors, though many wear "gangsta" styles and affect "gangsta" attitudes without actually being in a gang. Still, he didn't seem to be intimidated by the other's weapon. In fact, he seemed to be doing most of the intimidating. Whether or not he was actually affiliated, he'd apparently bought into the whole street hood ethos.

Of course, with the Oakland city line just a few miles south, and Berkeley developing plenty of its own gang problems, he could very well be a genuine 'banger.

But he didn't have a weapon visible, and the other one did.

Nick and I both pointed our guns at the knife-wielder. I said, "Police! Both of you stop right there."

They both stopped and turned to look at us.

"You with the knife," I went on. "Drop it right now."

He dropped it.

By this time Doris and Fred had joined us. In the next few moments we had the knife-wielder frisked and handcuffed. The 'banger-type was also frisked, but, for the moment, he wasn't in handcuffs, since he was the supposed victim.

Fred, as the handling officer, conducted the interviews with both men, and directed the three of us to talk to the witnesses.

As it shook out, it all seemed to be a misunderstanding, though one that the black guy, showing off for his date, did everything he could to aggravate.

As they waited outside of one of the upstairs theatres for a movie to end so they could enter for the next showing, Knife-Wielder had accidentally tripped and jostled 'Banger-Type who'd been standing in front of him.

'Banger-Type, deciding to play the badass street thug for his girl, had waved off Knife-Wielder's apology, grabbed a handful of Knife-Wielder's shirt, thrown him against the wall, and started advancing toward him.

'Banger-Type had the clear advantage in height and weight, and, as it seemed to the Knife-Wielder, the clear advantage in homicidal intentions, as well. To equalize things, Knife-Wielder reached into his pocket for the folding blade he habitually carried and started backing away. Facing the weapon slowed the 'Banger-Type's advance, but didn't stop it.

This had all the earmarks of a case that the DA would decide to kick "in the interests of justice." And none of us would be likely to object. But that would be the DA's decision to make.

Fred decided to book both of them.

***

The next day I walked into another felony arrest when I saw an illegally parked car near the entrance to the BART station at Shattuck and Center. The driver was still inside. I figured I could save myself some paperwork and him some money by just telling him to move along.

Before approaching him, I had the plate run through a computer check. The car came back stolen.

I ended the shift with a felony arrest and a recovered stolen car to my sole credit just for being alert for illegally parked cars.

God, I love this job!

TWENTY-ONE

On the evening of December 22nd I was sitting alone in the vestibule of a Mexican restaurant on Geary Street in The City. Stephanie, Louise, and I had made arrangements to get together for a private Christmas celebration, since we'd all be with our families on the actual holiday.

Both Steph's and Lou's folks lived in San Francisco, so it made sense to meet there for dinner rather than Berkeley. I was just about the last resident still at Roylmann that late in the semester break, and being all by yourself in a place that big was weird. I was happy for an excuse to get away for a night.

We'd agreed to meet at six o'clock, but it was already half-past and neither of them were there. Did I have the night wrong?

At a quarter to seven I was just about ready to leave, when they walked in.

"What are you doing here so early?" asked Lou.

"Didn't we say six?"

"Yeah," said Steph. "That's why we're getting here at six forty-five. We didn't really expect you for another fifteen minutes."

"Are you kidding me?"

"No. We figured what with coming across the Bay and everything, we could count on you being at least an hour late. We said six so we could be sure you wouldn't get here any later than seven."

"That's right," said Lou. "I mean, if you were us, would you have expected you to be on time?"

I suppose I had a right to be angry, but I couldn't claim I hadn't given them both plenty of reasons for taking precautions against my tardiness.

I decided to just take a deep breath and let it out slowly.

"Okay," I said, "let's just get a table, then."

"Are you mad?" asked Steph.

"Not really. Maybe a little annoyed, but I guess I brought it on myself."

"Well, we're glad you're not angry," said Lou, "and at least now you know how it feels."

"I never kept either of you waiting on purpose."

"We didn't either. We honestly didn't expect you to get here on time."

"It's an object lesson," I said, smiling. "I'll do better in the future. Let's get a table."

***

An hour later, I'd finished off a margarita, two bottles of Dos Equis, and a three-way combo dinner special that included a huge beef enchilada, a chili relleno, and a pork tamale. I was feeling considerably better. Steph and Lou had also finished their somewhat less generous dinners, and we were set to exchange presents.

"Here're yours," I said, handing them their packages. "Go ahead and open 'em."

Steph opened my present to her first. I'd gotten her a copy of *Hammett*, a novel by a private eye turned mystery writer named Joe Gores, in which Dashiell Hammett, also a private eye before becoming a mystery writer, solves a mystery in the San Francisco of the Roaring '20's. I'd also gotten her a DVD of *The Dain Curse*, a TV-movie version of one of Hammett's novels.

"Dan, this is great!" She held up the video. "Is this faithful to the book?"

"Pretty faithful. It was set in Baltimore instead of here. And obviously, with James Coburn in the lead, the Continental Op isn't being depicted as short and fat. And they give him a name."

"What do they call him?"

"Hamilton Nash. That's Dashiell Hammett spelled... uh... sideways. Sort of."

"And they picked a tall, slender, silver-haired actor with a mustache, because he resembled Hammett, I suppose."

"That would probably be a reasonable supposition."

Lou's present to Steph was a colorful scarf that had a kind of gypsy look that would go particularly well with Steph's dark coloring.

She gave Lou a hug and said, "It's gorgeous."

Lou's gift from Steph was a framed picture of the three of us at the Shakespeare Festival up in Ashland, Oregon, the previous summer. We were all standing on the stage of the replicated Globe Theatre, where we'd seen *The Merchant of Venice* and *Antony and Cleopatra*. We'd all enjoyed ourselves, but Lou'd had a particularly great time, and Steph thought, correctly, that she'd appreciate the memento.

It played well with my gift, which was a pair of DVDs, each a different version of *Henry V*, one from the '40's directed by and starring Sir Lawrence Olivier and the other from the '80's directed by and starring Kenneth Branaugh.

"It figures that, of all the Shakespeare plays you could've gotten, you'd give me *Henry V*," she said.

"How's that?"

"It's the closest thing Shakespeare ever came to writing the script for a John Wayne movie."

I chuckled and opened her present to me. It was an omnibus edition collecting seven of Mickey Spillane's Mike Hammer novels.

"I figured I had to get back at you for making me sit through *The Girl Hunters*," she said.

"Thanks, Lou. I'm sure I'll like them a whole lot more than you liked the movie."

Steph's present was three books, all of them autobiographies of famous police officers.

"You don't have any of these, do you?" she asked. She knew I had a small collection of cop memoirs that I'd been putting together, a bit at a time, since I was in the seventh grade.

"No," I said. "But I've been looking for all of them for a while. Where'd you find them?"

The first was *Nipper*, by Leonard "Nipper" Read, the Scotland Yard detective who'd nailed the Kray brothers, London's most powerful organized crime figures.

The second was a reprint edition of *My Double Life*, by Detective Mary Sullivan (no relation), who, way back in the

1920's had been the NYPD's, indeed America's, and probably the world's very first female homicide cop.

The third book was a particular Holy Grail of mine. I've wanted to add Harold Danforth's *The DA's Man* to my collection for years. Danforth had been the top undercover investigator for the Manhattan District Attorney's Office back in the racket-busting days of celebrity prosecutor and future presidential hopeful Thomas Dewey.

"They were at Moe's," she said.

"You're kidding," I said. "How did I miss them?" Moe's Books, on Telegraph Avenue, is one of the biggest, and one of the most popular, of the many used book stores in Berkeley. I'm in there frequently, but I'd never been able to find any of these three books.

"Firstest with the mostest," said Steph.

"Well, thanks both of you," I said. "I really appreciate these."

"What'd you get for Megan?" asked Steph.

"Nothing yet," I said. "I've kind of been wondering if I should."

"What's to wonder?" asked Lou. "You've been going together for weeks. Get her a present."

"Well, she's kind of on the rebound from some relationship that went sour back home. I just don't want it to look like I'm crowding her."

"Oh, honestly!" said Steph. "I didn't mean you should get her something ridiculously extravagant like diamond earrings. Just get her something nice and sweet and moderately priced. Believe me, she won't feel crowded."

"Absolutely," said Lou. "At this point in your relationship, not getting her a gift's a lot more likely to get you in trouble than getting her one. I remember back in high school getting a Christmas present for a guy I'd gone out with maybe a half-dozen times. It turned out he didn't get me anything 'cause he thought it was too soon and he didn't realize we were 'exclusive.' I never went out with him again. I'd be willing to bet Megan's already gotten you something, and, in that case, you don't want to be caught short."

"Okay, but I won't be seeing her before New Year's, so it'll have to be a Seventh Day of Christmas present."

"Well, then here's another tip," said Steph. "Don't get her seven swans a-swimming."

TWENTY-TWO

The last Holiday Foot Patrol Shift was on Christmas Eve. I dutifully patrolled Berkeley's downtown shopping area for eight hours, then signed off and headed across the Bay to the Peninsula to spend the holiday with my family.

We had a nice dinner together, then went into the living room to exchange presents. We always open our gifts on Christmas Eve instead of Christmas morning. When my brothers and I were little, Santa Claus always seemed to hit the West Coast early. The tradition continued after we'd gotten a little older and Santa'd stopped making personal visits.

I got two more books to add to my collection of police memoirs. My youngest brother, Pat, presented me with a paperback called *Witness Protector* by retired Deputy US Marshal John Harker, who'd spent two decades as the bodyguard of mobsters who'd agreed to testify against their old colleagues. I'd never heard of the guy, but the book looked interesting.

Dad gave me another book by a considerably more famous US Marshal named Joe LeFors, the frontier lawman who'd relentlessly pursued Butch Cassidy and the Sundance Kid. Copies of *Wyoming Peace Officer*, LeFors' posthumously published memoirs, are hard to find, and damned expensive when you manage to find one.

"Where did you get this?" I asked Dad.

"Client of mine's a western history buff," he said. "A few months ago I happened to mention your collection to him. He always brings around a bottle of Bushmill's every Christmas. This year he brought that book along with the whiskey and said he thought you might like it."

"Well, he was sure right about that."

After cleaning up the discarded wrapping paper, we got out the Bailey's Irish Cream, and sat around enjoying each other's company.

I noticed Dad wasn't drinking and asked why.

"I'm driving later tonight," he said.

"Where?"

"Midnight Mass at Mission Dolores."

Mission Dolores is the oldest building in San Francisco. It was built by the Franciscans who, along with the Spanish military, founded The City back in the 1700's, and it's still operated as a parish church. Dad's office is less than a block away from it, and he's been a daily Communicant there for years.

"Is that where we're going?" I asked. "Nobody told me."

"We're not all going," said Mom. "Just your Dad. Father Huerta asked him to usher tonight, and he couldn't really turn him down. The rest of us are going to St. Robert's tomorrow."

"You're going to Christmas Mass by yourself?" I said. "That's not right. I'll go along, too. I've always liked Midnight Mass."

"No, Dan, that's all right. You've been pounding a beat all day. Get a good night's sleep and go with everyone else tomorrow."

But I insisted. At eleven, after everyone else had turned in, we drove into The City together.

***

It was kind of hard keeping my eyes open, particularly after all that wine at dinner and the two glasses of Bailey's afterwards. But it was a beautiful service. In both Spanish and English, reflecting the ethnic make-up of the parish. I drifted a bit during the sermon, but managed to stay mostly awake from the first Sign of the Cross 'til the final, "Go in peace. The Mass is ended."

I kind of regretted that the whole family wouldn't be going to Mass together this Christmas, but, at the same time, it was nice to share the service just with Dad. In years to come, I thought, it would undoubtedly become a particularly cherished memory.

Dad and I finally got home at about one-thirty in the morning. By the time I finally climbed between the sheets, I was so tired I slept nearly twelve hours.

***

Between the 26th and the 30th, I did nothing but a four-hour evening tour in the Crimes Against Persons Detail answering phone calls. Those calls were becoming more infrequent with the passage of time. As the Christmas season had gotten closer and closer, the general public gave less and less thought to DeeDee Merryweather.

For that matter, I realized with a twinge of guilt, I'd thought about her very little myself, and she was supposed to be a friend of mine. At least a friendly acquaintance.

But, while the shift in Crimes Against Persons brought her back to mind, I was becoming increasingly convinced it wouldn't bring her back to life.

I guess I'd lost the last vestige of hope some weeks earlier. I hadn't had that much hope to begin with when she'd first gone missing, and that little hope(?) had flickered out altogether right after Megan went home for the holidays. Maybe there was a connection there, I don't know.

In any case, I was becoming more and more convinced that she was dead. And if she was dead, there was nothing I could do to help her.

So little by little, I was putting her out of my mind.

***

On the 29th, I met Megan at the Oakland Airport and drove her home. Her other two roommates weren't back yet, so we had her place to ourselves. We made a home-cooked meal together, and exchanged Christmas presents a few days late. She *had* gotten me one, confirming Lou's prediction.

We'd gotten each other videos. Big surprise. She'd gotten me *Casablanca*. I'd gotten her *His Girl Friday*.

We watched movies into the wee hours.

***

That New Year's Eve was the best one I ever had. We went into The City and party-hopped from one restaurant, nightclub, or hotel to another, just getting caught up in the excitement and the party atmosphere.

When midnight came, we shared a long, slow kiss that seemed

to last hours.

We'd expected to do more drinking than we were used to, so we'd taken public transportation over, avoiding the issue of driving under the influence. By two o'clock we'd been partying for eight straight hours. BART was no longer running, and neither of us felt like walking down to the Transbay Terminal at First and Mission and waiting for an "F" bus. I decided to splurge, and flagged down a cab.

Less than thirty minutes later, we'd pulled up to Megan's apartment building. I paid off the cab and walked Megan to her door.

"You wanna come in?" she said.

"Yeah."

I stepped through the door and gave her another long, slow kiss.

It lasted the rest of the night and most of the next day.

TWENTY-THREE

"Of course, when we consider that the hero of this film is an informer, Kazan's and Schulberg's real reason for making this movie becomes clear. It was meant as an apologia, if not an apology, for their testimony to Congress," said the professor.

It was the second week of the new semester, and I was in the lecture section of "The Gangster in Literature and Film," an English course that both Steph and Megan had talked me into.

A two-hour discussion section was scheduled at ten AM followed immediately by a two-hour lecture at noon. On Tuesday we used the discussion section to talk about the book we were reading for that week, then go to a lecture on the book. On Thursdays, we'd go to the Pacific Film Archives theatre and see a film, usually based on that week's book, then attend a lecture on the film.

The first week, there'd been no novel. We'd just seen two movies, both of them featuring James Cagney. *The Public Enemy* on Tuesday and *White Heat* on Thursday. I'd liked the movies fine, but the lectures struck me as so much pedantic, self-indulgent bullshit.

The second week we'd read *Waterfront*, Budd Schulberg's novelization of his Oscar-winning script for *On the Waterfront*, which we'd seen earlier that Thursday morning.

Now we were hearing about how director Elia Kazan and screenwriter Schulberg had sold their comrades out during the blacklist days and were using *On the Waterfront* to justify it.

Silly me. I'd always thought they'd been exposing labor racketeering.

***

147

Just before the semester had started, Megan'd told me about the class.

"It sounds like something you'd really enjoy, Dan. I need to take a genre course for my major anyway, and this would count. You could take it as a breadth requirement. Let's go together."

We were at Roylmann watching a cop movie called *The Big Combo* on cable. An honest police lieutenant, played by Cornel Wilde, tries to take down a major organized crime figure, played by Richard Conte, while becoming increasingly obsessed with the mobster's girlfriend, played by Jean Wallace (Mrs. Cornel Wilde at the time). The movie's gangster elements were evidently what prompted Megan to bring up the course.

I was not as enthusiastic as she'd assumed I'd be.

"Megan, the course sounds great, but it takes up so much class time. That's four hours on Tuesdays and Thursdays instead of only two. If I manage to find two other Tuesday-Thursday courses, I'd be going to class eight hours a day, plus the Board and committee meetings on Tuesday nights. Plus work."

"I think it sounds like fun," said Steph. She and Lou were watching the flick with us.

"Me, too," said Lou. "It's too bad it's at the same time as a major requirement I need."

I looked over the reading list. I had to admit, it looked like it was right up my alley. *The Big Heat* by William P. McGivern. *Scarface* by Armitage Trail. *The Desperate Hours* by Joseph Hayes. Budd Schulberg's aforementioned *Waterfront*.

What finally decided me, though, was one of the few pieces of non-fiction in the course, *The Untouchables* by Eliot Ness and Oscar Fraley. When I was about to turn thirteen, my dad took note of the fact that my interest in law enforcement, having lasted some three or four years, wasn't just a passing fancy.

He also noticed that I was particularly devoted to the old Robert Stack TV series that had been adapted from the book, which was being rerun on one of the local UHF channels.

For my birthday, he gave me a copy of Ness' book. That became the first entry in my collection of cop memoirs. It being included on the reading list seemed like a favorable omen.

"Okay," I said. "I'll sign up."

***

Now I was regretting my decision. As Ms. Remsberg noted during that "Male Roles" class the previous semester, I don't like having political rhetoric jammed down my throat, and I like leftist rhetoric even less, and Marxist rhetoric least of all.

The thing is, at Cal you've got to put up with a lot of that. And there's very little you can do except grin and bear it. At least that's what you have to do if it's a University requirement, or a requirement of the particular school you're enrolled in, or a requirement for your major.

But this wasn't any of those. This was supposed to be a fun class. This was supposed to be a way I could have a flick date with my girl and get academic credit for it. This was about movies, for Christ's sake. Not arty-farty, candy-ass foreign films, but American gangster movies. Why did this guy have to turn it into an avenue for political indoctrination?

Thoroughly stoked, Professor Ward suddenly left the subject of the movie altogether and launched into a history of the Hollywood blacklist that had cost so many in the film industry their jobs ("just for having a political opinion") and how Kazan and Schulberg had contributed to the "climate of fear" by appearing before the House Un-American Activities Committee as friendly witnesses.

He paused to take a breath. I raised my hand.

"Yes," he said, irritation at being interrupted evident in his tone.

"So are you saying that Terry Malloy was wrong to testify against Johnny Friendly?"

"I'm talking about the climate in Hollywood at the time the film was released," he answered.

"Yeah, but you're saying Kazan and Schulberg were wrong to testify against the Communist Party USA, so it follows that Malloy must have been wrong to testify against the Mob. And the real-life guy Malloy was based on must have been wrong for testifying against the real-life wise guy Friendly was based on, too."

"Real-life guys?"

"Yeah. Remember, the movie was based on a series of articles about the Mob infiltrating longshoremen's unions in Hoboken and New York. Those articles resulted in a crime commission getting set up to investigate the problem, just like the one in the movie. One of the people who testified was a longshoreman who'd once been a prizefighter, named Tony DeVincenzo. He gave evidence against Albert Anastasia. Anastasia was the Mob's top triggerman and the guy they put in charge of the docks when Lepke Buchalter got sent to the chair. For the movie script, Schulberg turned DeVincenzo into Malloy and Anastasia into Friendly."

"How do you know all this?"

"It's common knowledge, Professor. Which brings me back to my original question. Was Malloy, and by extension DeVincenzo, wrong to offer testimony against the Mob?"

"Malloy was testifying about criminals. He was trying to purge himself of his own guilt once he'd realized how wrong he'd been to go along."

"Weren't Kazan and Schulberg trying to purge themselves of their own guilt once they'd realized how much harm communism was doing in the world?"

"But they weren't testifying against criminals. And they helped contribute to the blacklist."

"Okay, so why was the blacklist such a terrible thing?"

"Are you serious?"

"I'm willing to admit that the blacklist *might* have been wrong, but I'm not going to accept it on faith just 'cause you say so. All I've heard is that some people lost their jobs. So what? The jobs didn't go away, did they? Somebody else filled the jobs they lost, right?"

Steph, on my left, was digging into my arm with her elbow, trying to signal me to shut up. Megan was just looking straight ahead, trying, to the degree she could without actually moving from her seat, to distance herself from me.

Maybe that was what it felt like to be blacklisted.

"Yes," said Ward, "I suppose other people did get the jobs that those on the blacklist lost."

"So if those people hadn't been blacklisted, the people who ended up getting the jobs would have been out of work, right?"

"I suppose."

"Well, frankly, Professor, that sounds pretty much like a wash to me. Somebody was going to be out of work no matter what happened. Why was it worse for one set of people to be out of work than another set of people?"

"Because they lost those jobs simply because of their political convictions."

"I see. So what you're saying is that if you lose your job for no other reason than because of your political opinions, that's wrong."

"Exactly."

"So if it had been ten years earlier, and a group of people in the film industry had been blacklisted for being Nazi sympathizers instead of communist sympathizers, that would have been wrong?"

"That's not the same thing at all."

"It's not? Why's that?"

"We were fighting a war against the Nazis."

"A war, huh? That little fracas in Korea was what, a pillow fight?"

"Hardly the same thing."

"I'm pretty sure it was exactly the same thing to the soldiers in the field, to say nothing about their families back home."

"But Nazism and communism were two movements at complete odds with one another."

"Were they? I think, for most people in the early 1950's, whatever distinctions could be drawn between Nazism and communism made no difference to anyone but academics. No offense meant, Professor."

"The distinctions are obvious to anyone who looks at them critically. No one can read both *The Communist Manifesto* and *Mein Kampf*, for example, without seeing the philosophical differences."

"That just proves my point. Nobody reads those books but academics."

"But even the average, ordinary person should have been able to see the differences between Marx's worldview and Hitler's."

"Really? I think what the average, ordinary person could do was look at the regimes of Hitler and Stalin and see a lot more similarities than differences. If you lived under one of those regimes, and you got sent away for not towing the party line, I don't think it mattered much whether they called the place they sent you a concentration camp or a gulag. And if you died there, I think it mattered even less whether it was for the purity of the Aryan race or for the principles of the great historical dialectic.

And I'm dead certain that it didn't matter much to any of those average, ordinary people you apparently feel so superior to."

"This is all abstract, anyway. There was no blacklist of Nazi sympathizers in the '40's that I know of. There was of communist sympathizers in the '50's."

"And your original point was that it was wrong because they were blacklisted for nothing more than their politics. But you know what? I bet if there had been a Hollywood blacklist of Nazis in the '40's, nobody'd care now. So it's not really about freedom of thought, is it? It's about whose ox is being gored."

***

"Did you have to do that?" asked Megan after class.

"I don't know, but it felt like I had to at the time. I'm sick and tired of hearing about how tough a bunch of Stalinist fellow travelers had it back in the '50's."

"They were making a stand on principle, whether you agreed with them or not. They were defending their rights."

"Nobody was denying 'em their rights. They still got to say what they wanted, and write what they wanted, and think what they wanted. But having the right of free expression doesn't mean having the right to be listened to. And when you boil down all the complaints, that's what it comes down to. Nobody wanted to listen to them."

"But innocent people were hurt. Like Aaron Copeland, the composer."

"Copeland wasn't a communist."

"What's that got to do with it?"

"Your point was that innocent people were hurt. That's true. But they were innocent precisely because they weren't commies. Innocent people get hurt in wars, even cold ones. It was wrong for us to put a bunch of loyal American citizens in relocation camps in the '40's just 'cause they were of Japanese descent. That doesn't mean it was wrong to fight fascism. And Copeland having a rough time doesn't mean it was wrong to resist communism. Anyway, Ward wasn't even talking about people like Copeland. He was talking about ardent, committed, passionately devoted communists. People who supported the enemy, then hid behind the Constitution, and what did they get for selling out their country? They lost their jobs. Big deal."

"Don't try to convince him, Megan," said Steph. "He manages to keep all that right-wing stuff suppressed most of the time, but now and then it boils over. Get him wound up and he makes Rush Limbaugh look liberal by comparison."

She turned to me and added, "Still, it would have been nice if you could have at least tried to look at it from another perspective. People did have their lives ruined. Maybe you didn't agree with their opinions, but did they deserve to lose their livelihoods because of it? Where's your sense of proportion?"

"Sense of proportion? Don't you read history? Look at what was happening! The Soviets had taken over virtually all of Eastern Europe after the War. They tried to starve out the non-Soviet part of Berlin, forcing us to airlift food in for almost a year. They stole our atomic bomb designs and then popped their own nuke just to show us they could. They invaded South Korea, or at least they encouraged North Korea to, which got us into a shooting war. They rolled tanks into Hungary and damned near leveled the whole frigging country just 'cause the Hungarians had the unmitigated gall to want to chart the course of their own lives. And I'm supposed to puddle up over a bunch of overpaid, professional narcissists whose holy martyrdom amounted to not being able to get jobs in Hollywood? And let's not forget that these were mostly ardent communists, and that the Communist Party USA was a wholly owned and operated subsidiary of the KGB. Sense of proportion, my ass!"

"What's that about the KGB?"

"The CPUSA was, at the very least, acting in concert with Soviet intelligence, and, at worst, controlled by them. That's all been proven, both by KGB records and CPUSA records that were made public after the Iron Curtain fell."

"But I'm just talking about trying to see the other side."

"I've had the other side jammed down my throat for as long as I can remember. I'm sick of the other side. Yeah, people did go overboard with the anti-communism back then, and some people got hurt who shouldn't have. Yeah, people were reacting out of fear. But the most salient point for me, and the one nobody seems to remember, is that there was plenty of reason for them to be fearful."

"Fine," said Megan. "You were absolutely right, and he was absolutely wrong. Are you going to take him on at every class session, now? This may be just an elective to you, but it's a major requirement for me. I need this class. Making him look stupid isn't going to turn him into a Republican. It's just going to make him want to get back at you. And if he takes it out on you, he'll probably take it out on Stephanie and me, too. Couldn't you have considered that before you went off on him?"

I had to admit that was a good question. And, just then, I couldn't think of an answer.

TWENTY-FOUR

At six that evening, I arrived at the Crimes Against Persons Unit to cover the phones 'til midnight. I'd brought a few textbooks to study and a copy of William P. McGivern's *The Big Heat*, the novel portion of next week's novel/film combo. Calls were falling way off, and I figured I could do homework during the down time.

I was still upset about Megan and Steph telling me off after class. It was going to require a massive effort to be courteous and attentive to the people calling in their generally useless tips. I'd have cancelled, but the detail was down to only one reserve officer an evening, and I didn't want to get a reputation for not following through on commitments.

I entered the office, shrugged out of my jacket, adjusted my shoulder holster, sat down at one of the desks, took a book out of my backpack, and opened it.

I was reading intently enough, or maybe just caught up enough in my own romantic problem, that I didn't notice Detective Sergeant J.B. Mills come up to the desk.

"Sullivan, isn't it?" he asked.

I looked up, noticing him for the first time, stood up, and said, "Yes, sir."

Mills, a slender, athletic-looking black man, ran the Crimes Against Persons Unit.

"Sergeant Cutter said you were one of the reservists I should be talking to," he said.

"Did I do something wrong, Sergeant?"

"No, no, nothing like that. Did you happen to see any of the papers this morning?"

I shook my head. He handed me a folded-up copy of the Oakland *Tribune* and pointed to a story on the front page.

Berkeley Chief of Police Sylvester Nolan had given a press

conference about the DeeDee Merryweather case. Goaded by suggestions a reporter had made that BPD wasn't taking the case seriously, Nolan protested that the Department had developed hundreds of leads and was in the process of following them up.

"A police officer will be personally conducting a full investigation into every single tip we've received," Chief Nolan was quoted as saying.

"Did he really say that?" I asked Mills.

"He sure did. On every front page in the Bay Area and every local TV news show. And now we're stuck. We've got to make at least a show of conducting a field investigation into all of those tips," he said, waving his hand at the huge pile of completed tip sheets on a table by the wall.

"But we haven't got the manpower," he went on. "And it's not like this is the only case CAP's got."

"And?"

"And what we're hoping is that you and a few other reservists will be willing to investigate these tips yourselves. I'll have one of my men go through the tip sheets and pull out the ones that look promising. Frankly, what we want you guys to do is follow up on all the unpromising ones. It's a shit detail, but thanks to the chief, we haven't got any choice."

"And he's cool with this?" I asked.

Nolan didn't really like reserve cops, so the scuttlebutt went. He was uncomfortable with the concept of part-time civilians doing police work, and he was particularly uncomfortable with the level of autonomy reserves had in Berkeley. Maybe that was what fueled his resentment over my contributions to the Stench case.

"He doesn't have a choice, either. He made a public commitment, and having unpaid reserve cops do the follow-ups is the only way we can afford to do it without going way over budget. And it's only March."

I knew that, as with answering phones, there'd be no shortage of volunteers for what Mills quite correctly called a "shit detail."

And I also knew that, despite my misgivings, I was definitely going to be one of them.

TWENTY-FIVE

I checked the street number against the address on my assigned tip sheet.

It was a big house up in the Berkeley Hills, Spanish-style architecture, with huge curved tiles on the roof, and an ornate, somewhat overproduced garden in the front yard. It was the sort of place you could imagine Don Diego de la Vega living in when he wasn't busy being Zorro.

I knocked on the door. The man of the house answered.

My eyes widened.

"Professor Ward?"

"Yes," he said. He apparently didn't recognize me.

"*You're* Russell Ward?"

"That's right. Is there something I can do for you?"

I showed him my star and ID and said, "I'm Officer Sullivan. Do you own a blue van, by any chance?"

"Yes," he said slowly, his eyes narrowing. "What's this about?"

"We're following up on tips we've received on DeeDee Merryweather's disappearance. I'm afraid somebody phoned in a tip on you."

"That's ridiculous. Why would anyone do that?"

"Have you ever worn a beard?"

"Yes, I shaved it off a month or so ago."

"Well, that's probably why. You're kind of a stocky guy. You own a blue van. When you still had a beard, you probably looked a lot like the guy who abducted her."

"Someone accused *me* of being the one who abducted her? This is just outrageous."

"Well, annoying, anyway. Look, Professor, I know there's almost no chance you're really the responsible. But the tip was

157

called in, and I've got to investigate it."

"Who'd report such a thing, anyway?"

"Whoever called didn't leave a name. He may have sincerely felt you ought to be checked out. Or he may have been somebody who just wanted to cause you some trouble and embarrassment. Either way, I've got to check it out."

"All right, all right. How can we clear this up?"

"Did you know DeeDee Merryweather?"

"No."

"Didn't have her for a class or anything?"

"Not that I remember," he said. He paused and looked at me closely. "Don't I have *you* in one of my classes?"

"Yeah, the gangster movie class."

"And you're a policeman?"

"As you see."

"Well, that certainly explains why you took up for Edmund O'Brien when we discussed *White Heat*."

"Yeah, I'm just a hopeless prisoner of my preconceptions. Look, I didn't know it was going to be you when I got assigned this tip sheet. Would you prefer I turn it over to another officer?"

"What difference would that make?"

"Just to avoid the appearance of a conflict of interest. I'm a student of yours, after all. If I report this tip as unfounded, it could be construed as angling for a better grade."

"That wouldn't work. I don't give grades on that sort of quid pro quo basis."

"And if I investigate more deeply than appears justified, it could be construed as payback for being slighted in your class."

"Are you threatening me?"

"Of course not. I'm suggesting I turn this over to another officer to avoid the situation altogether."

"No, never mind. That won't be necessary. Let's just get this over with."

"Do you remember where you were on September 4th. That was a Wednesday."

"Why should I?"

"It was the last day she was seen."

"Well, I suppose I don't really recall. Could you remember where you were on a given day more than four months ago?"

"Probably not. What was your regular schedule on Wednesdays last semester?"

"I had a morning class, afternoon office hours. Meetings occasionally, but I don't remember whether or not there were any that day."

"Do you drive the van to work?"

"No it's my wife's car. I drive a BMW."

"Do you own any other property besides this home?"

"No."

"Can I have your permission to look around?"

"You don't seriously think I'm keeping her a prisoner here, do you? My wife and kids live here, for God's sake."

"No, I don't think I'll find her here. But I won't know for sure unless I look. I don't have a search warrant, and I'll tell you honestly, there's next to no chance I could get one. Asking if I can search the house is just one of the things I'm supposed to do."

"What will happen if I don't permit a search?"

"Most likely nothing. I'll put down in my report, 'permission refused.' The report will be reviewed. And whoever reviews the report will decide that there are more promising leads to follow, and file this one away."

"Oh, hell. Just come in and get it over with, then."

I walked through the front door, and said, "Could you show me the basement?"

He took me on a tour of the house, anxious to prove that DeeDee Merryweather was not to be found there. It was a beautiful home, decorated tastefully and comfortably. There was a master bedroom with an attached bath. Three more bedrooms, one of which the professor had converted into a study. Kitchen, living room, den, dining room, and powder room on the ground floor. No basement, but a crawlspace under the roof and part of the large garage were both used for storage. Not unexpectedly, DeeDee was nowhere to be found.

As I left, he said, "Maybe now you realize why I'm so passionate about the blacklist."

"I'm just an undergrad schlub with a 'B-minus' average, Professor. I'm afraid you're going to have to explain that one to me."

"I'm the victim of an informer, just like the Hollywood Ten.

And, as a consequence, I've had to put up with a police invasion of my home."

"Professor, in the first place, I'm investigating a possible kidnapping, not vague allegations of political subversion. In the second place, I explained as clearly as I could that you had every right to refuse me permission, and that, in all likelihood, there'd be no repercussions if you did. I resent you characterizing it as an invasion, or this investigation as a politically motivated witch hunt."

"Well, I don't claim I've been victimized as much as those who were on the blacklist. I just understand their plight even better, now."

I nodded. "Okay. Thanks for your time, Professor."

I turned to leave.

"No response to that?" he asked.

"No."

"You always seem pretty passionate for your own viewpoint in the classroom."

"I'm a student in the classroom. I'm a cop here. It's not the time or the place to get into a discussion of politics."

"You do have an opinion, though, don't you?"

"You know what they say, Professor. Opinions are like assholes; everybody has one. But, like I said, it's not the time or the place."

"Nevertheless, I infer that your opinion is pretty much what it was in class. Can't you see the harm that this kind of back-stabbing does? Can't you see why Kazan and Schulberg were so wrong?"

"Kazan and Schulberg testified publicly. They didn't drop names anonymously. There was no back-stabbing there."

"They ruined lives."

"They gave up names that HUAC already had. So, if lives were truly ruined, they would have been ruined anyway, no matter what Kazan and Schulberg did."

"And you have no sympathy for the victims of the blacklist whatsoever?"

"Not nearly as much as I do for anyone forced to live behind the Iron Curtain."

"Well, I suppose as a policeman, being dependent on informers, your perspective is skewed."

"I've already said more on this subject than I should have. But think about this before you go putting down informers. If you *had* been the abductor, and DeeDee Merryweather *had* been hidden in your house, how do you think she would have felt about whoever dropped the dime on you?"

***

After leaving the professor's house, just to dot my i's and cross my t's, I went to Sproul Hall, the main administrative building for UC Berkeley, and checked DeeDee's academic record to make sure she'd never taken a class with Ward.

She hadn't. Ward just had the bad luck to resemble the sketch of the responsible.

That was what most of these follow-ups consisted of. I went up to an address where a possible suspect lived, asked a few questions, said thank you, and went on my way. That this particular suspect happened to be one of my professors was just sheer coincidence.

The fact of the matter was that even if, by some cosmic chance, I managed to stumble onto DeeDee's kidnapper, I'd probably never figure it out from the answers I was getting to the questions I asked. And how embarrassing would it be if it came out that an investigating officer contacted the responsible without having identified him as the responsible? Probably a lot more embarrassing than never having done the follow-up in the first place.

I was liking this whole assignment less and less. I wasn't a trained detective, for Christ's sake. If the Department wanted these follow-ups done why didn't they have them done by people who could do them right?

On the other hand, though I may have been uselessly spinning my wheels, it still beat the hell out of answering phones.

TWENTY-SIX

The next day, a Thursday, Megan, Steph, and I were sharing a late afternoon pizza at the Southside La Val's. Earlier we'd seen *Bonnie and Clyde*, with Warren Beatty and Faye Dunaway, followed immediately by Professor Ward's gushing lecture about it.

"I have to commend you for your restraint today," said Steph. "When he started in about 'the unconscionable police ambush of two people who could have easily been taken alive,' I thought for sure you were going to jump down his throat."

"I probably would have," I replied, "but I was pretty sure he was directing that at me personally, and I decided not to bite."

"Why should he be directing that at you?" asked Megan. "He doesn't even know you're a cop."

"He does now. I bumped into him yesterday when I was at work, and he wasn't pleased about it."

"What happened?"

"Nothing really. He felt his privacy was being invaded, and, to a degree, he's not altogether unjustified."

"What did you do," asked Steph, "pull him over and take his car apart?"

"No, nothing like that. I just interviewed him in connection with DeeDee's disappearance and he wasn't pleased about it. So now I'm probably going to get a heaping serving of his comments about jackbooted police tactics every time a cop so much as talks tough to a thug in one of these damned movies. Wait and see. By the time we get to *The Untouchables*, he'll be insisting that Al Capone's the hero and Eliot Ness is the villain. God, I wish I hadn't let you two talk me into this class."

"What does he have to do with DeeDee?"

"Not a single damned thing, as far as I know. That's why he's all pushed out of shape. But his name came up on one of those damned tip sheets, and I was assigned to follow it up."

I didn't really want to talk about it, but, little by little, the story of the previous day's encounter with Ward came out as Megan and Steph peppered me with questions.

"Are you enjoying the new assignment?" asked Megan.

"It beats sitting around the office answering phones. But mostly it's just a lot of wheel-spinning. I'm just looking at a lot of chaff so the real detectives can concentrate on the wheat."

"Well, it'll look good on a job application."

"That's why I volunteered when I was asked."

Steph asked, "What *did* you think of the movie, anyway?"

"I've never liked it," I answered. "Nothing but a glorification of a couple of kill-happy psychopaths who weren't even very good robbers. Do you know, for all the bodies they left behind, they only managed to put together a few thousand bucks the whole two years they were on the road? Dillinger got more than that on a single job. He and his gang racked up three hundred thousand or more in half the time it took Bonnie and Clyde to steal five or six grand. Of course, Dillinger's gang killed just about as many people. They may have gotten a bigger bang for the stolen buck, but they still left a lot of widows and orphans behind. Now, Willie 'The Actor' Sutton, *there* was a bank robber. He managed to steal something like two million dollars, and never killed a single person. Never even shot at one. Hell, to hear him tell it, he never even loaded his guns. It was all stagecraft. A point of pride with him."

"How many people did Bonnie and Clyde kill?"

"Best estimate's about a dozen. Most of 'em were cops, but the rest were people they were holding up or taking hostage. Basically Bonnie and Clyde were nothing but a couple of bullies pushing over small-town grocery stores or gas stations on backcountry roads, stealing from people who weren't that well-off to begin with. But the film makes it look like they were striking blows for the little guy against a bunch of rich fat cats. And on top of all that, it slanders a really fine cop."

"You mean Frank Hamer?" asked Megan.

"Of course I mean Frank Hamer. Hell, if just half the stuff written about him is true, he was the greatest American policeman ever to pin on a badge."

"Then why do you think the film treats Bonnie and Clyde as heroes, and Hamer as the villain?"

"The times. It was the '60's, and the basic situation appealed to the counter-culture sensibilities of the filmmakers. You've got two good-looking kids in love, rebelling against society, pursued by a middle-aged authority figure. So, instead of a couple of thrill-happy multiple murderers, Bonnie and Clyde get transformed into a Depression-era version of Robin Hood and Maid Marian. And if you've got a latter-day Robin and Marian, you've just got to have a Sheriff of Nottingham. That's what they used Hamer for."

"He couldn't have been that good if they got the drop on him like they did," said Steph.

"That's exactly what I'm talking about," I replied. "That never happened. They did use cops as hostages now and then, and that's probably where the writers got the idea for that scene. Once they nabbed a deputy sheriff down in New Mexico, for example, another time a city cop up in Missouri, and a small-town police chief in... I think it was Oklahoma. Clyde got a big laugh out of kidnapping cops. But they never captured Hamer. That was total invention."

"What happened to the ones they did kidnap?"

"They let 'em go. They were the lucky ones. Nine other cops were killed by the Barrow gang."

"You seem to know a lot about them," said Megan.

"Well, you know I collect cop autobiographies. I have one called *Ambush* by Ted Hinton. He was one of the members of the posse that nailed Bonnie and Clyde. The only one who ever wrote about it. Well, Hamer wrote a short article, but Hinton's the only one who ever wrote a book. And I've read a lot of other books about the case, too."

"Is there a movie that gets it right?"

"There's a cheapie from about ten years earlier called *The Bonnie Parker Story* with Dorothy Provine. Funny thing is, that movie changes Clyde's name. His brother's, too. Instead of Clyde Barrow and his brother Buck, they're 'Guy Darrow' and his brother 'Chuck.' Frank Hamer gets turned into a guy named Tom Steel. But in a lot of ways, for all the low budget and fictionalized names, it's closer to the real story."

"Any others?" asked Steph.

"Back in the '30's there was one called *Persons in Hiding*, about a pair of lovers on the run who robbed gas stations, partly modeled on Bonnie and Clyde. It was based on a book by J. Edgar Hoover, so it's the FBI who catches up to them at the end instead of the Texas Rangers. That book we read for the class on Tuesday, *Thieves Like Us*, there've been two film versions of that, *They Live By Night* in the late '40's and *Thieves Like Us* in the '70's.

"Wonder why he didn't show one of those?" said Megan

"The novel was inspired by the real-life Bonnie and Clyde, but the Beatty movie's a lot better known than either of the direct adaptations."

"Any more?" asked Steph.

"In the late '40's or early '50's there was a really fine gangster-on-the-run flick called *Gun Crazy*, about a couple of bank robbers who were also pretty clearly modeled on Bonnie and Clyde. Considered a film *noir* classic, now. At least two TV-movies and a direct-to-video film. Probably a few versions I'm not even aware of. *Anime*, musical comedy, who knows?"

"You think they'll continue making movies about them?" asked Megan.

"Oh, sure. It's like the gunfight at the OK Corral. One of those true-life stories they just have to make a movie about every twenty years or so."

"Well," said Steph, "you may be sorry you're taking the course, but I'm not. You're a regular encyclopedia about this stuff. The gangster stuff and the movies both. You're my main research source."

"You're sure right about that," said Megan. "In fact I have an idea for a term paper I wanted to talk to you about. Can you come over to my place after we're finished here?"

There was, of course, almost no place I'd rather be than Megan's, but I had a committee meeting that night.

"How about the next day?" she asked.

"I'm on duty all day," I said. "But I'll call you as soon as I get home and we'll plan something."

TWENTY-SEVEN

I pulled my ancient Toyota into the parking lot of Roylmann at about seven PM and was pleasantly surprised to find Megan waiting for me when I walked into the foyer.

She gave me a hug which I quite liked and suddenly collapsed which I didn't.

I caught her before she fell to the floor.

"Are you okay?"

She shook her head as though she was waking up from a deep sleep and said, "Yeah. It was just a passing thing. Could you get me a Coke? I probably just need a sugar transfusion."

She leaned against me for support as we walked into the dining room. I sat her down at one of the tables and went to a fridge in the corner marked "La Cantina." I pulled out a can of Coke for her and a Henry Weinhard's for me, dropped some money in a jar to pay for them, and brought them back to the table.

"I was just about to call you," I said. "What brings you here tonight?"

"Just wanted to see you, thought we could talk about that idea for a term paper topic I mentioned."

"Great. That's what I was going to call you about."

I stripped off my corduroy sports coat and saw her grimace when she saw the pistol snugged into my shoulder holster.

"Were you working today?"

"Yeah. I'm doing more follow-ups on some of those tip sheets. Listen, let me go down to my room and lock up Old Betsy here. Then I'll see what they saved me for dinner and be right back."

"Okay."

***

She was looking a lot better when I got back upstairs. Her idea for a paper was an examination of the interface between the cop picture and the gangster picture.

"I'm talking about gangsters in the 'big-time racketeer,' organized crime sense," she said.

"As opposed to bandits like Bonnie and Clyde, or Dillinger?"

"Exactly."

"And what sparked this idea?"

"Last week's movie, *The Big Heat*, kind of reminded me of the one we saw during the Christmas break, *The Big Combo*. Both of them featured cops who were dedicated, obsessed even, about nailing their city's top gangster."

"And you want to compare them for your paper?"

"Not exactly. The thing that struck me about both of them is that, unlike most detective movies, the problem wasn't figuring out 'whodunit,' because everyone already knows who's at the top of the criminal pyramid. The problem is getting enough evidence to convict him of something."

"And you want some more movies with that same theme?"

"Yes. Can you think of any others?"

"Funny you should mention *Combo* and *Heat*. 'Cause one that comes to mind immediately is *The Undercover Man*. It's about a federal agent trying to nail a Midwest city's top mobster on tax evasion."

"Like the way they got Capone?"

"It's based on that, actually. They change the names and it's set in the postwar era instead of Prohibition, but it's clearly the Capone case. Fact is it was based on the autobiography of the Treasury agent who put the tax case against Capone together."

"Eliot Ness?"

"Ness didn't work for Treasury. At least not during the Capone investigation. He was an agent of the Justice Department. Ness made the bootlegging case against Capone, and, on a few of his brewery raids, he seized some of the financial ledgers and documents that the Treasury guys used against Capone. Aside from that, though, he had nothing to do with the income tax prosecution."

"Who did?"

"Guy named Frank Wilson. He was the top criminal

investigator for the IRS. In the movie he's named Frank Warren and he's played by Glenn Ford, who also played the cop in *The Big Heat*. And the script was by Sidney Boehm, who also wrote the script for *The Big Heat*. And, just to tie it all together, the director was Joseph Lewis, who also directed *The Big Combo*. Lewis is kind of a film *noir* icon. He also made that movie I talked about yesterday, *Gun Crazy*."

"That's great! Do you think we could find a video of it?"

"Probably."

We talked some more. I also suggested a Warner Brothers flick from the '30's, *Bullets or Ballots*, with Edward G. Robinson as an undercover cop who infiltrates the New York mob, *Dragnet*, a feature-length version of the TV series from the mid-50's in which Joe Friday works the Day Watch out of LAPD's organized crime section, *The Racket*, with Robert Mitchum as an honest police captain trying to bring down mobster Robert Ryan, and two film versions of Eliot Ness's autobiography, *The Scarface Mob* with Robert Stack and *The Untouchables* with Kevin Costner.

"That should be plenty," she said.

"Good. We'll be seeing *The Untouchables* in class. I'll see if I can track down some DVD's or videos of the others on Friday. I'll be out in the field doing some more follow-ups. I should be able to steal a few minutes to find a few of 'em at a library or video store."

"You're working this Friday?" she asked.

"Yeah."

"Are you carrying your gun?"

"Of course I'm carrying my gun. When I'm on duty I always carry my gun. In fact, I'm required to carry my gun. You're not suddenly going to go all queasy about me being armed, are you?"

"Well, it kind of troubled me seeing you wearing it tonight when you came home."

"Why? I was wearing it the first time you ever saw me."

"You were in uniform then. This time you were in regular street clothes. It just seemed different. Besides..."

"Yeah?"

"You'll just think it's silly."

"No I won't."

"What would you do if you knew you were going to get into a shootout before you started your shift?"

"Call in sick," I said, chuckling.

"Well, that's what I want you to do. Don't go to work on Friday. Just call in sick."

"I've already committed myself. I can't just blow it off. What's the problem? Did you have a vision or something? Do you think I'm going to get into a shooting if I go to work?"

She looked away from me and nodded.

"I know you're a skeptic," she said, "but you've always admitted that it was possible I really had a gift."

"Was that what was happening when you collapsed? Did you have a premonition?"

She nodded again. "It was when I hugged you. I could feel your gun under the jacket. And I suddenly had a vision of someone shooting at you and you shooting back."

"And you're sure it's this Friday?"

"I don't know. But every premonition I ever had came true within a day or two. The ones that came true at all."

"So you've had some visions that didn't come to pass."

"Yes," she admitted.

"And aren't some of your visions of things that have already happened?"

"Yes, I suppose most of them are. But you've never been in a gunfight before, have you?"

"Actually, I've been in two."

"You never told me that!"

"Well, it's never really come up."

"Were you hurt?"

"First one got me in the leg. Second one just managed to pull his gun. He never got a shot off."

"What happened to them?"

"I wounded the first one. He survived. He's in the slam now. The second one died."

"You killed him?"

"I fired at him, but none of my shots were lethal. There were two other officers with me. They fired the fatal shots. But I was the first one to open fire, and as soon as I did all hell broke loose." I shrugged. "I guess you could say I created the situation that got him killed."

"I've always heard that most cops can go their whole careers and never have to use their guns."

"Most never do. And I'll probably never have to again. I'm not questioning your gift, Megan. But isn't it possible, if you saw anything at all, that you were seeing something that already happened?"

"Maybe. But I'd still feel better if you didn't go in on Friday."

"People are counting on me, Megan. The odds are way against anything happening. Trust me. I'll be fine."

"You see that you are," she said. "You just see that you are."

TWENTY-EIGHT

"You reported that you took a blue Chevy Astro as a trade-in for a new vehicle, but you didn't say who made the trade. Just that he was a big, heavyset man with a beard."

I was talking to Zac Putnam, a car dealer who operated a lot in Oakland. He'd phoned in a tip several months ago. It had been on top of the "unpromising" pile when I'd signed in that morning.

"Well," said Putnam. "I didn't feel right about giving out the guy's personal information over the phone. This way, I've seen your badge and everything, there's no question I'm turning the information over to the police."

He showed me the sales documents, which indicated that the previous owner had been Scott Kay, who lived in Concord out in Contra Costa County.

"See, he came in to make the trade right after that story broke about the bearded guy with the blue van kidnapping that gal up on Grizzly Peak. Seemed suspicious to me, like he might have been trying to get rid of evidence, so I called it in. But that was months ago. How come you're looking into it now?"

"We've been getting hundreds and hundreds of tips, Mr. Putnam. It's taking a lot of time to get to all of them."

"But this seemed so suspicious."

"We'll check it out thoroughly now. You can be sure of that."

The drive to Concord took about forty-five minutes. It took another fifteen to find the Concord police station on Galindo Street and make a courtesy check so they'd know a police officer from another jurisdiction was operating in their town. It took another ten to find Scott Kay's address, a typical suburban ranch-style house on Whitman Road.

I didn't expect him to be home. It was a weekday, and the likeliest place for him to be was at work. The problem was I had

173

no idea what work was. On the documents he'd filled out at the car dealership he'd simply put "self-employed" in the occupation box, and no address had been given. He'd paid cash, so Putnam hadn't quibbled.

I was hoping his wife might be home, assuming he was married, so I could be directed to his place of business. But even that was pretty unlikely, with both spouses working in an increasing number of households.

Consequently, I was mildly surprised when my knock on the door was met with a "Who's there?" and even more surprised that the voice was male. Maybe he worked at home.

"Police."

"What do you want?"

"Are you Mr. Kay?"

"Yes. What do you want?"

"I need to talk to you about the van you traded in a while ago."

I was standing to one side of the front door. This is a fairly common officer survival tactic, and it gets to be second nature after a while. There've been all kinds of cases of cops who got shot because they were standing right in front of a door they'd just knocked on. To avoid that, we're taught to stand to one side or the other. It's so relentlessly drilled into you that the first ten or twenty times you knock on a door, you half expect shots to be fired in response. After that, you stop expecting shots, but the habit remains.

That day, the habit saved my life.

Four sharp explosions sounded from inside the house and four holes appeared in the door.

I snatched at the nine-millimeter in my shoulder holster, crouched down to a squatting position, leaned my back against the wall, and stayed there frozen for a few moments.

I heard a door slamming in the back. I peeked around the corner and saw a big, burly man with a dark beard running toward the detached garage, a big pistol, probably a .45, gripped in his right hand.

I brought my nine up in a two-handed, isosceles grip and, keeping most of my body hidden behind the corner of the house, sighted carefully at the broad back of the bearded man.

"Stop!" I yelled.

He looked over his shoulder, and, still running, started to raise his gun. Focusing the front sight on his back, I began squeezing the trigger of my nine. It was a double-action weapon, but that would only be relevant for the first shot. The slide mechanism would cock back the hammer as it ejected the empty shell from that shot, making the second, and all subsequent shots single-action.

His pistol was now level with his shoulder, held sideways "gangsta-style." I forced myself not to hurry my trigger squeeze. Still running, twisting his upper body toward me as much as he could while continuing to run forward, he snapped off a shot that went wide.

My answering shot, carefully aimed and carefully squeezed, didn't.

The slug took him in the upper right back. His legs buckled. He fell to his knees, but managed to hold onto his gun. It was pointed down, but still gripped in his right hand, his forefinger still on the trigger, the hammer cocked back.

I stepped from behind the corner of the house, and, with my pistol still aimed at him, still held in the two-handed grip, started slowly walking forward.

"Put the gun *down!*" I shouted. "*Now!* Put it down *now!*"

Instead, still on his knees, his back still to me, he once more twisted around and started to raise it again.

As I continued walking toward him, I fired six more times. He swayed as he absorbed the impact of the slugs smacking into his back, then fell forward, his hand still gripping the cocked pistol.

The sudden silence was a relief. What's most surprising about a firefight is how loud the guns are. When we train and qualify on firing ranges, we wear ear protectors to muffle the noise, so we're not really exposed to the actual sounds of a firing gun. That sound can be paralyzing. I'd frozen for a few moments after Kay, if it was Kay, had fired at me, as dumbfounded by the noise as by the fact that I was being shot at. Now, having survived the encounter, I was frozen again, a reaction to the explosive, deafening reports that had issued from my own gun.

I shook my head, partly to rouse myself, and partly to clear the ringing noise in my ears, and slowly approached the man on the ground, and knelt down next to him, and turned him over.

"You shot me in the back," he croaked.

"Yeah? Your own fault for shooting at me while you were running away," I replied. "If you'd've turned and faced me, those holes'd be in the front of you. And, who knows? It might've even improved your aim."

Those were the last words he ever heard. He took one last breath, held it while he grimaced, his body stiffened, and his eyes widened. Then he exhaled. Or not so much exhaled, as that the air just left his body and his breathing stopped.

I felt vaguely guilty that I hadn't said something kinder to ease his passing. But, after all, I hadn't started the shooting, and I was disinclined to let his implied accusation that I'd violated some sacred ethical shibboleth of gunfighting go unanswered.

There were no exit wounds in his chest or stomach. In BPD we're issued what are referred to in official memoranda as "controlled expansion rounds," a euphemism allowing us to avoid the more politically charged, if more accurate term "hollow-point." It's precisely because hollow-points rarely exit the target that BPD went with them. Damage that might be caused by an exiting slug is minimized if the slug, expanding and slowing down once it hits the target, doesn't exit at all. In my semi-dazed state, I was still able to note that the "controlled expansion rounds" had performed as hoped.

His gun, a .45 as I'd thought, was still gripped tightly in his hand, likely the result of a cadaveric spasm, and still cocked. There might be no way to get it loose short of breaking his fingers. I didn't feel up to doing that. Instead I removed the magazine, racked out the round still under the hammer, then locked the slide back, all while it was still being held by the corpse.

Except I wasn't qualified to say he was a corpse. And if he wasn't dead, I was responsible for administering appropriate first aid until more qualified medical personnel took over.

This couldn't be happening. None of these tips were supposed to amount to anything. These weren't even the "promising" leads. Real detectives were getting those. I was just supposed to be spinning my wheels, looking into the ones everyone thought were just wild geese.

How had one of those wild geese turned out to be someone I'd had to shoot down?

A lady in one of the other houses on the street opened her door.

An older woman, in her late sixties probably, but trim and fit-looking, and still full of vinegar.

"What's all this ruckus?" she yelled.

I held up my star. "Ma'am, I'm a police officer. Call 911 for me. Tell them we need an ambulance for a gunshot victim. Tell them an officer in civilian clothes is already at the scene."

She stood there for a moment.

"Ma'am, I need you to do it *now*."

She retreated back into her house. My car's radio didn't work this far away from Berkeley, and I wasn't carrying a cell phone. I could only hope she actually was calling the police.

I felt for a pulse. Nothing. Still, better to be safe than sorry.

I went back to the car for the first aid kit. In the distance I heard sirens.

Good. She'd called.

***

In the immediate aftermath of the shooting, I didn't speculate about whether or not Kay firing at me might have anything to do with the Merryweather case.

The first arriving patrol units went through the house to make sure there were no other suspects inside. It probably registered subliminally that, if no accomplices were inside, neither was DeeDee, but consciously all I could think about was the shooting itself. Not what led up to it.

The hours following that immediate aftermath were a blur. I went through the story of what had happened with the Concord patrol units who'd been the first to arrive, then with the detectives from Concord PD, then with investigators from the Contra Costa County DA's Office, and finally with officers from my own department.

The questions seemed to be the same, no matter which set of cops was asking them. So were my answers.

How many shots did he fire?

Four through the door. One more while he was running away. Total of five.

How many did you fire?

Six, I think. No. Seven.

Did you identify yourself as a duly authorized law enforcement officer?

Of course I did.

How?

I said "Police."

Did you issue a warning before you fired?

Not specifically. I just ordered him to stop running.

How?

I yelled "stop."

What was his response to that?

He fired another shot at me.

That's when you fired the seven shots?

That's when I fired once. He fell to his knees. I started toward him, still covering him, and told him to put down the gun.

What did he do?

Raised it to fire.

How did you know he was going to fire?

No other reason for him to point a cocked pistol at me after I'd just ordered him to put it down.

That's when you fired the six shots?

Yeah.

Why weren't you working with a partner?

These were tips that were considered dead ends. Nobody regarded them as hazardous. Two officers working alone could cover twice as many tips as two officers working together.

Why didn't you radio for help?

I was out of radio range.

Why didn't you use your cell phone?

I didn't have a cell phone.

Why not?

The department doesn't issue them to reserve officers.

Why don't you have one of your own?

Because I'm a college student who's 100 percent self-supporting, and any money I have left over after paying for tuition, books, and room and board, I choose to spend on things other than a God damned money pit like a cell phone and what the hell is it to you, anyway, pal!

***

I was suspended from duty pending the outcome of the investigation. Standard procedure. Everyone assured me that it looked like a good shooting, nothing for me to worry about. But still that word.

Suspended.

I called my folks from the Concord police station and told them they might be hearing about me on the news, but not to worry, I was okay. I called Megan and told her the same thing.

"You're sure you're not hurt?" she asked.

"Yeah. I'm shaken up, but otherwise fine."

"You're *sure*?"

"Honest."

"Thank God."

"You sound even more relieved than my parents did."

"Your parents haven't been expecting to hear the worst since Wednesday night."

That's right. She'd actually predicted the shooting. It sounds odd, but I'd put it out of my mind after we'd talked Wednesday, and I hadn't actually connected it with today's events. While it was going on I was too focused on staying alive. Afterwards I was too focused on getting all the details straight. At no time did it occur to me that Megan had warned me in advance.

But she had. She'd been right on the money.

Right on the money.

***

I got home after eleven that night. Steph and Lou were waiting up for me, ready to provide moral support. I thanked them but said I just felt like going to bed, and went down to my room.

I slept about as well as you'd expect. Which was not at all.

At two AM, I got out of bed, pulled on a bathrobe, and went upstairs. I found some leftovers in the kitchen and fixed myself a sandwich, pulled two Henrys out of La Cantina, and went into the living room to see what was on the tube.

I've got a small portable in my room, but I don't have a cable hook-up. Anyway, I felt closed up in my room. Alone. I wanted breathing space, and Roylmann's expansive living room could provide that.

I channel surfed for awhile. Turner Classic Movies had already started *The Longest Day*. Yeah, three hours of gunfire and battle action was just what I needed, all right. RetroPlex was showing *The Detective* with Frank Sinatra. Hell with that; the last thing I felt like was a cop movie. I clicked it to Classic Film Network. *Sons of the Desert* with Laurel and Hardy was just starting.

That was more like it. Gentle, unchallenging comedy.

I took a bite of my sandwich and opened one of the beers.

***

I woke up in the chair the next morning. The TV was still on. *Sons of the Desert* had been followed by *The Awful Truth* with Cary Grant and Irene Dunne. I remembered seeing the beginning of that. I was on my third or fourth beer by that time.

I looked down at the empty bottles on the floor. Fourth beer.

Anyway, I'd seen the beginning of *The Awful Truth* but couldn't recall the end. I must have drifted off. That would have been around four or four-thirty.

I didn't have my watch on. I got up and went into the dining room. Saturday morning brunch was still being served, so it had to be before eleven.

Yeah, the clock on the wall said nine-thirty.

I usually have a big breakfast on Saturdays, but, slightly hungover, and still not well-rested, I couldn't work up any appetite for it. I just poured myself a tall orange juice.

Steph and Lou were seated at a table. I joined them, nodded, and took a long swallow of OJ.

"How are you feeling?" asked Lou.

I shrugged.

"We knocked on your door a little while ago," said Steph, "but you weren't awake yet."

"I was in the living room watching late movies."

"Trouble getting to sleep?"

"Yeah."

"You should have woken one of us up," said Lou. "We told you last night we wanted to help."

I shook my head. "Don't feel like talking about it yet."

180

"You should talk about it to someone."

"They'll send me to a shrink like the other two times. I'll get all the talk I need. And a hell of lot more than I want. Nothing against either of you. I just can't talk about it yet."

"Okay," said Lou, and left it at that.

Real friends give you distance when you need it.

***

That Monday I went in to see Sergeant Cutter.

"Dan," he said, looking up from his desk as I entered the office.

"Hi, Sarge." I looked at my name up on the roster of reserve officers. There was an adhesive red dot next to it, signifying that I was unavailable for duty. Instead of a date when I'd be available again, the words "Until Further Notice" were written next to the red dot.

"Come to see how things stand?"

"I suppose. I'm signed up for a couple of Marina details this weekend. Any chance I'll be able to work 'em?"

"Not likely things'll be settled by then. You can probably switch with a couple of guys who have the next weekend. You should be off the 'Red Tag' list by then."

I asked the question it hadn't occurred to me to ask on Friday.

"Did this guy have anything to do with DeeDee?"

"No," he said. "Nothing like that."

"Then why'd he come up shooting?"

"Kay was a drug smuggler. At least he used to be. Small-time but he did well enough he was able to afford that nice house in Concord. He used to run it up from Mexico. Turns out that van he traded in had a lot of secret compartments he'd hide the stuff in."

"'Used to be?'"

"Yeah. Apparently he'd decided to retire."

"Retire?"

"He had a pretty good pile in the bank. More invested. Enough to live comfortably, maybe not luxuriously, but comfortably, for the rest of his life."

"Then why'd he decide to shoot it out?"

"According to some of his associates, he was pretty paranoid.

That was why he got out. A lot of these guys like the risk, push it 'til they get caught. Not this guy Kay. He'd set a monetary goal for himself, and as soon as he made that goal he quit."

"Okay, so he was paranoid. But he was out of the business."

"Yeah. But according to the shooting team, you specifically said you wanted to talk to him about the van he'd traded in."

"That's right."

"Well, that's it. That was the van he used to run the stuff up. Once he got out of the business, he got rid of it. He probably figured you'd found some evidence connecting the van to dope, and had traced the van back to him, so he went nuts."

"Christ, if he'd just kept his head, I would've cleared him on the DeeDee thing and he would've been able to get back to his life."

"'The guilty flee where no man pursueth.'"

He looked at me more closely.

"Are you doing okay, Dan?"

"I'm having trouble sleeping. A couple of the guys called me 'Wyatt Earp' when they saw me come in. I'm starting to get a reputation as a gunslinger. And I don't think I like it."

"Well, get used to it or think about getting out of the Job, because it's probably going to happen again."

"Why do you say that? Most cops go their whole career without ever firing their gun. I've already beaten the odds three times. Doesn't that make it even more improbable there'll ever be a fourth?"

"In my experience, it doesn't work that way."

"What do you mean?"

"You know how they say that there're two kinds of cops, those who go their whole career without firing their weapon, and a much smaller group who do?"

"Yeah."

"Well, there are two kinds of cops, all right. But it should be those who never fire their weapon or else fire it only once. And those who fire it more than twice."

"I'm not sure I follow."

"Cops are hired to go in harm's way. So there's always a possibility, fairly remote, but still a possibility of suddenly finding yourself in a situation where you have to use your gun. It can happen to any one of us at any time. But the odds against it happening, by sheer chance, twice in one career are astronomical."

"And the other kind of cop?"

"The other kind of cop is instinctive. Has a nose for trouble. And he's proactive. Looks for crime instead of waiting to get called to it. Not that there's anything wrong with the first kind of cop. They just don't have as well-developed an instinct for finding criminal activity. This second kind of cop is going to find himself, or herself, getting into dangerous situations a lot more often because he's got a knack for finding those kinds of situations. When you got into your first shooting, I figured it was sheer chance. When you got into your second, I was pretty sure that, if you continued on the Job, there'd at least be a third, and probably more."

"How many cops like that do you know?"

"Besides you? Well, I'm one."

"You are?"

"I've been in four shootings. I'm a member of the 'shot-at-and-missed-and-shot-back-and-hit' club from way back. And that's nothing compared to some guys I know about."

"Like who?"

"There's a lieutenant over at the Sheriff's Department, Sam Dunnegan, he's been in eleven or twelve. An old-time FBI agent named Jelly Bryce was in nineteen or twenty. An officer in NYPD's stakeout squad, Jim Cirillo, was in seventeen shootings back in the '60's and '70's. There was a Cleveland beat cop named Jim Simone, he got in eleven shootings in 38 years, but only five of 'em were fatals. And, if the legends are true, Frank Hamer, the Texas Ranger who got Bonnie and Clyde, was in more than 50."

"Christ, it sounds like these guys were working in Dodge City back in the frontier days."

"Some bad guys still have a frontier mentality. That's why you need cops like Hamer, Cirillo, and Bryce. They're legends on the Job. You're in good company."

"I don't see myself as a legend."

"You're not yet. But it's something you've got the capability to swing for. Hamer, Cirillo, and Bryce weren't just great with their guns. They were great cops. Nobody wants to get into gunfights, not if they've got any sense. But being a great cop. Not just a good one, but a great one. That's something every cop should aspire to."

He was right. Everyone who ever pins on a badge dreams about being one of the greats. But if I had to go through any more armed encounters to achieve that status, I couldn't help wondering if it was worth the price.

TWENTY-NINE

I'd given some thought to staying with Pete and Pet for a few days in the rural home they'd retired to up near the Russian River, but I wanted something that felt more like it was personally mine, and hoped that my old bedroom would serve that purpose.

For two days I hadn't talked about the shooting. The first day I didn't feel up to it. The second I didn't want to burden Dad, talking about an incident that was bound to remind him of his bum knee and how he'd gotten it.

He probably sensed my reluctance and the reason for it. Thursday night he suggested the two of us go out to dinner together, a boys' night out, at a seafood place in Pacifica he likes. After finishing the meal, while we were waiting for his coffee and my tea, he brought the subject up himself.

Now I was telling him about Megan's uncannily accurate prediction.

"Are you mad at yourself for not listening when she warned you?"

"No. It wasn't like I was blowing her off. She just gave so few details. I didn't know what I should be avoiding. She wasn't even sure whether she was seeing a past event or a future one."

"What's the problem, then?"

"The point is, Dad, she was right."

"Maybe she was, but it still sounds vague enough that it could just be a coincidence."

"It's a hell of a coincidence, if that's all it is. I mean, someone tells you to beware, there's unspecified danger in your unspecified future, and you wind up in a car accident six months later, that's one thing. Someone says you're going to get into a gunfight in the next two or three days, and then you do, that's something else."

"So you're becoming a believer, now?"

"Well, I'm sure becoming a lot less skeptical."

"Has she made some other prediction? Is that why you're concerned?"

"Something like that."

"What's it about?"

"Remember me telling you about how we met at that football game?"

"Sure."

"That wasn't the first time I ever talked to her. When I was working that phone detail at CAP, she called in an anonymous tip."

"And she gave you psychic information about the disappearance?"

"Exactly."

"And in light of what happened last week, you're wondering if you shouldn't take what she said more seriously?"

"That's it."

"What did she say, exactly?"

"That she felt DeeDee getting buried. That she was already dead."

"That's interesting. And I can sure understand why you'd be looking at what she said in a different light. But even if she's right, where does it get you?"

"What do you mean?"

"Well, does she know where the body is, other than in the ground?"

"I guess not."

"So even if she's right, you really don't know anything you didn't know before. I expect, at this point, that most of the guys on the case are already proceeding on the assumption that she's dead."

"Yeah, but if she's right, it at least tells us that there's a body to look for. That whoever killed her didn't cremate the body or something like that."

"Did she give any other hints?"

"Well, there's this. I told you how she got the premonition about me when she brushed against my gun?"

"You did."

"She got her vision about DeeDee when she brushed against Chris Bridges' motorcycle."

"Bridges is the guy DeeDee was living with, right?"

"Right."

"So you're thinking that since it was property belonging to Bridges that sparked the vision of DeeDee being dead, Bridges might have something to do with that death."

"Essentially."

"Did she ever ride on it with him?"

"All the time."

"Then maybe it was DeeDee having ridden on the bike that sparked the vision, not that Bridges owns the bike."

I nodded. That had occurred to me, too.

"Anyway, you have that eyewitness statement from the woman, what was her name, Mrs. Taylor, who saw her getting kidnapped."

"I know. But I'm starting to wonder if Mrs. Taylor saw what she thought she saw."

THIRTY

The following Sunday, I was over at Megan's apartment. We were watching *The Godfather*, the film I'd missed during the week I was staying with Mom and Dad. It's not one of my favorites.

"I thought all guys liked *The Godfather*," said Megan.

"Can't root for any of the characters. I mean I'm supposed to admire the guy because he won't get into the narcotics trade..."

I stopped. That hit a nerve that was still pretty raw. Of course, strictly speaking Scott Kay had no longer been in the narcotics trade, but the memory of him stretched out on his driveway still came up unbidden. Funny, all the talk in the movie about whether or not the Mob should get into the dope business hadn't. Just my mention of it.

"Are you okay?" asked Megan.

"Sorry about that. I lost my train of thought. What was I saying?"

"You were talking about how Don Corleone didn't want to get into trafficking in narcotics."

"Right, and that's supposed to make us forget the prostitution, and the union racketeering, and the extortion, and all the other dirty stuff he's into."

"I think the point is that he's living in a corrupt world and he's just playing the cards he's dealt."

"We're all living in a corrupt world. What does Corleone do except make it more corrupt?"

"Didn't you feel sorry for him when he lost his son?"

"Who pushed Sonny into the business? He knew that his kid being in the Mob made him a potential target. What the hell'd he think Organized Crime was? Some kind of nice, safe family business like a mom and pop grocery or a medical practice? Something to take pride in when you passed it on to your son?"

"Police work's dangerous, isn't it?"

"Not a fair comparison. Dad and Pete never pushed me into the Job. Anyway, enforcing the law's an honorable calling. Breaking the law isn't."

"In this film it's not honorable. The cops are worse than the gangsters."

"Maybe that's another reason I don't like it."

One of Megan's roommates, Helen Bartley, came out of her room and went into the kitchen to make a sandwich. Helen's a pretty girl, a bit taller than Megan but not by much. She'd just put her shoulder-length honey-blonde hair up after washing it.

She smiled at us and said, "Hi, Dan. What are you guys watching?"

"*The Godfather.*"

"That's one of my dad's favorites. I've never really liked it, but that Al Pacino was dreamy-looking when he was young, wasn't he?"

"Yeah. Dreamy."

She went back to her room. I looked at her closed door for a few moments before turning back to Megan.

"What's so interesting about Helen's door?"

"It just occurred to me."

"What?"

"You and Helen are both blondes."

"So?"

"And you're both the same physical type. Same height, within a few inches. Same weight, within a few pounds. Similar build." I stroked her hair. "Similar hair style."

"Your point?"

"If someone was giving a capsule description of DeeDee Merryweather, it would fit you and Helen, too."

"You're still losing me."

"Think about it. Girls that fit that description aren't that unusual around here. It's California, after all. Maybe it's not Southern California, but it's California. Blondes aren't all that uncommon. And the build, and the size, I bet there're hundreds of girls on campus who match that description. Maybe thousands."

"So what you're saying is?"

"That the one up on Grizzly Peak wasn't necessarily DeeDee."

"I thought that witness, Mrs. Taylor, said she was."

"She said, and I quote, 'It certainly looked like her.' We just assumed it was her because she was in the right place at the right time. More or less."

"So it was some other girl getting kidnapped?"

"Who says she was kidnapped? Mrs. Taylor didn't think anything bad was happening when she passed them on the road. It was only after she read about DeeDee's disappearance that she thought there might have been something wrong."

"But that would mean that..."

"The investigation's been on the wrong track for months," I finished. After a pause I added, "It would also mean that you might have been right all along."

***

The problem was how was I supposed to broach the subject? Should I go into CAP and suggest that experienced detectives had followed the wrong lead?

"Excuse me, Sergeant Mills," I could say, "but has it occurred to you that the girl up on Grizzly Peak may have been somebody else? And that a driver who saw her while passing by at thirty or forty miles an hour probably couldn't be sure who she saw, anyway?"

Oh, right. That would go over really well, coming from a reserve.

But I couldn't just let it lie.

If DeeDee wasn't abducted, the profile was useless. And if the profile was useless, the most sensible thing we could do was bet the same way the smart money would, and the smart money would bet on the hot-tempered significant other. In other words, we were back to Chris Bridges as the prime suspect. And if Chris was the responsible, then the likelihood was that DeeDee never left the hills. That she was still up there somewhere.

But those hills cover a lot of territory.

***

Maybe I couldn't march into CAP and tell an experienced

191

detective sergeant how to handle an investigation.

But I could go to my own sergeant.

My period of suspension was over. The shooting had been ruled justifiable. My pistol had been returned to me.

The next morning, I showed up in the Reserve Office in uniform, signed in for a regular patrol tour, and turned to the Sarge. He was talking on the phone. As soon as he hung up I went over to his desk and sat down opposite him.

"Got a few minutes?" I asked.

"Sure."

I laid out my thoughts, pretty much as I'd explained them to Megan the night before.

"Now we've got so much time invested in this whole abduction theory," I said, "that any other possibility's been ignored."

"You make a pretty good argument. But what do you want me to do?"

"Well, what do you think would happen if I presented that argument to Sergeant Mills the way I presented it to you?"

"I think he wouldn't appreciate a reserve suggesting that he was making a huge error."

"That's exactly what I think. But he'd probably accept it better coming from you."

"Why me?"

"You worked CAP a few years ago before you made sergeant, didn't you?"

"*Many* years ago," he said. "They called it 'Homicide' back then."

"Point is you've got experience as a detective, and even if you didn't, it's not like you're some semi-amateur part-timer. And you're a supervisor, like him. He'd be a whole lot more likely to listen to you."

"He might, but I'd like to have a little more to take to him. You know this Bridges, don't you?"

"We're both on the Co-op board. And we used to serve on the same committee, but he switched to Finance this semester."

"Are you in any classes together?"

"No. We don't have the same major."

"Well, maybe if you started spending more time around him, dropping hints, he might start to get rattled. If he let something slip, that would be something to take to Mills."

"That sounds like fun. I always wanted to be Columbo."

"This wouldn't just be unpaid, Dan. It would be unofficial. You wouldn't be acting as a police officer. You wouldn't even be on duty. And you'd have to tread lightly, or you might blow the whole thing."

"But if I saw something suspicious?

"You could report it to me as a concerned citizen. And then I could bring it to Mills."

"And if I blew it?"

"I would, as usual, disavow any knowledge of your activities."

"And my career would self-destruct in five seconds."

THIRTY-ONE

The following Wednesday, I was seated in the dining room of Ridge House, waiting for the Finance Committee meeting to begin. Though my regular committee assignment is Personnel and Operations, I have the option of attending any committee meeting and casting a vote.

I rarely exercise this option, so Debbie Baynes, the VP for Financial Affairs and FiCom's chairperson, was surprised to see me.

"You've never come to a FiCom meeting before, Dan," she said. "Not since I've been chairing them, anyway."

"Roylmann had a house council meeting last night."

"What about?"

"Some new business my house wants addressed."

"That sounds cryptic, but I'll put you on the agenda."

FiCom's dull as dirt. Actually, I guess all committee meetings are dull as dirt. I didn't choose POpCom because I found the nuts and bolts of personnel management and corporate operations stimulating, after all. I chose it because it met on Tuesday nights.

But at least, after more than a year, I'm familiar with the issues that routinely come before POpCom. FiCom's seemingly endless swirl of numbers makes me dizzy. Debbie's in the Bus Ad school, majoring in Accounting, so it's right up her alley. I, on the other hand, barely manage to get my checkbook to balance every month, so I'm happy to leave the arcane world of corporate money management to others.

I was attending tonight because Chris Bridges had decided to make FiCom his committee this semester. I halfway suspected that he'd decided to switch just to get away from me. I didn't want to make it easy for him.

Two minutes before the committee was called to order, Sid

Eisbach entered the dining room.

"Hi, Sid," said Debbie. "This is getting to be a night for newcomers."

"Well, it's just around the corner from Northside, so I figured what the hell."

"Great."

Actually, Sid was there at my request. If it wasn't me Chris was trying to get away from, it might be Sid. He and Chris had never gotten along well. I thought Sid's presence might rattle Chris, if mine didn't.

Or if my issue didn't.

Chris arrived right after Sid. He was as surprised as Debbie to see Sid and me there. And not nearly as pleased.

Rich Merryweather was the last to arrive. Rich has served several terms on the Board, and was a regular FiCom member during that time. This semester he held no actual oligarchic office, but all Co-op members have the right to attend meetings, to speak, and to make or second motions. It's precisely to allow members to see their Co-op government in action that Board and committee meetings rotate from house to house.

Rich, like Sid, was there at my request.

I suffered through all the other agenda items, not participating in any of the debates, either voting with the majority when a motion was called, or abstaining. Finally it was my turn.

When Debbie gave me the floor, I said, "I don't normally attend FiCom, as most of you know. I'm here tonight because Roylmann's house council voted last night to propose that the BSC offer a reward for information leading to the recovery of DeeDee Merryweather, and the conviction of her victimizers."

Of course, the house council meeting had been called at my request, and I'd been the one who proposed the motion. I'd done it that way, so that when I took the proposal to FiCom, it would look like I was just following the wishes of my constituency instead of pushing my own agenda.

"Roylmann's willing to contribute 500 dollars to such a fund. If the other houses make similar contributions, and the central organization matches them, we could offer a substantial reward. I'll put that in the form of a motion."

"Second," said Sid.

"Okay, that opens the issue for discussion," said Debbie. "Dan, you still have the floor."

"Right. It's been four months since DeeDee's disappearance. Nothing substantial has turned up since the report that she was seen struggling with a bearded man up on Grizzly Peak Boulevard. I've been working on the case, along with several other reserve cops. I'm not at the center of the investigation, but I'm close enough to tell you that public interest has waned since before the holidays. The tip line is getting fewer than five calls a week now. A reward like this might get the media, and the public, interested in the case again. And this is the kind of case that needs public interest if it's going to be solved."

Sid spoke in favor of the proposal, saying we owed it to another Co-oper to do what we could. Rich talked about how much such a show of support would mean to his family. Geoff Korekt, the BSC's general manager, talked a bit about logistical problems, but had nothing to say against the concept. No one spoke against it.

Chris Bridges didn't speak at all.

It passed the committee unanimously.

Chris voted "aye," but he didn't look enthused about the idea.

***

The next step was the board meeting, but that wasn't 'til the following Tuesday. In the meantime, I wanted to keep the pressure, such as it was, on.

Chris Bridges was majoring in Political Science, and Mondays, Wednesday, and Fridays, he had a class on Constitutional Theory in Dwinelle Hall, Room 155, one of several auditorium-sized classrooms around the campus designed to accommodate the University's huge classes. Go to a class in 155 Dwinelle or Pimental Lecture Hall or one of Cal's other massive classrooms and you'll swear you're attending a course with at least a third of the entire student body, which meant I could audit it without drawing a lot of attention to myself.

There was only one person whose attention I wanted to draw. And I waited patiently until he entered the classroom and took a seat. Then I sat down next to him.

"Hey, Chris," I said. "How're you doing?"

"Are you in this class?"

"Just auditing. I'm supposed to do a term paper this semester on constitutional issues relating to law enforcement. Thought I might get some ideas here."

"Doesn't Legal Studies offer a constitutional law class?"

"Yeah, but it's focused on criminal justice. You know. Crime. Punishment. Like that. I wanted to get a broader view. Hoped sitting in on this class might spark some thoughts. And what a pleasant surprise finding you here. I'll make it a point to come here as often as I can now. Wouldn't that be great?"

"Yeah," he said. "Just great."

***

I audited the class that Friday, too. This time I sat directly behind Chris. Just before the class started, as he was settling into his seat, I tapped him on the shoulder.

When he turned around I said, "Hi, Chris."

The weekend I devoted to making a living. I worked Marina details on Friday and Saturday night and Sunday afternoon. I don't usually luck into a Marina trifecta during a single weekend, and twenty-four hours of paid work was most welcome. The football traffic details and Christmas foot patrols last semester had earned me just about enough to cover my school and living expenses for this one. But it had almost all been spent already. Details like these would provide a welcome financial cushion until June.

Monday I was back in class. This time I sat right in front of him so he couldn't avoid seeing me.

***

Tuesday night's board meeting was held in the dining room of Cloyne Court, one of the bigger Co-op dorms in the system. Committee meetings move all over the Co-op, but the Board can only meet in one of the larger properties. There are nearly forty directors, and most of the houses can't accommodate that large a group.

Add in the professional staff, like General Manager Geoff Korekt or Operations Manager Rikki Sterling, who both attend all

Board meetings, all the veeps, who give the committee reports, and any interested members who happen to drop in to watch "Their Co-op in Action," and it adds up to quite a crowd.

With so many people, virtually all of them bright and opinionated, Board meetings can be long, drawn-out, exhausting events. I'm as opinionated as any of them, and more than most, and I'm usually in there swinging with both rhetorical fists. Tonight I was saving my eloquence for the FiCom report.

It was the third committee report to come up. FiCom issues tend to bring out the parsimony of the directors. At least the small issues do. The Board will routinely approve expenditures of hundreds of thousands when the professional staff recommends them. The numbers are so large they don't even seem real to most of us, poor starving students that we are.

But line items that amount to no more than a few hundred dollars will generate hours of passionate debate. Should we spend money for a new printer for the Co-op newsletter, or make do with the old one for one more year? Do we really need to provide Rochdale residents with a miniature refrigerator when each apartment already has a full-sized one? Should it be the responsibility of the Co-op Central Level to make sure cable or satellite TV is provided to every property, or should that be left to the individual houses?

These are small-time issues. We can grasp small-time issues. What we can grasp, we can argue about. And we do. At great length. I remember another Board rep, who had a touch of Ogden Nash in him, describing it this way.

"The Board decides the Co-op budget at the meeting in Stebbins Hall. They'll spend a lot of time on every thinnish dime, but on thousands none at all."

Which was okay with me. Tonight a long debate suited me just fine.

* * *

It was eight-forty. The debate on the reward proposal had been going on for a half-hour. Once Debbie had moved the item out of committee, I'd spoken about the responsibility of the Co-op to look out for its members and its civic duty to help solve crimes, particularly when a Co-oper was the victim. It wasn't my best speech since becoming a Board member, but far from my worst.

So far, as BSC President Cathy Rolfe worked her way through the speakers' list, the sentiment seemed to be running in favor of adopting the motion. Of course the point wasn't really to post a reward for information about DeeDee's disappearance.

The point was to start a public discussion about DeeDee's disappearance. One that Chris Bridges, as a Board rep, would be right in the middle of, whether or not he chose to participate. And he couldn't feel comfortable about that.

I looked over at where he sat. He was looking down at the agenda, a sullen expression on his face, apparently trying to ignore the proceedings. But every time DeeDee's name was mentioned, he winced a bit and fidgeted in his chair.

Not everyone was for the motion. Some thought it was not the BSC's business to inject itself into an ongoing police investigation.

Others didn't like the idea of spending money without knowing exactly how much they'd be spending. Since the motion called for the BSC to match the donations made by individual houses, and only one house, Roylmann, had pledged any money to help fund the reward, there was no way to set an actual amount.

Still others questioned whether any amount that the Co-op could afford to offer was likely to generate any new information.

Sue Hedley, the rep from Sherman, who's a bit of a ditz, objected, as near as I could tell, on the grounds of courtesy.

"It just seems wrong to me," she said, "to be discussing poor DeeDee with poor Chris sitting right here at the table, and poor Rich," and at this she pointed to Rich Merryweather, seated just outside the inner circle, "here tonight, too. How do you think they feel having poor DeeDee talked about like this?"

It happened that Rich was next on the speakers' list. Though not a member of the Board this semester, he'd come to the meeting tonight, as he had to FiCom, because he knew this issue would be discussed. And, like all Co-op members, he had a voice, though not a vote, on the Board.

He got up from his seat when Cathy recognized him.

"First of all," he said, "I just want to assure you all that I take no offense whatsoever at this issue being discussed here tonight. On the contrary, I'm very moved that some of DeeDee's brother and sister Co-opers feel strongly enough about her to make this proposal."

He took a long breath, nodded at me, and continued.

"I don't know whether offering a reward would help find DeeDee, but I don't think it would hurt. This all happened months ago. Most people have forgotten about it. Just the publicity that news of the reward would generate might be valuable. And if no useable information develops, well, the BSC isn't out anything. I know that my family and I would appreciate the gesture, whether or not anything came of it."

He paused and took another breath.

"That's all I came to say, except that the one person you should be concerned about here isn't Chris or me. It's DeeDee. So, don't worry about causing either of us to relive painful memories. All I'm concerned about, and I'm sure all Chris is concerned about, is finding out what happened to DeeDee, and getting her back safe. Thank you."

Chris fidgeted a little more during Rich's speech than he had during the others.

I got the floor after Rich.

"Rich brings up a good point," I said. "In fact, it was the main reason I made the proposal. The key to breaking this case is going to be publicity. Rich knows this, and Chris knows this."

Chris looked up at me when I mentioned his name. I looked right back. Right in the eye, as intently as I could, and as I did I said, "Somebody knows exactly what happened to DeeDee."

I paused to let that sink in.

"And the trick is to get that person to tell what he knows."

I sat down, and leaned over to Sid Eisbach, a master manipulator of parliamentary procedure, and whispered, "Chris doesn't seem to be enjoying this at all. Is there a way we can delay a vote so the discussion gets spread out?"

"Leave it to me," he said.

When his name was called he got up and started speaking.

"The main justification given for this motion is the publicity it'll generate. If it does nothing else, offering a reward will get the case back in the public eye. 'DeeDee's Fellow Students Putting Meager Financial Resources on the Line to Get Her Back.' It's a human-interest natural. There'll be newspaper coverage. TV coverage."

He paused while the notion of media coverage sank in.

"If it only generates a week's worth of publicity, then the police'll get a week's worth of new tips phoned in. One of those tips could be the one that breaks the case."

He paused again, then switched to a new subject.

"However, the objections of some of the directors that we shouldn't commit funds without knowing just how much we're committing are well-taken. So I propose we table this motion and return it to committee. In the meantime, all the directors should take the issue back to their individual house councils and see how much, if anything, each is prepared to contribute to the effort. Once we have a total of the amounts pledged, we'd know what Central Level is going to have to match. Consider that a motion."

"Second," I said.

It made me look reasonable and open to other points of view to second a motion tabling my own proposal. But the real beauty of the motion was that, if it passed, it assured that Chris would have to endure two more long discussions on the subject, once at the next week's FiCom meeting, and once more when the Board met again in two weeks.

"Okay," said Cathy, "there's a new motion on the floor, to table the main motion, and return it to committee. In the interim each Board rep is to determine what amount, if any, their house is willing to contribute to a reward fund. I'll continue with the same speakers' list."

Kevin Webster, Cloyne's rep, was next up.

"The current motion is to table the main motion?" he asked.

"That's right."

"Okay, I move the previous question."

"Second," Sid Eisbach said.

"The question has been moved and seconded," said Cathy. "This is not a debatable motion. There are still ten persons on the speakers' list. All those in favor of coming to an immediate vote?"

"Aye," came a chorus of voices.

"Opposed."

A few stray and uncoordinated "Nays," sounded.

"Discussion on this motion will now end and we'll proceed to voting. If this motion fails, we will continue discussion on the main motion."

Not all of the nearly forty directors are as conversant as Sid with Robert's Rules of Order, and when things get sort of complicated, with substitute motions, and amendments to motions, etc., Cathy tends to take them by hand so they'll all understand what's going on.

"All in favor?"

Another loud chorus of "ayes."

"Opposed."

More scattered "nays."

"Motion passes," said Cathy. "The main motion will be returned to committee and an updated report will be made to the Board at the next meeting."

Two more weeks of DeeDee being at the forefront of both FiCom's and the Board's affairs.

Chris couldn't be pleased about that.

THIRTY-TWO

I sat in the same row as Chris at his Poli-Sci class the next day, but a dozen or so chairs to his right. I waved at him, winked, and gave him the pistol forefinger with the wagging thumb hammer, just to make sure he'd be aware of me. And to let him know he was in my sights.

The lecture subject that day was "probable cause," as it was used in the Fourth Amendment of the Bill of Rights.

The professor started the lecture by explaining what would be regarded as sufficient grounds to establish probable cause for either an arrest or a search warrant.

"The classic standard," he said, "is known as the 'two-pronged test.' The first prong is the quality of the informant. If a police officer can show, for example, that his informant has given reliable information on previous occasions, he's proven the quality of the informant. You should have all read the chapter. Can anyone tell me what the second prong is?"

This wasn't my class, so it wasn't really my place to intrude on the professor's Socratic dialogues, but no one else was responding. Finally, I raised my hand.

"The informant's basis of knowledge," I said.

"Correct. Can you explain what that means?"

"The officer has to provide a reasonable explanation for how his informant knows what he's passed on to the police."

"Correct again. If the officer can demonstrate the quality of the informant and reasonably describe the basis of knowledge, he should get the warrant he's applying for."

He paused to give the class time to ask questions, then pressed on.

"More recently, courts have begun issuing warrants based on a looser standard of what constitutes probable cause. It's called the 'totality of circumstances.' Suppose an officer gets an anonymous tip. He can't prove the quality of his informant, because he doesn't know who his informant is. And he can't give the informant's basis of knowledge because the informant didn't stay on the phone long enough to explain it. Suppose, though, that in subsequently investigating that tip he discovers that everything the informant has told him is correct. On that basis, his objective investigation of the tip having verified the allegations of the informant, he might be able to get a warrant based on the 'totality of circumstances' standard."

I raised my hand and was recognized again.

"A hypothetical case, Professor."

"Go ahead."

"Suppose a woman has disappeared. There's no trace of her. She has no history of dropping out of sight like this. She's got family and friends who care about her and who she cares about."

"All right."

"The last person to see her alive was her husband. He reports that she's left him, at least temporarily, and gone back to her parents, but her parents have no idea what he's talking about. And there's a history of domestic violence against the missing woman by her husband."

I looked over at Chris to see how he was taking it. "Would those facts alone, considered in their totality, justify an arrest warrant?"

"For what?"

"For murder."

"It's very doubtful," he said. "There have been cases of successful murder prosecutions without a body actually being produced, but they're very rare. And at least some proof of death, if not physical proof, would have to be offered before a murder charge could stick. He might be arrested on suspicion in the hopes that he makes an incriminating statement, but once he's in custody, his Miranda rights come into play, and if no further evidence was developed he'd have to be released."

"Okay, suppose there isn't enough evidence to prove the case beyond a reasonable doubt. Not even enough to justify an arrest warrant. Leave the evidence aside. Just on the circumstances as I've described them, how would the smart money bet?"

"Personally, I'd say the smart money would bet on the husband being his wife's murderer."

***

After class, Chris, face red and eyes blazing, caught up with me in the hallway outside of the classroom.

"What the hell was that all about?"

"Probable Cause."

"Don't give me that. If you've got something to say, come out and say it to my face."

"I'm afraid you've lost me."

"That so-called hypothetical case. That was me and DeeDee you were talking about, wasn't it?"

"What makes you say that?"

"It was obvious."

"I doubt it was obvious to anyone else. Look at all the differences."

"Like what?"

"In the first place, you and DeeDee aren't married."

"We were living together. Same thing."

"It's not the same thing. It's a difference, a big one, and not the only one. A second one is DeeDee didn't just disappear. She was kidnapped. Isn't that right? She was kidnapped?"

He seethed for a few seconds, then muttered, "Yeah. Kidnapped."

"And this guy has a history of slapping his wife around. You've never done anything like that, have you? A sweet-natured, even-tempered guy like you, I bet you never even let a cross word pass your lips the whole time you were with DeeDee."

He just stood there fuming.

"And finally, and here's the big difference, you didn't kill DeeDee and then try to conceal your crime, did you? The guy in my story did, but not you. Or are you saying that's *not* a significant difference?"

His fists clenched at his sides and the backpack he had slung over one shoulder slid down to his wrist. Cursing, he pulled it back over his shoulder, then secured the other strap over his other shoulder to keep it from slipping again. His eyes widened and he started to take deep breaths, snorting through his nose like a bull preparing to charge.

"Slow down there, pal," I said. "You're going to hyperventilate."

"If you think I killed her, say so."

"Why would I think that? I already told you, DeeDee was kidnapped."

"You know she wasn't kidnapped."

"I do? How do I know that? For that matter, how do you know that?"

He paled a bit, apparently realizing his gaffe. But he recovered quickly.

"You're acting like you think I had something to do with DeeDee's disappearance. I just figured you must have some information that discredits the kidnapping theory."

"Ah," I said nodding. "'Discredits the kidnapping theory.' Good choice of words. No, I have no hard information that 'discredits' the kidnapping theory. At least I didn't 'til just this minute."

He stalked off.

***

In his office, Fred Cutter listened to the cassette tape intently. He replayed Chris' comment about knowing DeeDee wasn't kidnapped several times.

"Close," he said. "But it's not enough."

"Not for an indictment, maybe. But it ought to be enough to get Sergeant Mills and the rest of CAP to concentrate on him."

"I don't know. Maybe it should. But I think Mills would want more than an emotional outburst that it probably wasn't even legal to record in the first place."

"I was recording the lecture. I just forgot to turn the thing off."

"Yeah, a part-time cop, working on the case, attending a class he's not even enrolled in, just happens to forget to turn off his recorder."

"If it was all a ploy to get him on tape, how'd I know he'd try to talk to me after the class?"

"Either he would or he wouldn't. You'd be ready if he did."

"Anyway, it's legal if at least one party to the conversation knows it's being recorded."

"Yeah, theoretically. But try convincing our candy-ass DA."

"But that just brings me back to my original point. Even if it's not useable as evidence, it should be enough to set CAP on the right track."

"Maybe it should be, but it's not. I'll put a tag on it, book it into evidence. Keep on it for another week or so. Then I'll take everything you've developed to Mills."

"I'm still way out on a limb, Sarge."

"You're not by yourself, anymore. I don't think you'd convince Mills but you've convinced me. I'll back you if this goes south. I've got my thirty in. I'll take the heat if there's any heat to take."

THIRTY-THREE

At the next FiCom meeting, the other houses reported pledges amounting to two thousand dollars. With the five hundred originally pledged by Roylmann, and a matching pledge put up by Central Level, the BSC would be able to offer a 5,000 dollar reward. The motion passed easily.

Chris wasn't there.

And he hadn't been coming to the Constitutional Theory class at Dwinelle.

He was also absent from the next Board meeting. Apparently, I was getting to him, but as long as he made a concerted effort to avoid me, I'd gotten to him as much as I was going to. I couldn't very well stake out the door to his room at Rivendell.

All I'd done so far was audit classes, which I had every right to do as a registered student, and attend meetings, which I had not only a right, but an obligation to do as a Board rep. Anything beyond that could be construed as harassment. Hell, anything beyond that would *be* harassment.

I said as much to Sergeant Cutter in his office, the day after the Board meeting.

"He's rattled, Sarge, but he's deliberately avoiding situations where he might get more rattled. He's cutting classes and blowing off meetings just to avoid running into me. I could try for a transfer to Rivendell, but I think he'd just transfer out. If it comes to it, he might just transfer to another school."

"Doesn't your girl live near him?"

"You don't think he'd go after her, do you?"

"That wasn't what I meant. I just meant spending time at her place puts you in the same neighborhood as him. Maybe you could run into each other occasionally."

"Yeah, but it's no way to keep up steady pressure. It's hit or miss. It's not like this is some old cartoon where I'm Droopy Dog and he's the Wolf. I can't just pop up wherever he is."

"Droopy Dog and the Wolf?"

"You know. They were cartoon characters back in the '40's. Droopy was always the good guy and the Wolf was always the bad guy, and no matter how hard the Wolf tried to hide, Droopy was always there..."

"I know who they are!" he interrupted. "Jesus, if you could plug your ears into a pair of speakers and put some light bulbs behind your eyeballs, I bet you could play back every movie you've ever seen, frame for frame."

"Thanks. I think."

"Anyway, you're right. You can't just do a rough tail. He's not an organized crime figure. He'd complain. And the complaint would stick. Well, it was worth a try. Too bad we couldn't find her body."

"So we're just giving up?"

"What should we do?"

"You said you'd turn whatever I developed over to Sergeant Mills. I think the time has come."

"I guess it has. But I don't think he'll buy it."

***

As if to put the lie to my comments to Cutter about the unlikelihood of accidentally coming across Chris Bridges at strategic moments, I actually did bump into him, quite by chance, at Doe Library that same night. We were both looking for a book in the constitutional law stacks.

He saw me first.

"Are you going to turn up everywhere I go?"

"I'm just looking for a book, same as you."

"I don't believe that."

"Well, that'll keep me awake nights."

He grabbed my shirt and pulled me toward him.

"Get off my back! I'm not kidding!"

I grabbed his thumb with my left hand and pulled it back. His grip on my shirt immediately loosened, and he grimaced in pain as I brought my right hand up, used it to turn the thumb lock into a twisting wrist lock, and forced him onto his knees.

"Don't ever try that again," I said through clenched teeth. "I'm not some girl half your size. I'll fight back and you won't be able to leave me buried in some lonely canyon."

"What are you talking about?"

"You were right. I do think you killed DeeDee. Why don't you tell me about it?"

"You're not going to advise me of my rights?"

I turned him loose. "You're not in custody," I said, as he got to his feet. "I'm not on duty. Hell, legally I'm not even a cop right at this moment. Miranda doesn't apply. So satisfy my curiosity, just between friends. Tell me how you did it."

"You think I did it," he sputtered. "Prove it!"

We were starting to attract the attention of some of the students cramming in study carrels on the same floor. As they began to shush us, he pushed passed me roughly and stomped out of the area.

Maybe I shouldn't have braced him head-on like that, but, like I said, it really was a chance encounter, despite what he thought. And I didn't think I could count on many more chance encounters. So I'd impulsively taken what seemed to me to be the only shot I had left.

And I'd missed.

***

Like Sergeant Cutter said, the key was finding the body. There'd been a search of the area back when DeeDee was first reported missing, a full-court press with special equipment and dogs and the whole shebang. But it's a large area, and they weren't necessarily looking for a body at that point.

A body.

DeeDee was dead. That was my premise. So if she was dead, there had to be a body.

Well, there didn't *have* to be. There have been cases where the murderer disposed of his victim's body, or most of it, but those were premeditated, planned murders.

Given Chris' personality, killing DeeDee was a lot more likely to have been a crime of impulse. You can't dispose of a body without a plan, and you can't plan to dispose of a body if you're not planning on having a body to dispose of.

So, the body must still be up there somewhere.

Which brought me back to my original problem.

The hill area is a big place.

I couldn't find her alone.

THIRTY-FOUR

"It really is a beautiful view," said Megan. "Especially on a clear day like this."

"Yeah, it is. I guess I kind of take it for granted, growing up in the Bay Area like I did. Need to look at it through new eyes every now and then."

I was conflicted about what I was about to do.

And what I was about to do, basically, was use Megan without her knowing about it. Without getting her permission first. I had a good reason for this, but it still seemed like a betrayal, and I was afraid our new, still-fragile relationship might not withstand the strain.

It was late in the morning, maybe ten or ten thirty. I'd suggested we share a sort of picnic brunch while enjoying a gorgeous view. We were seated in my old Toyota, parked at the outermost hump of an S-curve on Grizzly Peak Boulevard, looking out over the hill at a huge chunk of the Bay Area. Below us we could see most of Berkeley and Oakland. Across the Bay, the one-of-a-kind skyline of downtown San Francisco. Off to the side, the Golden Gate Bridge, one of the most photographed structures in the world, leading to the southernmost tip of Marin County.

I reached into the glove box and pulled out a pair of binoculars. Not the huge, high-powered military type, but more substantial than a pair of opera glasses. I looked through them, adjusting the focus.

"Can I see?" asked Megan, exactly as I'd hoped she would.

"Sure," I said, handing the binocs to her.

She held them up to her eyes and suddenly her whole body went rigid. She stayed that way for a few seconds, then put the binoculars down on her lap.

"Where did you get these?" she asked.

"From Rich Merryweather. I asked him if there was anything of DeeDee's his family would be willing to let me borrow. He gave me those. Seems she was an avid bird-watcher. I never knew that about her. Chris Bridges gave 'em to her for Christmas."

"Why didn't you tell me?"

"You always said that your visions came unbidden, when you weren't expecting them. That when you tried to summon a vision, it didn't work."

"And you thought if you sneaked something of hers on me I might get some sort of reaction."

I didn't like her use of the word "sneak," but there really was no other that applied. I looked away from her, feeling a little ashamed, feeling a lot ashamed, and nodded.

"She's out there, Meg. Somewhere in this area. I'm sure of it. You said you felt her being buried after just brushing against a motorcycle. I thought if you touched something else of hers, something she'd handled a lot, something you grabbed a hold of instead of just brushing against, you might get a sense of where. We've got to find her body. It's the only way we'll have a chance of nailing her killer."

"'We' being you and me?"

"I meant we, the police department, actually. Right now I'm acting as a cop, not as your boyfriend."

That was actually true. I was signed in and on duty. Officially, I was following up on one of the thousands of tip sheets. Specifically, the tip sheet I'd filled out when Megan had called me months earlier. As expected, it was near the bottom of the "unpromising" pile.

She stared me, disbelief, disappointment, and bitterness in her eyes.

"Well, congratulations, Officer," she said. "It worked."

***

At her direction, I drove to the intersection of Grizzly Peak and Centennial Drive, then downhill on Centennial to the beginning of the Strawberry Canyon Fire Trail, and parked.

She got out and said, "This is it."

She started walking. I went to the trunk and got out a small spade and followed her.

About a hundred feet into the Trail, she stopped, bent down, and felt the ground.

"It's like a rising thermometer," she said, and continued on, walking faster now. She continued the pace for what must have been at least a mile, then turned off the trail and into the hill.

I continued to follow trying to note landmarks, so I'd be able to find my way back by myself if I needed to.

She kept a steady pace, moving without hesitation as though she knew exactly where to go. Then, abruptly, she stopped.

"Somewhere near here," she said.

She got down on all fours and carefully felt the ground, like she was a bloodhound guided by touch rather than scent. She'd crawl, stop and feel the ground carefully, then crawl some more. Suddenly, she gripped a handful of ground tightly with both hands, and came bolt upright, still on her knees. Her face grimaced in pain, and she let out an anguished cry.

"She's here! Oh, God, she's here!"

I pulled her away from the spot and sat her down some distance away. I looked down at the spot where she'd dug the two tiny holes with her hands.

It was hard to tell if the ground had been disturbed, but it had been just a few weeks shy of a half a year since DeeDee had gone missing. Any signs of disturbance would long since have disappeared, unless you were some kind of expert tracker out of James Fenimore Cooper.

I started to dig.

A little less than a foot down, I hit something. I got down on my knees and started digging with my hands.

It was a piece of fabric. Yellow cotton, or some kind of cotton mix.

It was faded and dirty, and I hadn't exposed enough to see any kind of insignia, but it looked a lot like a Cal t-shirt, the kind anyone can buy at the Student Union store.

I pushed down on the fabric. Whatever was underneath felt like a rib. My heart had already been racing. Now it felt like it was breaking the sound barrier. I stood up.

I'd found her. After all these months I'd found her.

Except I hadn't really. She was gone forever. All I'd found

were her remains. But that was a philosophical bone I didn't feel up to picking at that moment. Her remains were all I'd really expected to find.

I resisted the urge to dig deeper. It was better to leave the rest of the digging to trained crime scene specialists.

I straightened up elated, and disappointed, and saddened, and angered all at once.

What a waste. What a stupid, lousy waste.

"'The obscure grave,'" I said.

"What's that?" asked Megan.

"Last summer Lou, Steph, and I went up to Ashland, Oregon, for the Shakespeare Festival. We saw a production of *The Merchant of Venice*. I remember some line about 'the obscure grave.' Seeing her here reminded me of it."

"You've found her." It was less a question than a flat statement.

"Yeah. Let's get back to the car, and I'll get you home."

"You'll have to use my name now, won't you?"

"I think I can still keep you anonymous. I'll try to, anyway."

***

Megan didn't say a word on the drive back. After walking her to her door, I went back to my car, opened the trunk, pulled out a belt radio I'd signed out when I went on duty, and turned it on.

"Dispatcher, 673."

If I specify "Dispatcher" in a radio communication, it means I want to talk to one of the assistant radio operators instead of the one in charge, who is designated as "Control."

"*673 from Dispatch*," came the reply.

"Could you have someone from CAP meet me on Channel Two?"

"*10-4*."

I switched the selector the Channel Two, which is BPD's frequency for non-emergency communications between units.

"*72 to 673*," came a transmission a few minutes later. 72 is the badge number of Officer Hal Bocatelli.

"673."

"*What's up, Sullivan?*"

"I think I've found DeeDee Merryweather's body."

THIRTY-FIVE

I guess I have as much of a sense of the dramatic as anyone, and that flat announcement had the desired effect. Stunned silence followed by a request to repeat what I'd just said.

What followed was less dramatic, and much more slow-moving. An army of forensics investigators, and photographers, and pathologists, and detectives, and a host of other crime scene specialists would have to be assembled, which would take some time. And before that process could even be started, we had to figure out where DeeDee's body was.

I mean we, or at least I, knew where DeeDee's body was, in the sense of being able to find the right spot. What we didn't know, and had to find out, was who had responsibility for policing that spot.

Grizzly Peak Boulevard runs east and west, sort of. To its south is the University's wilderness preserve, which is under the jurisdiction of the UC Police. To its north is Tilden Park, the huge recreational area that comes under the East Bay Regional Park District's Department of Public Safety. But some of Tilden bleeds over to the west side of Grizzly Peak, so, conceivably, DeeDee's body could be the responsibility of either the campus cops or the park cops.

Where the University's property line ends, the City of Oakland begins. Some parts of the Canyon on the Oakland side are simply undeveloped parts of Oakland. Others are owned by the East Bay Municipal Utilities District, which is responsible for providing law enforcement to its own property, though I think it may contract those duties out to either Oakland or the Park District.

To make it even more confusing, the border between Contra Costa County and Alameda County runs in a straight line through part of that same area, with Grizzly Peak S-curving back and forth across it, making a tiny sliver of the Canyon west of Grizzly Peak unincorporated county area, the bailiwick of the Contra Costa Sheriff's Office.

And, of course, it might have been in a part of the Canyon that was an undeveloped section of Berkeley.

So, before the crime scene could be processed, we had to determine exactly whose crime scene it was.

And even determining that might not settle the case. Suppose it turned out to be outside of BPD's jurisdiction. On the one hand, BPD had been the lead agency on the case from the beginning, and it might be deemed more efficient just to let us finish the investigation that we'd started.

This often happens, for example, when a victim is killed in one jurisdiction but dumped in another. The police agency responsible for the area in which the body was found usually handles the case. Once it's discovered where the actual crime was committed, it doesn't make sense to turn the investigation over to a different police force. For the sake of continuity, it's more sensible just to let the agency that began the case finish it.

On the other hand, it wasn't as if BPD had been investigating it as a murder. For practical purposes, this was now a brand-new case. If the body was outside of our geographic area of responsibility, the department having actual jurisdiction would probably want to take over.

***

After some map consultation and discussion and buck-passing, the burial spot was determined to be Oakland. And it turned out that Oakland wanted the case.

An OPD Homicide detective interviewed me at the burial site while the grave was slowly being uncovered and the rest of the scene carefully processed for forensic evidence.

"How'd you know where to find the body?" he asked.

"Confidential informant."

"Confidential informant, huh? How'd your confidential informant know?"

"Does that matter? This isn't any place where a private person could have a reasonable expectation of privacy. I didn't need probable cause to search."

"No, but I'd kind of like to make sure your informant didn't know where she was buried because he put her there."

"She," I corrected. I wasn't giving anything away, there. In the original tip sheet I'd listed Megan's gender as "female," though that was the only personal information I'd had at that time. He'd get a copy of that tip sheet anyway, so I'd gain nothing by using awkward phrases like "he or she."

"Okay, I'd like to make sure *she* didn't put her there."

"She didn't. She was out of town the week DeeDee went missing. She was visiting a relative in the hospital. Gone for more than a week. I've already verified that."

"Then I'd like to know so I can put it in my report so my lieutenant doesn't ask me the same question I'm asking you."

"When she called in her initial tip, which you'll be getting a copy of, she said she had a psychic vision that DeeDee had already been buried. When I did the follow-up, I contacted her personally. She was able to get another psychic vision that led me here."

"If she called in that tip anonymously, how did you know how to contact her?"

"She's a student at Cal. I bumped into her, by chance, in the course of a University event, and recognized her voice. I told her who I was and asked her if she was the person who'd called in the tip."

"Why doesn't she want to be identified?"

"She's not really at ease with being a psychic. Nobody knows about it in Berkeley except me. I told her I'd try to keep her out of it. She cooperated, and she's not a viable suspect herself. We couldn't have found this body without her. I think we owe her."

"All right. I'll leave it like that for the moment."

"By the way, when you get done here find my sergeant, Fred Cutter."

"Why?"

"He has a tape recording you might find interesting."

***

I stuck around while the scene was getting processed, though I really had no role to play there.

The body, now completely uncovered, was in a pretty advanced state of decomposition. What skin was left had tightened around the skeleton. A lot of her had been consumed by insects and worms.

I felt a little queasy. Hell, I felt a *lot* queasy. I'd seen dead bodies before. I'd seen one last year that had been dismembered. It had given me nightmares for weeks. But I'd never seen the natural process of decomposition so well advanced before.

And this wasn't just any random body. It was the body of someone I'd known and liked.

When my stomach started gurgling, I walked away from the crime scene as quickly as I could. I didn't want my puke disturbing any physical evidence.

And I didn't want anyone to see me puking.

***

When my stomach settled I returned. I talked to one of the techs.

"Do they know what happened?"

"The side of her head's caved in," he answered. "They've found an old hubcap with dried bloodstains on it. They should be able to match it to the skull fracture. It looks like whoever did her might have used the same hubcap as a makeshift shovel to dig the grave."

"'The obscure grave,'" I said again.

"Not obscure enough. You managed to find it."

"With help."

"That's how most cases get made. With help."

"Anything pointing to the responsible?"

"We didn't find any prints on the hubcap. And the crime scene's old. I think they like her boyfriend for it. He was the last one to see her alive, right?"

"Yeah."

"Well, it looks like they both came up here together, he got mad and smacked her upside the head with the hubcap, and then buried her. Crime of passion, most likely."

"What are the chances you can find something that definitely ties him to the murder?"

"After all this time, not good. If we'd gotten to the scene right after it happened, it might be a different story, but all these months later, a lot of the physical evidence has degraded. They'll most likely bring him in for questioning, but if he just keeps quiet, he might dodge this bullet altogether."

Knowing it and proving it are two different things.

***

Sergeant Mills was also on the scene. He beckoned me over.

"Sullivan, you know the victim's family, is that right?"

"I know her brother."

"I've got another shitty detail for you. You don't have to take it, but I think it would be better coming from you."

"You want me to notify the family?"

"Yeah. Hear that?" he said, pointing up.

I looked up where he was pointing, aware, for the first time, of the sound of a motor overhead. There was a helicopter hovering over the scene, a little off to the west. There were call letter signs along the aircraft's side.

"TV copter," said Mills. "They probably heard something on the police scanners. Even if we don't make a public announcement, it shouldn't take them too long to associate all this activity with the Merryweather girl. It would be better if someone from the department notified the family first. And it would be a lot better if whoever notified them was a friend."

THIRTY-SIX

One of the hardest things I ever had to do was tell my Mom that my Uncle Mike, her younger brother, had passed away.

In some ways, though, entering Rich's apartment to break the news that we'd found his sister buried in some remote part of Strawberry Canyon was even worse. The news about Uncle Mike was unexpected, so Mom's pain, while immediate and shocking, was not the terrible culmination of some long painful ordeal.

But Rich and his parents had spent the last five months fearing the worst, and coping with that fear by hoping for the best. I'd killed the hope. I'd confirmed the worst.

"Are you sure it's her, Dan?"

"Yeah. I'll be honest with you, she doesn't look good after all this time. But it's her."

Not to a forensic certainty, perhaps. But holding out a glimmer of hope until after DNA matches could be made or dental charts compared would be cruel.

"If you can, you should try to spare your parents seeing her like that," I said.

"Poor Mom and Dad. They loved her so much. And now she's dead."

He began to weep. And not manly tears blinked back while an outward mask of stoicism was maintained. He collapsed onto his couch and started bawling like a baby.

I went over and sat down next to him. I patted his back and tried to say something comforting. He turned around and buried his face in my shoulder.

It didn't take too long for him to regain his composure. He apologized for the emotional outburst.

"Nothing to apologize for," I assured him. "It's your sister we're talking about. You're not made of stone."

"Do my parents know?"

"I don't think so. If you don't feel up to it, I can call the local police and have them make the notification. Is that Menlo Park or Palo Alto or what?"

"Atherton," he said.

"I'll ask the cops there, if that's what you want. Or I can try to get a friend or a priest or somebody like that. But it would probably be better if you told them. I'll drive over with you, if you'd like, and answer any questions they have. But they're going to need you now."

"Should we call them first?"

"It's not the sort of news you should get over the phone. That's why the Department sent me personally."

"When can we go?"

"Right now. I don't think it'll be long before the story breaks in the news, and we ought to make sure your folks know before that happens."

***

After I told Mom about Uncle Mike, she had the infinitely more difficult job of telling Pete and Pet. I'm not a parent, but I can't imagine anything worse than outliving your own kids.

And Rich's job wasn't just to tell his parents that their baby girl was dead, but that she'd been murdered, and then left in some shallow, hidden grave by her killer to slowly decay in the hope that no one would ever know what happened to her.

He handled the job about as well as a job like that can be handled.

Mrs. Merryweather collapsed. Her husband and son helped her to her room. Mr. Merryweather came back after a few minutes. He was old school, holding his emotions in strict check when outsiders were around. Rich, he told me, was going to stay with his mother until she calmed down.

"It was Chris, wasn't it?" Mr. Merryweather asked me.

"I don't know, Mr. Merryweather. I'm sure he'll be talked to. That's all I can say."

He nodded.

"When can we claim her body?"

"I don't know that either, sir. I'm sorry." I reached into my pocket for a business card one of the coroner's investigators from the Alameda County Sheriff's Office had given me. "Here's a number you can call to find out."

"Do you know who found her?"

I hesitated briefly before saying, "I did."

"Thank you," he said. "It may not seem like it to you now, but you've taken a big load off of all our minds."

He'd been standing all this time. He looked at an easy chair as if noticing it for the first time, and suddenly realizing that he could sit down if he wanted to. He went over to the chair and did just that.

"It's terrible knowing what happened, but it would be worse not knowing."

"Just doing my job."

I winced at the triteness of my comment. That's right, Dan, I told myself. Stick with the clichés. The clichés are your friends.

"How did you find her?"

"I was just following a lead I got from a confidential source."

"Will you be talking again to whoever gave you this lead?"

"I think so. I hope so."

"When you do, tell him thanks, too."

"Her," I said. "And I will."

THIRTY-SEVEN

By the time I left Rich at his folks' house and started back, rush hour was in full swing. I'd already called Sergeant Mills on his cell and told him that I'd made the family notifications, so there was no official reason I had to get back. I was pretty tired and I gave some thought to just heading south to San Bruno and spending the night at Mom and Dad's.

But I still had unfinished business in Berkeley.

Traffic was so bad that it took me nearly an hour just to get across the Dumbarton Bridge, which connected the Peninsula city of Menlo Park to the East Bay city of Fremont, and another hour and a half to get from Fremont back to Berkeley.

I stopped in at the station, signed off duty, then headed up to Megan's apartment building, where it took me fifteen minutes to find someplace to park.

I knocked, heard steps on the other side, and saw the light go out in the peephole as someone looked through it.

A few seconds passed, and I'd just about decided that she wasn't going to let me in. Or even acknowledge that I was there.

"Come on, Megan," I said to the closed door. "Open up. We need to talk."

Still no response. I was turning to leave when the door opened.

"You might as well come in," Megan said.

I followed her into the living room. She sat down on a chair. I sat down on the couch.

"DeeDee's family said to tell you thanks," I said.

"You told them about me?"

"Not your name. Just that you gave me the lead."

"Is that what you said in your report?"

My report. Damn. I hadn't done any paperwork on the day's events yet. I guess I'd have to head back to the station after Megan and I finished our discussion.

"It will be when I get around to writing it. I just wanted to get some things settled first. Where do we stand? Am I another ex-boyfriend?"

"I haven't decided yet."

"Well, are you leaning one way or the other?"

"That sounded a little curt."

"I'm sorry. I just want to know what my position is."

"I don't know. I understand why you did what you did. I was angry at first, but after I thought about it, I could see you were in a tough position."

"So what's the problem?"

"The first time we went out I told you that one of the things that attracted me to you was that you weren't interested in my being a psychic. That's changed now."

"And I told you then that my attitude might be different if I was less skeptical. When you predicted that shootout, you converted me. At least you made me less skeptical."

"You began to think that what I told you about DeeDee might be true?"

"Yeah, I did. But it was such an incomplete description. I needed more details. I thought if we were in the general vicinity, and you were handling something of hers, it might induce a vision. If it didn't, no harm, no foul. You'd never even have to know I tried. If it did, well, I thought there was an even chance you'd understand. And I thought DeeDee's family had a right to bury her properly."

"I do understand. I'm not mad at you. Not anymore. I just don't know if I still feel the same way about you."

The phone rang. Megan went to answer it.

"Hello... Yes... Yes, he's here."

She handed the phone to me. It was Louise.

"Dan," she said. "Have you seen the news yet?"

"How did you know I was here?"

"You don't have class today. So you're either here at Roylmann, or you're down at the station, or you're there at Megan's. How hard is that to figure out? Now answer the question. Have you seen the news yet?"

"No."

"Did you know they found DeeDee's body?"

"Yeah, I heard something about that."

"Well, turn on Channel Two. There's a press conference going on right now."

I told her okay, hung up, and turned on the TV. Chief Nolan was answering questions from reporters. He was flanked by Oakland Chief of Police Dick Kreed and Supervisory Special Agent Steve Betz, head of the FBI's Oakland Resident Agency.

I vaguely wondered what Betz was doing there. Now that the kidnapping theory was completely debunked, there wasn't so much as a whisper of a federal interest in this investigation. Well, Betz and his agents had walked off almost as much shoe leather as anyone in BPD. I guess the Bureau was entitled to a share of the spotlight now that there was a break in the case.

"No, at this point the Berkeley Police is no longer the lead agency," Nolan was saying. "Miss Merryweather's body was found within the city limits of Oakland and, apparently, that's where she was killed. That makes it the responsibility of Chief Kreed and his department. We will, of course, be cooperating in every way we can."

"How was the body found, Chief?"

"One of our officers had been assigned to conduct follow-up investigations of phone tips we had received. As you'll remember, I pledged over a month ago that a police officer would personally investigate every such tip that had been made. The officer received information from an informant who prefers to remain anonymous and was able to use that information to find the dump site. That's as much information as I can give you at this time."

"Have her parents been notified?"

"Yes."

"What was the name of the officer who discovered the body?"

Oh, jeeze, Chief, don't give that up.

"I don't have that information here," he said.

Thank God for that.

"We've heard rumors that the officer who discovered the body is the same one who was involved in that gun battle in Concord several weeks ago. Is that true?"

Oh, great.

"I don't have that information available here," Nolan repeated.

"Chief Kreed, could you tell us if there are any suspects at this time?"

Kreed stepped up to the mike.

"Yes, I can. Earlier today two investigators from Oakland PD's Homicide Section, Sergeants Paul Lyons and Ed Procter, visited Riverdale Hall to inform Miss Merryweather's boyfriend, Mr. Christopher Bridges, of the latest developments in the case. He wasn't there. News of the discovery had already become public by this time. Several other residents of Riverdale Hall..."

He stopped as aide whispered something in his ear.

"I'm sorry, Rivendell House. Several of the other residents of Rivendell House informed the investigators that as soon as he heard the news of the discovery on television, he rushed up to his room, packed a bag, and hurriedly left the house. His departure preceded the arrival of Lyons and Procter by less than fifteen minutes. It's precisely for reasons like this that we try to control the time and manner of public announcements."

"So you're saying Bridges is your main suspect?"

"Mr. Bridges was the last person to see Miss Merryweather alive, and his behavior after her disappearance was quite suspicious. Alone, this might not make him our primary suspect, but his having run indicates a guilty conscience. In fact, legally, as many of you know, flight is evidence of guilt. On the basis of these circumstances, a warrant has been issued for the arrest of Mr. Bridges. If he's listening, we strongly encourage him to turn himself in."

A chorus of voices from the reporters. Kreed looked around the room for a few moments, then picked one.

"Do you have any idea why he killed her?"

"We don't absolutely know yet that he did kill her. We have no information as to motive. It appears to have been done in a state of rage. What might have generated that rage is unclear."

"Agent Betz, is the Bureau going to continue to be involved in this investigation?"

"Now that it's clear that Miss Merryweather wasn't the victim of a kidnapping, the Bureau has no jurisdiction over this case. However, Mr. Bridges is now a fugitive. If information should turn up indicating that Mr. Bridges has crossed any state lines in his attempt to avoid arrest, a federal warrant for unlawful flight to avoid prosecution will be issued and the Bureau would be able to re-enter the case at that time."

"What about the man who was seen with DeeDee up on Grizzly Peak."

Chief Nolan took that one.

"It now appears," he said, "that the woman seen with the bearded man on Grizzly Peak may not have been Miss Merryweather at all. It's not clear that what Mrs. Taylor saw involved any criminal activity whatsoever."

"So basically the BPD and the FBI have been conducting a wild goose chase for nearly half a year?"

"That's not really fair, Roger. The information seemed compelling at the time. And it wasn't only law enforcement that ran with it. It was the news media as well. If we've been on a wild goose chase, so have you. Now that's about all we have time for. Before we leave we'd like to show a picture of Christopher Bridges."

A photo of Chris filled the screen. Kreed was now doing a voiceover description.

"Mr. Bridges is a white male, 21 years old, five ten, a 160 pounds, with dark brown hair and brown eyes. If you see him please notify the police as soon as possible. Thank you."

The station returned to regular programming. All these months and DeeDee's case still managed to command that much attention. Of course, Channel Two was an East Bay station, so DeeDee's story might loom a bit larger than it would for stations on the other side of the Bay. Even so, interrupting the scheduled broadcast for a press conference instead of just showing highlights during the nightly news show was highly unusual.

I stood up.

"I better get going," I said. "I've got to get back to the station and do my report. I'll see you tomorrow in class."

I was at the door. She came up to me, with the binoculars in her hand.

"Don't forget these," she said.

"Thanks," I said, taking them from her.

"Dan."

"Yeah."

"Remember when you said that a psychic insight about water

isn't particularly helpful?"

I nodded.

"Well, then you might not find this particularly helpful, but when I picked the binoculars up I got an image of water."

"Okay."

"You did say that he gave her those as a gift, right?"

"That's right."

"So he would have handled them a lot, too, wouldn't he?"

"Yeah, I guess he would."

"It's probably not even worth mentioning, but I thought I should tell you."

"Thank you." I bent down and gave her a quick kiss. No hugs, no tongues. Just quick but, hopefully, meaningful lip contact. "Listen, your gift doesn't mean that much to me one way or the other. It doesn't affect how I feel about you."

"But it's become a lot more important than whether I'm right-handed or left-handed, isn't it?"

"If you being left-handed was, somehow, the key to solving a case, then, sure, I might use your left-handedness in an investigation. That's doing my job. But you being left-handed wouldn't have anything to do with my feelings."

"Okay. I'll think about what you said."

"Do that. See you tomorrow."

On that note, I left. Apparently, the smart money was betting against me.

THIRTY-EIGHT

The next day was Thursday. The scheduled gangster movie was the original *Scarface*, with Paul Muni as Tony Camonte, a fictionalized doppelganger of Al Capone. I'd seen it several times before, and had always enjoyed it, but I paid little attention that morning. Megan made a point of sitting away from me. Steph couldn't make it to the movie section. I sat through the whole feature alone. Little of it penetrated.

Neither did Ward's lecture following the flick. Now and then some particularly offensive Marxist screed trickled through, but I was too preoccupied to care.

Megan sat apart from me in class, too.

The smart money wasn't just not betting on me. It was avoiding me like the plague. In one day I'd gone from front-runner to thousand-to-one long shot to glue factory material.

***

I had a Marina detail the next night. It gave every promise of being particularly uneventful. It was cold and misty, which was keeping people away. Comparatively few folks were patronizing any of the restaurants. Judging by the number of cars in the parking lot, there weren't all that many guests registered at the hotel. And nobody was on the Fishing Pier. Driving aimlessly around the Marina was boring me stiff. My beat buddy, Bob Bower, patrolling the Marina in his own car, was probably just as bored.

I drove through the parking lots adjacent to the entrance to Docks H and I, checking for expired registration stickers. I usually regard that as petty chickenshit. That I could find nothing better to do is an indication of just how bored I was.

Dock H was where the Merryweathers' boat was moored. For no particular reason, I looked over at their boat and was surprised to see it bouncing. The water was very calm, so there was no reason for the boat to be bouncing, unless someone was on board. Rich was still staying with his family over in Atherton. Who else would be there?

Megan's comment about Chris being near water came back to me.

I picked up the car radio mike.

"673 to 645."

"*645.*"

"11-98 at the gate to Docks Ida and Henry."

"*10-4.*"

I parked the unit, got out, walked over to the gate, and waited for Bob. He arrived in less than a minute.

"What's up?"

"See that fifth boat down?"

"The one that's bouncing?"

"That's the one. It belongs to DeeDee Merryweather's family. There shouldn't be anyone using it."

"And you're thinking that..."

"Yeah."

"Let's check it out."

I keyed the shoulder mike on my belt radio and informed Control that we'd be checking out suspicious activity on Dock H, then unlocked the gate. We started down the dock.

"Ahoy the boat!" I yelled.

The bouncing stopped.

"It's the police. We need to talk to you."

No movement.

"Come on out or we're going to come in."

I unsnapped my holster. Bob did the same thing.

A figure slowly climbed up from below-decks. When he turned to face us the dock lights illuminated his face. It was Chris Bridges. He was holding a steak knife in his right hand, the point of the blade was pressed against his neck.

"It's all over, Chris. There's a warrant out for you. Come on down from there."

Bob got on the radio and informed Control that Chris had been found. Control started rolling some cover units, including a supervisor.

"It would be you, wouldn't it, Sullivan?" he said.

"Didn't plan it that way. Just where ball landed when the wheel stopped turning. Now put the knife down."

"What happens if I don't?"

"Come on, Chris. You watch TV. You know what happens. Back-ups are already rolling. If they decide that's not enough, we call for more. If you continue to hold yourself hostage and it gets really hairy, we get a SWAT team down here. But the end result'll be the same. You'll be leaving that boat and coming with us to jail. Let's make this low-key and do it easy."

"I don't feel like making it easy for you."

"For me? Hell, I get paid by the hour, Chris. If this takes a long time, then all you'll be doing is making it possible for me to pay the entire Fall tuition fee off of one shift. And make yourself look even guiltier than you already do. Give it up, and you'll probably get off light."

"How light?"

"The minimum on voluntary manslaughter's only three years. That's what you'd probably get for a first offense. You wouldn't even be 25 when you got out. You'd still have your whole life ahead of you. Smart lawyer might be able to plea bargain you down to involuntary, and the minimum for that's only two years. Hell, this is California. You might even get off altogether."

When we started talking, I'd unobtrusively slipped my pistol out of its holster, and held it at my side. Bob had done the same. If Chris changed his mind about who he was going to use that knife on, and started to charge one of us, I wanted to be ready. Bob and I were standing six or seven feet apart from each other, flanking Chris on the deck of the Merryweathers' boat. All he'd have to do was jump from the boat to the dock and he'd be within arm's reach of both of us. He could do that in less than a second, giving us no time to draw our weapons and defend ourselves. I didn't want to give him that advantage by leaving my gun holstered.

But I also didn't want to aggravate the situation by bringing the gun to bear.

He slowly lowered the knife from his neck. I started to think that maybe this was going to be a nice, peaceful surrender. Then I saw the cords of his neck becoming visible as the muscles tightened. His face started to contort. His eyes widened. His mouth pulled back to show his tightly clenched teeth.

All this happened in a fraction of a moment. I remember thinking that this must have been the face DeeDee saw before he smashed the hubcap against her skull.

He vaulted over the side of the boat, landing cleanly on the dock between Bob and me. He wheeled toward Bob and slashed at him in a wide, swinging arc.

Bob stepped back to avoid the attack, but the slashing motion cut a clean rip in his uniform shirt, exposing, but not penetrating, the Kevlar vest he was wearing underneath. He stumbled and fell back onto the dock.

Chris turned toward me and took a step, his knife hand held high over his shoulder for a downward slash. I backed away and started to bring up my nine.

He took another step.

I continued to shuffle back, trying to keep the distance more than an arm's length as he continued his advance. He suddenly rushed forward, slicing down toward me as he moved. I fired a single shot, one-handed. It caught him in the chest, dead center. He clutched at his wound with his empty hand, and fell.

**

I must've known, at least at some subconscious level, that he was dead.

I stood there paralyzed, looking down at him and thinking, it's too soon. Too soon since the last one.

And I recalled that conversation I'd had with DeeDee all those months ago, when she'd asked me if I could conceive of a situation in which I might have to arrest another Co-oper. In my wildest nightmares, it had never occurred to me that the Co-oper I might have to arrest would be her boyfriend, that it would be her murder I'd be arresting him for, or that I'd have to shoot him dead for resisting that arrest.

Bob was running back to the cars to get a first aid kit, and calling for an ambulance on his belt radio.

I shook myself out of my trance and bent down to examine him for signs of life, knowing it was going to be little more than an empty gesture.

***

And it was all so pointless. I hadn't been lying to him. If he'd just given up, he probably wouldn't have been looking at more than two years. And, as the crime scene tech told me, given the paucity of physical evidence conclusively linking him to the crime, he might even have been acquitted if he'd simply submitted to arrest and kept his mouth shut.

So why had he attacked Bob and me? He seemed intent on taking his own life when he first showed himself to us. Had he changed his mind about the method? Had he opted for suicide by cop?

Was it just that lethal temper of his, the same temper that apparently led to DeeDee's murder?

Did he have some personal grudge against me for the unofficial harassment campaign I'd mounted once I'd become convinced he was DeeDee's killer?

Some combination of all the above, more than likely. He's not alive to tell us, and who knows whether he'd be able to explain it if he were?

THIRTY-NINE

The shooting was ruled justified, but unlike the exchange of gunfire with the retired drug trafficker, this one generated a lot of bad publicity.

Chris' parents threatened to bring a wrongful death suit against both the Department and me.

"My son was shot down for nothing more than holding a kitchen implement," his father was quoted as saying in a front page story in the *Tribune*. The University's campus newspaper, the *Daily Californian*, was even more critical.

And it didn't help that the Concord shooting had been so recent.

Of course, I didn't have to read the papers if I didn't want to. What I couldn't avoid were the face-to-face denunciations.

At dinner, a few nights after the shooting, one of Roylmann's residents dropped some remarks about "trigger-happy, fucking pigs."

He didn't mention any names, but everyone knew who he was talking about. I took my meal out of the dining hall and ate it down in my room alone.

At the next Board meeting I was confronted by Rivendell's substitute rep, Greg Howley, who'd been pretty close to Chris.

"I know he had anger management problems," he said. "That was no excuse for you shooting him down like a dog."

"Anger management problems?" I said. "For Christ's sake, Greg, he was attacking me, trying to cut my throat. I was protecting myself, not administering therapy."

He wasn't convinced. The other reps were pretty supportive, though. Chris' mercurial nature hadn't made him many friends on the Board. And DeeDee had been very well-liked.

***

The Tuesday after the shooting, in Professor Ward's gangster class, we were discussing Eliot Ness's autobiography, *The Untouchables*, preparatory to screening the 1987 film version the following Thursday.

Ward got a little of his own back during his lecture.

"You may not know it, ladies and gentlemen," he said, "but we have an actual modern-day gangbuster right here in this class. That's right. Mr. Sullivan, the fearless defender of middle American values, is a member of our city's police force. I believed I noticed in the papers over the weekend that you'd killed your second man in less than a month, Mr. Sullivan. Have I got that right?"

I nodded, and said, "Yes."

"Don't believe in bringing 'em back alive?"

"Sure I do," I said. "Just not as much as I believe in bringing myself back alive."

"And I'm sure you followed all the rules set down for such encounters, didn't you?"

"Well, I certainly followed Sean Connery's rule," I answered. "The one he talks about in the movie."

"Which rule is that?"

"Don't bring a knife to a gunfight."

He frowned. Maybe he thought I wasn't acting embarrassed enough to suit him.

"Do you really think it's fair to bring such a superior level of force when trying to apprehend an obviously distraught individual, *Officer*?"

"A guy'll usually surrender when he's faced with superior force. And if he doesn't, what am I supposed to do? Ask him to hold on a second while I get a knife of my own? Or just let him stab me to death 'cause it's not fair to shoot him when all he's got is a knife? Like I said, Professor, I really do prefer to bring 'em back alive. But they've got to meet me halfway. They've got to be willing to be brought back alive."

He smiled and went on with his lecture. Maybe he hadn't scored any rhetorical points. Then again, maybe he had. I wasn't keeping a flow chart.

But I don't think his real satisfaction was in delivering the ultimate verbal riposte. It was simply in being able to embarrass me publicly.

***

Like all tempests, this one settled down eventually. Mr. and Mrs. Bridges discontinued their legal action when they were shown the steak knife that Chris had used, the shredded uniform shirt that Bob had been wearing, and the legal document that informed them that the Merryweather family was filing a wrongful death suit against the estate of Christopher Bridges.

Accompanying that document was an unofficial notification that the Merryweathers' suit would be dropped if and when Mr. and Mrs. Bridges dropped theirs against me and the Department.

The news media went on to other stories.

The loudmouth at Roylmann moved out when it became clear that the other residents intended to rally around me.

Rivendell elected a new permanent Board rep who, unlike Howley, wasn't a particular friend of Chris Bridges.

Ward never brought the issue up again in class. When the semester ended, I actually wound up getting an "A minus." Maybe he wanted to prove to himself that he was being fair. Of course, there was that "minus." I guess he couldn't keep his personal biases out of it completely.

***

Megan and I got back together, or maybe she decided that we hadn't actually broken up. It wasn't precisely clear to me. What was clear was that it wasn't the same. Though she said she understood, and I think she really did, I'd killed something special between us when I'd used her like that. Maybe I was too focused on the job to consider how that would affect our relationship. Or maybe, in the back of my mind, I had considered it, and decided I was willing to take the risk. In any case, I'd blown what we had, and though we never admitted it to each other, there was no getting it back.

When the summer break started, she went back home to San

Diego. By the time the summer ended, she'd transferred back to UCSD and gotten back together with her old boyfriend.

Girls are like buses. If you miss one there's always another in a few minutes. That's what I told myself.

***

We never did find out who the girl and guy were up on Grizzly Peak, the ones Mrs. Taylor saw and mistook for DeeDee and her presumed abductor. Maybe they were a couple who, despite all the publicity, were completely oblivious to having been taken for the missing girl and her supposed attacker. Maybe they were the victim and perpetrator of a completely separate crime, though, since no other girls who fit that description were reported missing, that seems unlikely. Maybe they were a couple who would've faced severe embarrassment if they came forward. If one or the other was married, for example.

I like to imagine that it was Professor Ward and some student with whom he was enjoying a little extracurricular slap and tickle. I've got absolutely no reason for believing that's the case, but pretending does give me a certain visceral satisfaction.

***

The nightmares are less frequent now. Usually I'm able to sleep the night through. Occasionally, though, I'll still jerk awake screaming when Chris comes at me swinging his knife while my gun just snaps on empty over and over again.

None of the other three shootings have haunted my dreams as much. Not even the first, and I was wounded that time.

Maybe my subconscious depicts him as a frightening figure in my dreams as a way of assuring me that I shouldn't have any regrets.

Or maybe it's just that, unlike the other three men I've shot at, he was someone I personally knew, and I haven't been able to come to terms with that.

But, as I say, the nightmares are less frequent now. Maybe, in time, they'll disappear completely.

Stephanie and Lou both say I need to find another girl to fill my dreams with something besides violent death.

And that shouldn't be hard. Girls, after all, are like buses. If you miss one, there's always another in a few minutes.

But, for the moment, I seem to still be stuck at the corner, waiting for the next one to arrive.

AUTHOR'S NOTE

Given my personal background, it seems more than normally prudent for me to make the usual disclaimer about *An Obscure Grave* being nothing more than a work of fiction, a mere product of the author's lively imagination, a harmless piece of artifice meant only to entertain, etc., etc., etc. Consider that disclaimer made.

That's not to say, however, that there are no references to actual places or institutions. There really is a University of California at Berkeley, for example, and, for all the unforgivably left-wing bias of most of its faculty, it really is one of the finest institutions of higher learning in the land.

La Val's, Top Dog, the UA Theatre, the Pacific Film Archives, Moe's Books, and many of the other student-supported businesses mentioned in the novel actually do exist.

There's also a real Berkeley Students' Cooperative which really does provide low-cost housing to Cal students, and really has done so since the Depression. On the other hand, there are no actual Co-op dormitories called Alexander Hall, Roylmann Hall, or Rivendell House (though persons familiar with the BSC might, if they are particularly discerning, be able to detect real-life counterparts).

As everyone knows, there is no such place as the City of Berkeley. That mythical town is, of course, nothing more than the fevered, drug-induced, leftist fantasy of a bunch of burnt-out radicals left over from the '60's. This plainly evident reality hasn't kept a great many people from insisting that Berkeley is, in fact, an actual locale. The best thing for you to do if you happen to meet such a person is simply to humor him.

A first novel doesn't get written without lots of help. At least mine didn't, and I'd like to thank a few of the people who helped me with this one.

First and foremost, of course is Katy, who, when she married me, had no idea that the vow was actually "to love, honor, cherish, and *edit*."

And there are my ultra-supportive friends at the Mystery Writers Forum, especially Jerry Peterson (author of the Sheriff James Early series) and Steven Torres (author of the "Precinct Puerto Rico" series), who both did line by line edits of the manuscript.

I also owe a huge thank-you to the British Crime Writers Association, whose Debut Dagger contest was the impetus behind this book being written. Special thanks to former CWA Chairman Mike Jecks, author of the Puttock and Furnshill series of medieval mysteries, and to Kay Mitchell, author of the Inspector Morrissey series of police procedurals, the Debut Dagger Coordinator the year I was a finalist.

My brother and sister officers at the University of California Police Department and the Berkeley Police Department continue to provide me with inspiration. Years ago, while still an undergrad at Cal, I started my law enforcement career, first as a civilian employee in the UCPD, and later as a reserve officer in the BPD. It's a bright, shining, fourteen-carat gold memory in my mental scrapbook of police experiences.

The encouragement of award-winning novelist and filmmaker Max Allan Collins, friend and mentor, has always been a source of strength.

John Weagly, who started in the same writing group as me, and who made his first sale at about the same time as me, critiqued this book's opening chapters when I first started writing it, and kept me convinced that I was doing something worthwhile.

Scottish *noir* specialist Al Guthrie, my brother Rare Bird, whose first novel, *Two-Way Split*, was a also a Debut Dagger finalist, critiqued the 500-word plot summary that was part of the contest entry, and his assurance that it was "a cracking synopsis" was a much-needed confidence builder during the early stages of writing this book.

Finally, two people who I can only thank in memory.

The first is Jean L. Backus, a fine lady and a fine novelist, who, before her too-early passing, was the instructor of a Mystery Writers of America-sponsored crime writing class that I was privileged to attend years ago. Some of the other writers Jean taught over the years include MWA Grand Master Marcia Muller, whose Sharon McCone was one of the first credible female private eyes in crime fiction; Julie Smith, who became the first American woman in over thirty years to win an Edgar in the category of Best Mystery Novel; and Sue Dunlap, who used the well-researched activities of the Berkeley Police Department as grist for her fictional mill years before I ever pinned on my own BPD star. I'm clearly the runt of that litter, but I'm very proud to be the latest of Jean's "graduates" to break into the ranks of published novelists.

The second is Captain Hugh Holton, Chicago Police Department, a great cop, a great writer (and author of a great series of cop novels featuring CPD Chief of Detectives Larry Cole), and a great inspiration, who died way too young. His suggestion that I move to the Midwest led to a multitude of blessings, personally and professionally, the most important of which, of course, was meeting Katy.

Thank you all.

ABOUT THE AUTHOR

Jim Doherty, currently the chief of police in a small Midwestern town, has served American law enforcement at the federal, state, and local levels, policing everything from inner city streets, to suburban parks, from college campuses to military bases, from rural farming communities to urban railroad yards. He is the winner of a WWA Spur Award for "Blood for Oil" which appears in his fact crime collection *Just the Facts*, published by Pro Se Press. Dan Sullivan, the protagonist of the CWA-Dagger nominated *An Obscure Grave*, has already been featured in a number of short stories that have appeared in magazines like *Mystery Buff*, *Mystery Tribune*, and *Writers' Journal*, and anthologies like *The Race Is On* and *Tales from the Red Lion*. From 2013 to 2017 he was the police technical advisor for the legendary cops-n-robbers comic strip, *Dick Tracy*.